FLYING IN THE FACE OF NATURE

Flying in the
Face of Nature

A YEAR IN MINSMERE BIRD RESERVE

Simon Barnes

PELHAM

PELHAM BOOKS

Published by the Penguin Group
27 Wrights Lane, London W8 5TZ
Viking Penguin Inc., 375 Hudson Street, New York, New York 10014, USA
Penguin Books Australia Ltd, Ringwood, Victoria, Australia
Penguin Books Canada Ltd, 10 Alcorn Avenue, Toronto, Ontario, Canada M4V 3B2
Penguin Books (NZ) Ltd, 182–190 Wairau Road, Auckland 10, New Zealand

Penguin Books Ltd, Registered Offices: Harmondsworth, Middlesex, England

First published in 1992
Copyright © Simon Barnes, 1992
Illustrations © Ian Wallace, 1992

Typeset in Photina $11\frac{1}{2}/13\frac{1}{2}$ pt
Printed in England by Clays Ltd, St Ives plc

A CIP catalogue record of this book is available from the British Library.

ISBN 0 7207 2005 2

The moral right of the author has been asserted.

This one can only be for
C L W
Hikkaduwa 1981
and all that

... on every blasted knollyrock (if you can spot fifty I spy four more) there's that gnarlybird ygathering, a runalittle, doalittle, preealittle, pouralittle, wipealittle, kicksalittle, severalittle, eatalittle, whinealittle, kenalittle, helfalittle, pelfalittle gnarlybird. A verytableland of bleakbardfields!

JAMES JOYCE

Twit twit twit
Jug jug jug jug jug jug

T. S. ELIOT

Kluut!

JEREMY SORENSEN

CONTENTS

ACKNOWLEDGEMENTS

THANKS are not enough for what I owe Jeremy Sorensen, chief warden at Minsmere. He made this book possible, and made its research a constant delight and a perpetual education.

More thanks to everyone else I met at Minsmere, in particular: Geoff Welch, Ian Robinson, Rob Macklin, Doug Ireland, Neil Gartshore, Kathy Archibald, Susan Ireland, Mike Sorensen, Joanne Lewis, Eileen Pinder, Robin Moore, John Denny, Eirwen Edwards, Anna Geach and Mike Barton.

I also owe thanks to the people at the RSPB headquarters in Sandy, especially Bob Scott, Sylvia Sullivan, Chris Harbard, Sue Steptoe, Derek Niemann, Mike Everett.

There should be a Campaign for Real Pubs: thanks to Dave and Dawn Drain at the Eel's Foot in Eastbridge, one of the last real pubs left, for hospitality and the Slimmer's Lunch.

Thanks to Mary Midgley, for permission to quote from her excellent book *Animals and Why They Matter*, published by University of Georgia Press.

Thanks to Roger Houghton at Pelham and to John Pawsey, as ever.

I would like to add thanks and greetings to many birding friends, especially Tim Goodwin, John Kier, Carolyn Orde, Jeff and Kay Vowles and Paul Harrison. Finally, special thanks to the person who bought me my first bird book, *The Observer Book of Birds*, rather more than thirty years ago – my father, of course.

MISTLE THRUSH
AND AVOCET

MINSMERE is a special place and it is full of special birds, but now I think of it, I don't want to write about special places and special birds at all. I want to write about all birds and all places. In fact, this book is as much about the mistle thrush that has just flown past my window as I sit here at the wordprocessor, as it is about the glamorous avocets and marsh harriers that people Britain's most spectacular bird reserve.

You might well ask, then, what I was doing at Minsmere. I was there, I suppose, because Minsmere has a quality of vividness. It is a place that opens your eyes and ears, your heart and mind to birds: and to everything else that lives as well. There is a magic quality about Minsmere that inspires a delight in life, all kinds of life: wildlife of every sort and, as an added bonus, your own life as well. The place is almost outrageously life-enhancing.

Minsmere is special all right. But the trick is to take Minsmere with you when you leave. Familiarity with Minsmere was only one of the great treats of my year of work on this book. Thanks to the people of Minsmere, and to the magic of the place, I learnt to carry a part of Minsmere away with me. After a while, the scruffy patch of British Rail scrub near my house acquired a touch of Minsmere. It filled up with birds that were not there before. It is, of course, just possible I hadn't noticed them. But Minsmere was the key: it unlocked the treasury door.

Minsmere is not just a bird reserve where you can see rare birds. Minsmere tells you how to understand life better, and thus how to enjoy life more.

Minsmere is an education and a delight: it is also a cause. The cause is not the maintenance of Minsmere: it is the maintenance of the world. Conservation. There are two kinds of conservation activity, very closely linked. One is the stopping of destruction. The other is the care and the creation of wilderness. This last sounds like a contradiction, but it is not. We have destroyed so much, we need to start recreating what is gone. More than anything else, and more than ever, we need wild places full of wild things. Destruction is a dramatic, frightening business, and it happens all the time. Sometimes it irrupts as a good newspaper story, sometimes it takes shape as a long, boring, slogging and often losing public inquiry, and most often of all, it takes the form of piecemeal destruction, the sort of thing that leaves you waking up one morning to find that something beautiful or important or meaningful has gone, and you never noticed. Campaigners oscillate from elation to despair. The answer is to concentrate on solutions: and this book aims to do that – and to enjoy a little tempered elation while we are at it.

But even at Minsmere, the depressing part of conservation cannot be avoided. Just south of the Minsmere River stands the massive folly of Sizewell nuclear power station. I turned my eyes to it a thousand times during the year: its rattles and groans were never out of my ears. I paid a memorable visit there and watched the teeming destruction taking place there in the company of a most charming chap who was convinced that Sizewell was going to Save the World.

But the antidote to Sizewell despair is Minsmere life. At Minsmere they are pushing back the boundaries: regenerating reedbeds, growing new oakwoods, planting out new tracts of heathland, directing more freshwater into a mere; and with painstaking delicacy in a roaring bulldozer, they are making profound and subtle improvements in the saline lagoon. This is the Scrape, Minsmere's pièce de résistance, where the avocets breed.

Learning the birds, and getting on terms of daily familiarity with such delightful things as avocets was one privilege of my work on this book. Another was daily familiarity with the people who make Minsmere work. They are, to put it as gently as I can, an *unusual* bunch. Well, some might call them eccentric or pretty well batty. If working in very difficult conditions for not very much money because of a deep, ferociously entrenched belief in what you are doing is a definition of eccentric, every warden who works on the green front line is a raving lunatic.

You do not need to be the world's most acute observer to spot the underlying sanity beneath all the paraphernalia of Help The Aged working clothes, state of the art binoculars, screaming chainsaws and red-rimmed eyes from the standard Maytime eighteen-hour day. These people have a purpose. They do not question the value of what they do, for they can see the effects of it all around them: squeaking in the tree tops, flying over the reedbeds, hooting and honking on the lagoons.

They are beyond fanaticism. Fanaticism is for amateurs, on the whole: for the twitchers who chase all over the place in search of lost, windblown rarities, trying to tick them off before they disappear. For there are two kinds of rare birds, and it is important not to get them confused. Some birds on the British list are rare because they should not be here at all: American warblers, for example, that took a drastic wrong turn on migration. These birds are frightfully common in their right and proper places. But some British birds are rare because there is something wrong with their right and proper places. It is birds of the second category that are the cause for concern. They are also a call to action.

The wardens are not fanatics for rare birds: they are just very determined to create a better place to live in. Mainly, a better place for birds to live, but that, quite incidentally, creates a better place for people as well. Birds are the focal point, at least where the wardens on the RSPB reserves are concerned, but to create a bird reserve you must create a place that teems with all kinds of life. You cannot have a wood full of blue tits unless it is also full of caterpillars. And so the wood must support the right kind of leaves for the caterpillars as well. And if you have a thriving population of blue tits, you will then attract sparrowhawks: four links in the chain. Every aspect of practical conservation involves the protection of a vast range of life. The conservation of birds means the conservation of habitat. Conservation of anything involves the protection of absolutely everything, because the world is a web of interconnected species.

Minsmere teaches more about this principle than anywhere else in the country: mainly because it has such a range of habitats. Different habitats have different superstar birds, different ecologies and different problems of practical management. At Minsmere, you can walk from oakwood, the climax vegetation of the place, to reedbed: fragile and everchanging. Minsmere is an education in many of the different habitats of England: it is at the same time both unique and the most typical place in the entire country.

I wanted to write about Minsmere because it had always seemed to me an enchanted domain: a special part of the world set away from the horrors and disasters of the real world; a place where life could be lived as it should be; a ghetto of sanity. But as I worked there, spent time with the wardens and spent time with the birds, my views changed. Minsmere became Everyplace. Each aspect of Minsmere became a generalisation: a template for conservation: a clue as to how life should be lived.

Minsmere gives its visitors the chance to reach a better understanding of the way life works. This is something hard to communicate in words: and it is this small task I have set myself with this book. I remember chatting to Jeremy Sorensen, Minsmere's chief warden, when we were having our by-then-traditional midday meeting, the Slimmer's Lunch: a pint of Murphy's and a chip butty at the Eel's Foot. Jeremy lobbed one of his bombshell questions into the conversation: 'What's this book of yours going to be about then?'

Brought up short, I fell back on facetiousness. 'The whole meaning of life itself, really.'

He laughed. 'That shouldn't be a problem then.'

'You know how at airports, every book you see has a sticker on it that says: "Few books will change your life. This one will"? I'm thinking of asking the publishers to put one of those stickers on mine. Because writing the damn thing certainly changed the author's bloody life.'

Perhaps I was overstating my case, but that is nothing new. A year in Minsmere was not, after all, a new world: it led to a better understanding of the one I already knew. Every second I spent at Minsmere was a re-affirmation. I had believed before that conservation was important, but now I *knew*. Every flutter and honk reinforced that knowledge.

It was the search for this kind of reinforcement that brought me to Minsmere in the first place. Minsmere is a place of legend: famous for avocets. Avocets had gone extinct as breeding birds in this country, because of mankind's destruction of their habitat. They returned because of mankind's taste for the destruction of himself: in the Second World War, areas of the East Anglian coast were flooded to provide obstacles for the invading force that never came. Thus, quite unwittingly, an avocet habitat was recreated. By the 1960s the avocet had become a symbol of successful conservation.

But the main reason I chose Minsmere is Minsmere's magic. It is an odd person that doesn't feel a sense of privilege here: more, you feel like a trespasser. The place, teeming with life, is quite overwhelming. I remember stepping from the car in the carpark on my first visit, some years ago, and at once I found myself in front of a large sand martin colony. The air was filled with birdsong: mainly nightingale, had I but known it then. I walked towards the Scrape, and on the way, saw skulking birds like wrens flaunting themselves from the tops of bushes. Minor rarities like Cetti's warbler stood and posed while I checked them feather by feather in the field guide. It was plain to anyone with a scientific turn of mind that I had entered an enchanted domain. The birds knew they were safe from me. The birds trusted: the people were trustworthy. This was as near as I was likely to get to Eden: I almost expected to come across a lion stretched out on the tussocky slopes behind the carpark, contentedly cropping the grass in the company of his friend, the lamb.

I made my way to one of the hides overlooking the Scrape. For the first, but not for the last time, I laughed aloud in delight and

Flying in the Face of Nature

disbelief as I did so. For everywhere I looked I could see birds of myth and legend. You could not bung a brick without hitting an avocet. It was as if I were looking at a field of unicorns.

KINGFISHER

GALES, gales, gales. There was a time, not so long ago, when I used to enjoy freak weather. A really good blow, making the bridges sway, slinging tiles to the ground, stopping traffic, and forcing all the rules of normal life to be suspended: these were stimulating reminders of the power of the natural world. A storm said that mankind, for all the boasting, was in the end never quite in control. That has always seemed to me a profoundly reassuring thought.

But we have been deprived of this luxury. When we are treated to a burst of unseasonal warmth, we now must wonder about the greenhouse effect. New Zealanders get terrible sunburn: they know this is because of the hole in the ozone layer. A drought, a gale: has mankind done something to cause these climatic extremes?

Ever since the invention of agriculture, mankind has earned a living by fighting nature. The trouble is that by the last decade of the twentieth century, it had become clear that victory has been complete. There is not a square inch of planet that we have not got our hands on. If something is wild, it is wild by mankind's express permission: like the great game plains of Africa: like Antarctica: like Minsmere Nature Reserve. Yes: this is a victory, and a pyrrhic victory if ever there was one. Another victory like this and we are done for.

These were gloomy thoughts that assailed me on Ipswich station in February. I was on my way to Minsmere, changing trains here from the Intercity to the little rattler that goes to Saxmundham. The overhead signs were swaying, trying to tear themselves free in the third big blow of the year. The third, for God's sake: what had gone wrong now? What had The Bastards – this being a kind of anonymous bunch of hate figures cultivated by all conservation-minded people at moments of depression – done to create this world of swirling chaos? 'British Rail regret to announce that due to debris on the line all trains are running late. British Rail apologise for the delay, and regret the inconvenience this will cause.' The human race regrets to announce that it is in the throes of killing off its own biosphere. Humanity apologises for this cosmic disaster and vaguely regrets any inconvenience this will cause.

Gloom and doom! Is it really that bad? Well, maybe it is. But I was, at least, on my way to Minsmere.

All the same, I was horribly late. This was to be my first meeting with Jeremy Sorensen, the chief warden of Minsmere; I feared that so desperately late an arrival would have a disastrous effect on our relationship. I was planning to work with this man for a year: his goodwill was slightly crucial. I had written to him, letting slip in the letter that my thoughts tended sometimes to stray in pessimistic directions. 'I don't get depressed,' he replied, surprising me for the first, but not for the last time. 'Certainly there are plenty of substantial problems.' For example, when the gale of 1987 blew down half his reserve. Or the year when the reserve failed to raise a single avocet. 'On the other hand, we get some fine fruit from some of our work.' I read, and wondered: how can you be a conservationist and not get depressed?

Sorensen? I imagined some hawk-faced Scandinavian throw-back: terrifyingly tall, immensely fair, rain-lashed face, eyes forever focused on the horizon, a man of silences, moody and intense. An unapproachable man: his keynote would be ferocious dedication. I was, as it happens, absolutely right about the dedication. But when I met him, he was wearing an incongruous Russian *shapka* on his head. You will never find a humourless Englishman in a *shapka*: by their hats ye shall know them.

At last, my train reached Saxmundham. I then made the acquaintance of Eric the taxi driver, and he agreed to take me to Minsmere. The way to the heart of Minsmere lies through a long wooded road invitingly called Sheepwash Lane. Once it was a dirt track, but the reserve now gets so many visitors that it has been tarmacked and peopled with sleeping policemen. Once this was a fine avenue of limes, but the '87 gale saw to them. Eric left me at Jeremy's bungalow.

Jeremy was aged fifty-four when we met, and straightaway my ludicrous notions of The Silent Scandinavian vanished. It was clear at once that all he needed was a brown habit to become a very good monk: a Franciscan, of course, because he would talk to the birds, the vowels of Manchester ringing in his speech. He could have been a classic jolly friar of legend: a man forever smiling and *chuckling*. Chuckling is something seldom performed outside the pages of Enid Blyton, and Jeremy is the only real chuckler I have ever met: a chuckling monk. He seemed already to possess a tonsure, and he had that untroubled cast of countenance that you find in people who have lived by an unresented vocation, and who live apart from the comforts and vicissitudes of domestic life. A genuine taste for celibacy is not exclusive to the religious life. Or perhaps it is: Jeremy is a man with a vocation, without a doubt.

It was a vocation that came late and capriciously. These days, most people come into conservation with degrees in biological science; Jeremy came via the wallpaper trade. He managed a string of twenty-four shops. 'Very useful experience it was,' he will say, without a shred of irony. He had long been a passionate weekend birder, but was content – reasonably content – to finance his passion by working in retail. He was involved in the trapping and ringing of birds for scientific purposes. This was where his heart was, and when he was invited to take part in an important ringing project, he applied for six months' leave of absence. This was refused. Jeremy promptly quit. His firm then offered him six months' leave of absence. So Jeremy still quit. Jeremy is as amiable a man as you could ever meet, but he was always been morally decisive. He does not suit morals to convenience, especially not his own convenience. He could not accept somebody else's moral compromise. 'It wasn't right, behaving like that,' he said.

It happened that wallpaper's loss was conservation's gain. After his six months of ringing, he applied for a job that had been advertised by the RSPB. His application was late, but the Society still gave him the job. He has been in the profession of conservation ever since. He has been chief warden at Minsmere since 1973; he inherited something wonderful and made it still better. It is a fiendishly difficult place to manage, and he has guided the place through a fiendishly difficult time. The difficulties stem from Minsmere's greatest asset: its huge diversity of habitat. It is not the largest, but it is unquestionably the most complex reserve the Society possesses. Every habitat requires a different form of intensive management for, as I was to learn, reserve management is not about putting a fence around a lovely place and letting nature get on with it. Minsmere has its centrepiece, the Scrape, which is a saline lagoon; it also has reedbed, a freshwater lake (Island Mere), a stretch of seashore, heathland, deciduous woodland and conifer. Each attracts different birds, each attracts different problems, each problem has numerous different possible solutions. It is an endlessly difficult, as well as an endlessly fascinating task. Endlessness is the point, rolling on from season to season, and from year to year: attracting birds, rearing birds, seeing bumper years and years of deprivation, years of drought and years of flood, years of feast and years of famine.

The enormous range of habitats makes for the enormous range of birds. At the beginning of the year, there had been 327 species of birds sighted on the reserve since its foundation in 1949. More importantly, there had been ninety-eight different species actually breeding on the reserve. Minsmere is, more than anything else, a place where birds breed. And let us not be narrow-minded: this is a nature reserve, not a mere bird reserve. There are otters in the reeds and the dykes, and there are red deer – the only truly shy creatures in all Minsmere – lurking in the woods.

Strange, then, to arrive, to start this book, on a day when there was nothing to be seen. The gale had bullied every bird on the reserve, bludgeoned them into keeping their heads down, staying out of sight and out of trouble. No bird with any sense starts flying around in a sixty-knot breeze. Hold tight, roost all day, and wait for easier weather. Conserve energy. Survive. Birds do not live by defying the elements, but Jeremy and I decided to do just that. Jeremy took the lead, *shapka* crammed hard on his head. The Scrape was not quite birdless: a small gathering of ducks was sitting the storm out in full view. 'Gadwall,' Jeremy pronounced. 'Observe the black sterns.' It was hard to see much: the wind wafted our binoculars around impossibly. Jeremy counted the birds: if a black stern is diagnostic of gadwall, then counting is diagnostic of a serious birder.

But I got distracted. I kept raising my eyes to look beyond the Scrape: the horror rose before us: the monster from the Black Lagoon. Well, if you wanted to build a nice nuclear power station, why not put it next to Britain's number one nature reserve? And if you wanted to build another, why not whop that one next to the nature reserve as well? The vast construction site of Sizewell B, with its dozen or so towering cranes – crane cranes, not *gruidae*, or bird cranes – lies just a short walk beyond Minsmere River. Beyond it lies Sizewell A, a fully operational nuclear power station. This juxtaposition is not one of life's more subtle ironies. Every time I got over-optimistic, all I had to do was turn my eyes south to Sizewell. Far in the east lies Chernobyl; to the west, Three Mile Island; to the north, Windscale.

Optimism and despair were to become cyclical over the course of the year. Every time Sizewell made me pessimistic, I could turn my eyes back to the Scrape, and tell myself again that despair helps no one and nothing. Jeremy and I marched along the beach, wind tearing at the *shapka*. A black sea heaved restlessly. A ringed plover crossed our path, portly, and with that ever-busy air that species always has. It was completely unafraid: a Minsmere bird all right.

We ducked into one of the hides for a breather. Surprisingly, we were not alone: a brave couple were staring bemusedly at the twenty-two gadwall. They had no binoculars, so the black sterns were invisible to them, even had they wished to see and interpret them. Not birders: passers-by. Many dedicated birders hold such people in contempt.

'Now the thing to do here is to think bird,' Jeremy said. 'What would you do on a day like this, if you were a bird?'

Flying in the Face of Nature

'Shelter,' I said. This was a flagrantly anthropomorphic approach, but I have no problems with that. Especially not when it works. Jeremy was scanning away with his binoculars: 'Ullo!' he said suddenly. 'Ullo mate. That's nice. That's smashing. Fabulous. Fabulous bird.'

He directed my binoculars: directing people to a bird you have spotted is the second most frustrating thing in birding. The first is being the person directed. In a deep wood otherwise intelligent people will suddenly yell at you: 'There! In the tree! On the branch!' The Scrape is the easiest place in the world to direct people to a bird, because every one of the tiny islands that litter the lagoon has a number. Even so, it is amazing how hard it can be to see a bird sometimes. 'Track along to the *fourth* post,' Jeremy was telling me. 'Now directly below it, and a yard above the bottom of the ditch. Sheltering like you said. Got it? Nice, innit? Fabulous things.'

Kingfisher. Of all birds, perhaps the most exotic in the minds of the non-birder. Like the avocet, a kingfisher seems to be a bird of near-mythical status, the sighting of which is not granted to ordinary mortals. In truth, kingfishers are common enough, in the right place. They are just hard to see: but there is a knack to it, as Jeremy was demonstrating. 'Would you like to see a kingfisher,' he asked the sheltering couple, proselytising, offering them a rare gift.

'A *kingfisher*?'

We both lent our binoculars, and Jeremy directed their eyes, '*Fourth* post. Down to the ditch. Just above the water: yes?'

'No. No. Can't see it.' There was resignation in the girl's voice: she knew she was not *supposed* to see kingfishers.

'Start again. Fourth post. And down. Three feet above the water – and tiny. Really tiny.'

'No. No – *oh!*'

Then silence for a long time. Eventually, and reluctantly, she passed the binoculars back. 'That's the most beautiful thing I have ever seen,' she said.

'Fabulous, innit?' said Jeremy. 'Have another look.'

Even in the teeth of a gale, Minsmere had not failed us. And soon enough, the Scrape, grey, uninviting, and almost deserted, would be heaving with life. Soon the avocets would be back. Hard to believe, as the windblown hide creaked like a three-master going round the Horn, but spring was just around the corner. Soon the avocets would be back.

PASSENGER PIGEON

SAVE the avocet. That was the battle cry of the RSPB in the late '50s and early '60s. We needed a flag we could rally to: the avocet became, if you like, the strange device on the banner of conservation. Avocets are odd, striking, beautiful, exotic: a walking logo. They represented an unqualified success story: they represented hope. They might have been designed as a symbol of conservation. In 1955 they established themselves as an emblem on the RSPB tie; by 1961 they had migrated onto the Society's writing paper; by the mid-'60s they had irrupted as a full-blown logo.

Conservation movements of the time tended to centre round a single species: an animal that was, to use an appropriately outdated term, truly sexy. Wildlife organisations set up appeals based around appealing animals: cuddly (Save the Panda), majestic (Save the White Rhino), strange and lovely (Save the Avocet). It was a perfect way of grabbing the attention: give us lolly or these lovely things will go extinct on us. Extinction is not a hard concept to grasp, for every extinction foreshadows our own.

In previous ages, when there were fewer people and more wilderness, there were no conservation movements, and no need for them. Or so it seemed. People killed, often profligately: and why not? Earth was a place of plenty. In one hunting competition in the United States, you could not win a prize with a bag of fewer than 30,000 birds. The bird in question was the most numerous bird on earth: the passenger pigeon. Supplies of passenger pigeons seemed quite inexhaustible: the bird went extinct in 1914, when Martha, the last passenger pigeon, died in Cincinnati Zoo on 1 September.

Reports of passenger pigeon flocks baffle the imagination: flocks four miles long and a mile broad passed overhead, and the sky would turn black with migrating birds. They nested in long strings of adjoining colonies of quite colossal size: colonies that covered thirty square miles. Sometimes these strings of colonies reached 100 miles in length. They all went. Forest clearance was against them, also, it has been suggested, imported avian diseases. But mainly, they were just shot. The enormous, inexhaustible flocks were shot to bits, mostly for commercial reasons. Once the huge flocks were destroyed, the pigeons plummeted to extinction: they had adapted to living on this enormous scale, and were, it seemed, incapable of hanging on in small pockets.

If mankind can cause the most common bird in the world, perhaps the most common in the history of the world, to go extinct, there is nothing beyond his range – especially when you remember that the technology of destruction has marched on apace since 1914. Look at Sizewell, just for a start.

In the nineteenth century, the thought of a Save the Passenger Pigeon campaign just would not have occurred to people. You might just as well campaign to Save the Sparrow or Save the Cockroach. But by the time we reached the middle years of this century, the thought of saving individual species was galvanising. And now, thinking has moved on. We have realised that if you wish to conserve icebergs, you have to do rather more than campaign to Save the Iceberg Tip. The idea of saving individual species is out of date. It is now clear that if you want to Save the Avocet, you must also Save the Ostracods, Copepods and Cladocerans. These last three are among the invertebrates – inverts, in conservationist jargon – that avocets eat. Or you might campaign to Save the Various Micro-Organisms and Plants on Which Ostracods and Their Pals Feed.

You must also campaign for the saline lagoon, the shingle bank and the mud island. And you must save the river estuaries where avocets spend their winters. And then you must – well, it goes on and on. This is what life is all about: the Great Chain, the chain of interdependence. Everything depends on everything else. This is expressed in the science of ecology. Ecology is largely understood as the science of remembering to take your bottles to the bottle bank, but to a scientist, ecology is the study of the Great Chain: avocets and ostracods and everything else. Its sister science is mathematics: enough to put anyone off. It examines the links in the chain: some of them robust, some alarmingly fragile. And we all know how strong a chain is. We should concentrate on the Great Chain as if our lives depended on it: and for the best of reasons.

The Great Chain is the guiding principle in the management of a nature reserve. Minsmere began because the avocets chose it. Had the RSPB simply bunged a fence round the place and told the avocets to get on with it, Minsmere would no longer be worth a damn to avocets, or to conservationists. This involves a rather baffling contradiction: Minsmere works because Jeremy has spent fifteen years in defiance of nature. Paradoxically enough, this is now the only way to keep the Great Chain intact.

For change is life. Even death is part of life's perpetual motion: devoured or rotted down, every corpse, animal or vegetable, nourishes life, and allows it to continue. Nothing stays the same: nothing stands still. You may have a habitat that is ideal for avocets, but it will not stay that way. Life, nourished by the succession of deaths, marches on, and it changes the landscape as it goes. At Minsmere, you see the avocets pacing across shallow pools: that pool is straining every sinew to become an oakwood.

I found this a difficult concept to grapple with. But when you take it step by step, it is not only comprehensible, it is inevitable. For, at the edge of the Scrape stand the reeds, the pioneer plants that move into open water. They colonise the edge, and then begin to inch forward. They grow and die, and grow and die, and as they do so, the corpses rot and become humus. At the front edge, new reeds push outwards. But at the back, where the ground is now more solid, where humus has built up for the longest, more plants come in. A green underlayer of sedge strikes up. The ground must, therefore, get still more solid, and soon you have outposts of willowscrub: willow is a plant that likes to have its feet in water. The willows will cause a further drying out. More scrub and vegetation advances, dies, and more follows. Finally, the oak moves in, at first in single spies, ultimately in battalions, growing up, closing its canopy, establishing dynasties of trees that will live and die, ever-changing and regenerating, replacing each other as far into the future as we can see. The process of change from open water to oakwood is called natural succession: the oakwood itself is the climax of the succession.

Every habitat in the world will go through a natural succession until it reaches its climax. A climax vegetation has been discovered in a jar of water – a kind of horrible green scum. Any aquarium owner knows about that. And any gardener knows a good deal about natural succession. Ignore a patch of bare soil in a garden, and at once the succession begins. The pioneer plants are fragile little annuals. They have adopted the strategy of broadcasting hundreds and thousands of seeds, in the hope that the odd one or two will find a toehold somewhere. They arrive, bloom, bolt to seed and die, all in a season or less. Gardeners know all about how rapidly these fragile opportunists can arrive and sprout. They call them weeds.

These ephemeral pioneers are followed by tougher plants that plan for a longer stay. They are perennials: perennial weeds if you prefer. They can store food to tide themselves over a winter or two: they can bloom and broadcast seed more than once. They are half-permanent, half-opportunist: daisies and dandelions. If your open space is big enough, the perennials will be followed by pioneering shrubs. You can see this happening on any building sight as bramble and buddleia take a hold. Eventually, the shrubs themselves will be upstaged by trees, for your patch of bare soil is straining every sinew to become an oakwood. A gardener is perpetually fighting the natural succession; so is the warden of a nature reserve.

A week or so after the day of the gale, I was back at Minsmere. Jeremy was fighting nature that afternoon by drawing the curtains, making me coffee and sitting before the fire. Winter is the quiet time: practical wardening needs daylight. He was taking time off from the incessant demands of the wordprocessor –

Flying in the Face of Nature

keyboard bashing being yet another of the essential skills of the nature reserve warden – and we were talking about life and birds, as we were to do all year. We were talking about nature, and how to fight it.

'A mature woodland doesn't need much in terms of day-to-day, or even year-to-year management,' he was saying. 'The rate of change is much slower at the climax. But at the beginning of the succession, it's different. The nearer you are to the beginning, the faster the changes are taking place. Or trying to take place. In a reedbed, you are fighting the succession all the time. We cannot let it do what it wants to do, what it *should* do. Because we want to keep our reedbeds as reedbeds.'

Two or three hundred years ago, the world kept itself intact without any human intervention. There would have been no point in fighting the succession in a reedbed. New reedbeds would be creating themselves all over the place: open water, floods, bursting rivers. In a dozen locations on land adjoining Minsmere, the succession would be starting from scratch in open water, beginning its long journey towards climax. But today, with every square inch of land under cultivation or built upon, there are no new reedbeds being formed. 'We must make the succession mark time,' Jeremy said. 'And at the moment we are in the happy situation of being able to raise our waterlevels.' Minsmere is locked into the system of sluices and dykes and bunds (ditches and raised banks) that gave mankind the control of waterlevels in East Anglia. The sea has been pushed back, land claimed from the sea, and the country squeezed like a sponge. The arable land of East Anglia is every bit as much a product of man's ingenuity as Manhattan. Minsmere itself stands on reclaimed land. If you stand at the Eel's Foot pub in Eastbridge and look east, you can see where the sea was pushed back and back again in a series of waves. Vast areas of East Anglia are now lifeless green deserts: in Minsmere this has been put into reverse. Water is going back onto the land.

'Obviously we can't go on forever opening the sluices and pouring water on. In the end, we will have created a kind of wetland table mountain: we will reach a level when the water will just run off. So then we'll get in some fancy machinery and get down to a lower level again. Still – that's not something that need worry us right now. There'll be different technology available in fifty years' time: it'll be up to them to work out the best and cheapest method of doing the job.' In fifty years, Jeremy and I will presumably be dead, and our corpses nourishing future life. Minsmere will, I trust, go marching on. Conservation must be like the papacy and think in terms of centuries rather than years. Centuries at the very least: in the late '70s Jeremy planted a belt of oakwood that should reach its full stature somewhere around the year 2200.

To fight the succession is to work in direct opposition to nature; that involves, as you might expect, acts of gross destruction. If you walk a nature reserve, you will generally come across someone destroying something. He, or she, might be assaulting a ditch with a chrome, which is a horrible kind of rake; or taking out vegetation with the whirling blade of a strimmer; or wearing a hardhat and ear defenders and carving trees into matchwood with a howling chainsaw. Such people love to emphasise the destructive side of their jobs, as if the guiding principle really were one of gungho mayhem. But every piece of vandalism is an act of loving care. It is performed after, and with, great thought. And every time, the thought is bird.

Think bird: that is the Sorensen catchphrase and the unspoken motto of all wardens. 'It's a complicated business,' Jeremy said. 'At the moment, when it's light, we are pushing the reeds back at the edge of the pools, to stop the pools getting swallowed up by reed. That's simple enough – but if you think right, you can improve the pool at the same time. A crooked pool will hold more birds than a perfectly round one. In a round pool, you will probably get one pair at each end. If you have a pool the same size, but with lots of inlets and little peninsulas, you could end up with a bird in each bay. So you let the reeds come in here, and cut them back there, and make a nice wobbly shape – and you're adding to the wildlife. You can't just take an academic approach. You've got to be simple; you've got to be practical; you've got to be intuitive. You've got to think bird.

'The Society – I mean the RSPB, obviously – backs up the wardens with academic research, and that is part of the Society's strength. Because if you wait for the results of the academic research to come through, you might wait for twenty years. And by then, it could be too late.

'In a properly run world you wouldn't be doing this. You'd let things go through to their climax, because there'd be new habitats coming up all around. But that doesn't happen. Land is always being grabbed for one development or another. If we don't fight like crazy to keep what we've got, we'll soon have nothing left at all. We've got to fight nature. It's the only way.'

Conservation, it becomes clear, is not a piecemeal business. You cannot protect rare birds at the expense of the boring common ones, or pretty birdies at the expense of ugly things like worms. We are not talking about the Royal Society for the Protection of Birds, but the Royal Society for the Protection of Absolutely Everything, the Royal Society for the Protection and Strengthening of the Great Chain. But birds are in one way more important than anything else: they are visible, audible and mobile. They tell us, more clearly and more immediately than any other creatures, what is happening with a particular habitat, and what is happening with the world. If you have a good collection of waders on a river estuary, then you know that you must have a substantial population of thriving, wriggling invertebrates in the estuarine mud. And that means that your estuary must be good and rich and poison-free. When the sparrowhawks went extinct in East Anglia, it was clear that there was something badly amiss with East Anglia: there was. When sparrowhawks returned, it was obvious that East Anglia was a cleaner place than it had been.

Avocets have become an institution at Minsmere. As we sat in Jeremy's bungalow anticipating the coming spring, he told me, in unexcited terms, what he was expecting and hoping for: something that would have been a miracle fifty years ago. It was routine now: he wanted a good, solid breeding performance from the avocets. Perhaps forty, maybe fifty, chicks to be raised. There were four other species whose progress he would monitor with particular attention: marsh harrier, bittern, nightjar, little tern.

Marsh harrier: birds of prey that nest in the reeds and hunt by sailing over the reedbeds in a sinister, leisurely glide, their wings uplifted in a shallow vee. They have recovered from extinction in this country to something close to respectability – at least around Minsmere. They are, in their quiet way, utterly spectacular.

Bittern: the skulker, the secretive pacer of the reedbeds. This is a bird seldom seen. It can be heard in the spring, mostly at night, when its voice carries over the marshes. It is a quiet, but eerily penetrating sound: the word 'boom', traditionally used to describe the sound, is altogether too noisy and explosive a word. It is more a sort of humming grunt. Bitterns are almost impossible to observe, their habits are elusive, and very little is known about them. They have been extinct in this country once already: they made a comeback and fell away again. This is a devastatingly rare breeding bird: any result at all from Minsmere would be a triumph.

Nightjar: the spookiest bird in Britain. A bird of the nighttime heathlands, it swoops about like a giant nocturnal swift. It is another bird of mystery: another bird more often heard than seen. In May it calls, and it makes a wild and bewildering sound: like that of a moron trying unsuccessfully to tune a radio.

Little tern: my favourite British bird. The competition for that accolade is pretty intense, but they are, as Jeremy would say, *fabulous* birds. Elegant, fast and utterly reckless, they hover and dive, scream and quarrel, perform the most spectacular aerobatics you could wish to see, and they come in the nattiest white-picked-out-with-black plumage. They have the ugliest voice of any bird in the country, and I could spend a day birding and see nothing but a single little tern and come away happy.

Five birds: four habitats. Avocet: lagoon. Marsh harrier and bittern: reedbed. Nightjar: heath. Little tern: beach and dune. Let us not be too dogmatic: there are a few overlaps here. But these are the five keynote birds of the Minsmere year. If you prefer, five canaries down the coal mine testing the air of the late twentieth century. I hoped they were not really passenger pigeons.

NIGHTINGALE

ERIC stopped the taxi outside Jeremy's bungalow, and I stepped out into the wildest din you have ever heard. Opening the car door was like opening the door to a disco: a sudden violent gust of pure sound.

Spring doesn't arrive at Minsmere, it explodes. This was a firework display of birds: light the green touchpaper and stand well clear. Jeremy, *shapka*less in the May sunshine, chanced to be standing at the roadside as we pulled up. 'Dreadful racket!' I complained. 'Can't you get the birds to sing more quietly?'

'Fabulous, innit?' said Jeremy. 'Nightingale, mostly. You can hear four of them going off at once.'

The air was full of the throbbing, unceasing song of the nightingale. Of course I had heard nightingale before, but I had never been able to *listen* to it. Now the song came to me with perfect clarity for the first time: *twit twit twit jug jug jug* – the traditional written rendition of the nightingale's song. The bird sings, off and on, through the pages of T.S. Eliot's *The Waste Land*, and at one point Eliot scoffs:

Nightingale

> *yet there the nightingale*
> *Filled all the desert with inviolable voice*
> *And still she cried, and still the world pursues,*
> *'Jug jug' to dirty ears.*

This has been interpreted by some as a comment on the depraved senses of the fallen human race: a species that has fallen so low that the best it can do to transliterate the sweetest sound in nature is a coarse 'jug jug'. There are also fairly unambiguous sexual connotations; jug is an archaic slang term for mistress.

> *Twit twit twit*
> *Jug jug jug jug jug jug*
> *So rudely forc'd*
> *Tereu.*

You can argue about this on literary grounds as much as you wish, but right from the first moment that I was able to listen wittingly to a nightingale, it seemed clear that you could hardly transliterate the song more accurately. This unbelievably loud song is full of variations and complexities: it seems to move from simple ploughboy whistling through to the more advanced electronic thoughts of Stockhausen and back again. It mixes a series of rising whistles, notes that get more and more intense till you think the bird might burst with the passion of it; follows this with tumbling bursts of song and then a series of thunking, resonant drumming notes. Jug jug has it to a tee. Did T.S. Eliot ever listen to a real, as opposed to a literary nightingale, I wonder? But certainly, the song is fairly unambiguously about sex: this is May, and the woods are full of the sweet song of sex. On every bush and brake, sex rears its comely head.

Minsmere is famous for its waterside birds: avocets and marsh harriers. But the nightingales are just as much a feature of the place if you have ears as well as eyes. I had walked Minsmere on many a May before this year, and walked through tunnels of jugging nightingales: and I had never heard a single one. Now I will always hear them. Jeremy was to unseal my ears and my intuitive understanding of the woods of England and the world over the course of a single Minsmere May. You can turn a jar of certain supersaturated liquids into a jar of crystals by adding a single tiny grain of the right stuff. I felt as if exactly the same thing had happened to my understanding: one minute I was listening to an agreeable cacophony of noise, the next I was hearing a thousand individual birds singing their hearts out, acclaiming their territories, singing out for females, affirming each and every individual life from one end of the reserve to the other.

'They have decided nightingales nest in coppice,' Jeremy said, as the birds jugged on all around us. Coppicing is part of traditional woodland management: a tree is cut down, but left living, and from the trunk spring poles which can be harvested every fifteen years or so. People used the poles for fuel and for building, for woods were managed for people over centuries. That is what woods were *for*. But as the coppice-poles grow up, they make a nice dense thicket, and many birds find their privacy enticing. 'So, naturally, they always want to see woods tidied into coppice,' Jeremy continued. 'They' is Jeremyspeak for academic researchers and people from the RSPB headquarters at Sandy. Jeremy is pretty well-disposed towards 'them', for the most part, but like everyone who works at the sharp end of a business, as opposed to the back-up, he has a different perspective on the problems.

'So they have decided that that's where nightingales breed. It amuses me, it really does. Because none of our nightingales breeds in coppice. We haven't *got* any coppice. So they're not supposed to like it here – but they do. As you can hear, eh?' You certainly can. Once you have isolated that jug jug jug from the background, it seems to follow you everywhere, like the eyes of a portrait following you round a room. The nightingale was the first stage of my entry into the undiscovered country of birding: song. You go bird*watching*, not birdlistening. Professional bird people, and serious amateurs, understand song. Song is a vital tool for serious census work. The top twitchers find song a marvellous aid in separating the common birds from the super-rarities that make their hearts beat so fast. But for most rank-and-file birders, for most tyro twitchers, song is a closed world. To have this world opened to me was, perhaps, the greatest privilege I was to enjoy during my year at Minsmere. I made a great deal of effort at repaying Jeremy for this matchless gift. Time after time, we would meet for lunch in the Eel's Foot for the Slimmer's Lunch – a pint of Murphy's and a chip butty. I tried to express my thanks by buying him beer, but it would take the entire brewery to express my thanks properly.

Jeremy is nothing less than a genius when it comes to song. 'He doesn't just identify birds by their song, but I swear he can tell them by the way they suck in air between notes,' wrote David Tomlinson in *The Great Bird Race*. Jeremy is so attuned to birdcall that he automatically wakes in the night when the birds on the Scrape sound the alarm. This is the man who slept right through the 1987 hurricane, which brought trees down all around his bungalow. The alarm on the Scrape often means that a fox has got in among the avocets and must be seen off. That makes it a very handy ability to possess: many a time, Jeremy has heard the alarm call, got up, dressed and gone down to the Scrape, while the volunteer on fox-spotting duty in one of the hides had not noticed a thing.

It is the avocets that normally wake him. Their voice is very clear and distinctive: the Dutch call them *kluuts* for that reason. So does Jeremy, mainly because he likes the name. It follows then that most of the Minsmere staff and volunteers have adopted the term as well: 'Two more kluuts started sitting on the East Scrape,' they will say to each other. Kluuts have a quality that penetrates dreams.

'The alarm call is the same as the normal kluut call,' Jeremy said. 'But there is a difference in tone. It's the same with the black-headed gulls: they start to make a different noise when there is real danger about.'

On 1 May, Jeremy was woken by the mass alarm call. He charged down to the Scrape and found that the alarm was a false one, or that the fox or whatever it was had already gone. Jeremy has done a fair amount of birdsong recording, as you might expect from someone with his ear. This is a pursuit that becomes a mania with some people, though Jeremy has always been fairly relaxed about it. But after the early morning false alarm, he decided it wasn't worth seeking out further sleep, so he got his recording gear out, aimed it at his scrap of garden, sipped a cup of coffee and listened. Within half an hour he had twenty species on tape. 'Nightingales and blackcaps and lesser whitethroats and willow warblers and green woodpeckers and carrion crows and blue tits and great tits and long-tailed tits, and you know, it was just *brilliant*. I just sat there. You feel you're getting somewhere. We must be getting somewhere, the amount of sparrowhawks we're getting this spring. There are at least three pairs out there. Just the other day I was putting some rubbish out into the dustbin, and bang! a sparrowhawk dropped on a blackbird, right here in front of me. I watched it kill and fly off.'

All avian life is here. And the better your ears, the more you understand it: you can hear the high yowling of a sparrowhawk and the laidback fluting of a blackbird. More than with any other habitat, the woodlands became a new land to me, as I walked the woods with newly awakened ears. Woodland birds are invisible: you can't birdwatch in a place where you see only leaves. But a walk in the woods in May, especially if the woods happen to be in Minsmere and you happen to be walking with Jeremy Sorensen, will bring a glorious collection of birds that flaunt themselves invisibly before your ears.

There are two popular errors about birdsong. Cockbirds sing throughout the spring, and the songs are lovely. The songs are not art for art's sake: they are used to acclaim a territory and to attract a female. The first error is the Madeleine Bassett Error; the second is the Adolf Hitler Error. Madeleine Bassett is the soppy girl in P.G. Wodehouse who loves the sound of birdies singing, and who believes that the stars are God's daisy-chain and that every time a baby laughs a wee fairy is born. The Madeleine Bassett Error is to think of birds as Beautiful Things.

The second error is a simple reaction to Madeleine Bassett. If birds are not noble, beautiful and generally wonderful examples to us all, then they must be bad examples: telling us that nature is red in tooth and claw. The 'viciousness' or 'selfishness' of the creature is emphasised: robins get a particularly bad press here. They are seen as vicious machines: 'the Adolf Hitler of the bird world,' I remember one newspaper columnist saying. This is because robins hold territory throughout the winter, unlike most songbirds, and they proclaim that territory in the traditional robin style: by singing. It is a lovely song, different to the spring song, and traditionally described as 'wistful' or 'sad'. Its meaning is that other robins should clear off: but the bird is no more a bully than it is wistful. 'That a behaviour is not altruistic should not make it any less special,' wrote Mark Owens in *The Cry of the Kalahari*.

'That a birdsong has a function does not make it any less beautiful.'

But people do get dreadfully confused about song. The fact that song has a 'function' leads them to the idea that birds are no more than feathered mechanisms, responding helplessly to certain stimuli. This is hopelessly depressing stuff. It is a straitjacketing line of thought, whether you believe that man is the only creature that is *not* a mechanism, and which possesses a will of his own, or whether you understand mankind to be just another mechanism floundering in the Darwinian maelstrom. The Madeleine Bassett Error and the Adolf Hitler Error are equal and opposite: action and reaction. Both are over-emotional. Both reduce birds to things: Beautiful Things for mankind's delectation, or Mechanical Things to dissect. I don't think either notion is helpful in trying to understand life: not birdlife, not the life of man, not the life of any other animal.

Science traditionally rejects emotion and intuition: science, in one view, was always a haven for tough guys, all thinking tough, crystal-clear thoughts, purged of all emotion. But some of the greatest advances in recent understanding of the way life works have been conducted by people who are nothing less than passionate about the animals they work with. The science of ethology, or animal behaviour, depends from the very start on recognising creatures as individuals. It involves major investments of time and energy, and the employment of great analytical and intuitive skills. This does not make the results wishywashy or sentimental or unacceptably anthropomorphic. But it is truly amazing to realise how many of the understandings in ethology have been acquired in the last two or three decades. African elephants have been observed for getting on for two centuries, and only very recently has it been realised that bulls do not maintain harems. The truth is that elephant society is at heart matriarchal. It is no coincidence that many of those ground-breakers in ethology have been women: Jane Goodall with her chimpanzees, Cynthia Moss with African elephants, Dian Fossey with gorillas. Women are always less worried than men about dealing with such terribly unmanning things as emotion. They have occupied, triumphantly, the no-man's-land between Madeleine Bassett and Adolf Hitler.

With a sensible, unstraitjacketed perspective, it seems quite obvious that no animal is a mechanical contrivance. Anyone with the eyes and the patience to spend time in the wild can see quite clearly that Pavlov's dogs have had their day. Minsmere gives you the easiest way in the country of understanding that: an hour in a hide on the Scrape will allow you to watch the avocets feed and fight and bicker and defend their nests and act out the traditions of their society. As you watch, the first glimmerings of an understanding of avocet life will come to you.

Or walk the woods at Minsmere. The great tit has nine territorial songs: some say that the male with the most variations gets the best mate. I have read that the nightingale that sings loudest and longest wins the best female. The world in the canopy is neither one of saccharine sweetness nor one of mindlessly vicious mechanical contrivances locked in endless battle. It's life, that's all.

Jeremy was, as ever, the ideal companion: calling the birds for me as Peter O'Sullevan calls the horses. Blackbird. Song thrush. Robin. Willow warbler. Chiffchaff. Great tit. Blue tit. Get the common birds sorted out: it is like learning the instruments of an orchestra. A pattern emerges from the chaos. It is like one of those trick drawings in a child's puzzle book: once you have seen the hidden objects you can never not see them again. 'There!' said Jeremy. 'Redstart. Got it?'

'Nope.'

'There . . . and again.'

'Nope. I can't pull it away from the background noise. Didn't I tell you to get these birds singing more quietly?'

Redstart are thoroughly English thrushes in shape, and wildly foreign-seeming things in colour, decked out in preposterous reds and blues. In their unabashed exoticism, they are very Minsmere birds.

'There!'

A fragment of song. Not over-stated: almost thrown away: a careless scrap of song. Very simple, very lovely. With, of course, an important function. The song was about territory and, equally unambiguously, about sex. *Chirrup.* 'Fabulous sound,' said Jeremy.

BLACK-HEADED GULL

ALL through May and even beyond, I felt a weird sense of dislocation every time I opened the wooden shutter of a hide and looked out across the Scrape. It was somehow never quite as I remembered it. The birds were further away: less recognisable: indistinct shapes and bewildering movements. It was a while before I got used to that first feeling of acute disappointment and confusion.

I felt as if all the previous pleasures and insights I had gained at Minsmere were illusion. I had achieved these insights because I wanted to acquire them, not because I had actually done so. I had replaced the reality of the place with a fantasy of intimacy: you seem to remember that opening a shutter puts you right in the front parlour of an avocet family. But when you arrive and march down to a hide there seems no intimacy available at all: you feel agoraphobic, alien, unwelcome. Almost every time I felt a sense of bafflement. The air was filled with nothing but black-headed gulls: why were there so many of these blackheads? What was the point of a reserve for one of the commonest and most streetwise birds in Britain? There were maybe 300 pairs, filling the air with their calls: *Quark! Quark!* The Scrape looked incomprehensible.

Flying in the Face of Nature

I would then feel an upsurge of panicking boredom. How long was I going to have to sit here? I am not a scientist, not a twitcher, not a trained taker of notes, not even a good observer. What on earth was I going to *do* here? I would check out the black-heads again: *Quark!* Scan the Scrape for avocets: yes, a few there. Now what? Many a time, I just sat there in confusion, peering out at all the muddle, all those white birds, listening bemusedly to the sounds: a fusillade of quarks mixed up with the occasional kluut.

And time after time a small miracle occurred. I would recollect myself with a start and realise that I was going to have to sprint if I was going to find Eric the taxi and catch my train. Somehow, I had mislaid an hour, staring out over the Scrape, lost in the domestic lives of the birds. It seems that a special rule operates here: you either see nothing or you see an awful lot. There is no in-between stage. It is a little like following the tennis at Wimbledon: you can watch the odd match and be mildly entertained, or you can watch every ball struck and get completely sucked in by the ebb and flow of personalities and fortunes across the full stretch of the Wimbledon fortnight. You see practically everything or virtually nothing.

At both Wimbledon and the Scrape, you must get your eye in before you do anything else at all. You must accustom yourself to the very special demands of either place: on the Scrape you must get your eyes used to the shapes and sizes and movements of the birds. This is true of all kinds of birdwatching, and it is especially true of a confused and crowded expanse like the Scrape. This is because your mind sees what it expects to see: this is a phenomenon called cognition. A football reporter going to watch a team he has seen only once or twice will be struggling when it comes to identifying the player that scored in a goalmouth scramble. But a reporter who follows the same team every week will be able to recognise every player in the side from a hundred yards away in driving rain with his number covered in mud. He knows the man from the way he moves, from the cut of his jib, what birders call *jizz*.

The etymology of jizz is obscure, though it has been suggested it comes from 'guise'. To recognise a bird by jizz is to recognise it despite seeing it badly. You might see a black shape skim low over the water. The person unaccustomed to such sights sees a black shape: the person with his eye in sees a kingfisher in all its glory. Vision must be educated.

For me, the first few minutes in a hide was always a confusing process of re-education in the first principles: the picture slowly coming into focus. The more you see, the more you see. You scan an island you have already scanned a dozen times and discover that two avocet chicks have appeared on it as if by a conjuring trick. The arrivals and departures and interactions slowly form a pattern: slowly assume the furtive fascinations of a soap opera.

The re-education process doesn't exist for those who live on the reserve. These include Jeremy, two fulltime wardens working under him, another warden on a six-month paid contract, and a shifting population of volunteers, staying on the reserve for weeks, sometimes months, sometimes even longer. Though the truth is that people who work on the reserve do not spend every second of the day birdwatching. The popular fantasy of a warden's job is that it involves sixteen daily hours chasing birds and an obsessive policy of keeping all the rarities for himself. The truth is otherwise: most of the year they are involved in hard, bruising physical labour, or hammering the keys of the wordprocessor. But in spring at Minsmere the rhythm changes: in this month of May almost every move a bird makes gets watched. Wardening makes demands of contradictory sides of a person's nature: still, contradictions come naturally to a person like Ian Robinson.

Ian was one of the two fulltime wardens under Jeremy: his number three. At first sight, he was forbidding: unsmiling, speech full of flat northern As. All wardens wear old and scruffy clothes: Ian dresses in the clothes the other wardens give to Oxfam. His Barbour looked like a garment worn by a beggar in a fairly safe and conventional production of a Shakespeare play. Thin-rimmed, metal-girdered spectacles gave his face a glare that might seem hostile; a pair of missing front teeth added to the impression that he was a reckless bruiser with a Bogart sibilance in his speech. Wardening is a profession that attracts unusual people, but Ian is unusual even by the standards of the trade.

His physical strength is legendary. He is a master of the chainsaw, a skill that was honed to fierce perfection when he was clearing the fallen giants of Minsmere after the hurricane of 1987.

Flying in the Face of Nature

When I got to know him better, I called him 'the Dirty Harry of conservation' – you don't assign him to a habitat, you just turn him loose. But that was after I discovered his sense of humour: not something that is buried terribly deep, in fact.

He arrived at Minsmere after a long spell at Abernethy, the great, rambling mountain reserve in Scotland. Ian took to the hills as a duck takes to water: long days in remote places seeing no one, scarcely speaking: long days alone in the mountains. It was an event to see someone, and there was seldom any need to do anything daft like talk to him. Solitude is a drug, especially solitude in wild and beautiful places. A view of the Scrape would suck me in for an hour of silent vigil: on the grand scale of Abernethy, the landscape sucks people in for days and weeks at a time – or whole lifetimes. It is the sort of thing I have seen happen to people in Africa: love of the bush becomes all-consuming. People lose the habit of civilisation. Many an African marriage has been concluded with the words: 'It's me or the bush.' Not a fair contest.

The longer you are alone in these wild places, the more you understand. The understanding and the solitude itself work on the system until they create an addiction. There is a deep, solitary streak in Ian: when he arrived at Minsmere from Abernethy he was, Jeremy said, comprehensively 'bushed'. It was a hard transition: to leave one of the loneliest and loveliest places in Britain and to come to the RSPB's most peopled reserve. Minsmere racks up more visitor hours than any other reserve in the country, Jeremy claims, and no one disputes that. Ian had to re-learn the art of being sociable.

In fact, there is a gregarious streak in Ian. He had just lost the practice of talking. He is a much-welcomed man at the Eel's Foot: he doesn't walk into social gatherings like a Martian having his first look at earthlings. But it was not simply that he lost the habit of people: it was also that part of him was quite content to do so.

At Minsmere Ian had to re-enter the world: he had to be obliging to visitors, polite to them when they told him they had seen golden eagles flying over the Scrape ('well, it's possible . . .'), and instructive to the ambitious young volunteers. Not every stage of the adjustment was easy, but despite his forbidding appearance and his laconic nature, he is a great communicator.

Black-headed Gull

His own intensity is the key. Ian gets so absorbed by the task at hand that people are just swept along.

He is indefatigable at the mundane tasks of management: the scrub clearing, the chroming of the dykes. He attacks a task: he loves to see a job completed. His approach is dynamic and aggressive. But that is only one side of the nature of a complex man: Ian also possesses the gift of stillness. He can be absorbed by the aggressive energy needed to control and bring down a potentially lethal crack willow and to carve it into kindling with a chainsaw, and equally enthralled by the demands of stillness required for intensive observation of the birds.

You meet him with a chainsaw, and you feel that he could carve his way clear across the face of the world, devouring anything in his path. You see him in a hide on the Scrape, you think he is a man who could sit still forever: unblinking, missing nothing of the birds living out their lives in front of him. He likes to take his favourite position in a hide at first light. He sets up his 'scope – no birder owns a telescope, it is always a 'scope – and just sits. Occasionally he takes a note, but mostly he stores it all in his head. He has a further gift of enviable mental clarity.

'Loads of avocet chicks,' Ian was saying. 'Eighty hatched so far. Not a record, but there's a long way to go yet.' Ian's task was to make an exact census of birds breeding on the Scrape. That is not easy. To me it looked quite impossible: a nursery of seventeen hectares of screaming chaos, in which the 300 pairs of blackheads were simply the eye-baffling start. You can't see all the birds from one hide, but you can see the same bird from many different hides. Birds are easy to miss, and just as easy to count several times over. The avocets dominate the thoughts, but they do not dominate the breeding. It is the blackheads that are the champions: the ubiquitous blackheads, Britain's commonest gull. There are reckoned to be 300,000 of them breeding in any one season in this country, and around three million of them overwintering here. They are birds that make their presence felt: incessantly screaming, quarrelling, hawking for insects, creating confusion for any observer who lifts up the shutter of a hide.

They get on pretty well with the avocets, if birds as quarrelsome as blackheads can be said to get on with birds as aggressive as avocets. They are much of a size, so we have a stand-off. It is part of the Minsmere strategy to get the blackheads and the avocets breeding alongside each other across the Scrape. Despite the quarrels and the friction, it actually makes life easier for the avocets. For a start, the black-head chicks make a more tempting target for predators: they are more of a mouthful, easier to grab and, of course, there are more of them. Avocets can, to an extent, hide among the black-head flock, rather than stand alone. The Scrape offers the same strategy as the game plains of Africa: the individual can find safety among numbers.

'You always miss birds,' Ian said, pulling back from the 'scope after a long, hard, Paddington Bear stare at the island in front of him. 'The vegetation has got up very fast lately, since we had that bit of rain. I missed an oystercatcher's nest with two young: where the hell did they come from, I thought. I've counted thirty-two avocet nests, but you can't be there counting twenty-four hours a day. So you miss little bits of behaviour: the avocet may be off her nest feeding, or may be making an interchange with her mate. You don't see it, because you can't see everything. And so you assume that the nest has been deserted. I try to eliminate that sort of mistake by checking twice a day: very early in the morning, before the reserve is open for visitors, and again late at night, when there are fewer people about and visibility is often a lot better, too. That way, the errors should cancel themselves out.'

Avocets are territorial, but not in a precise way. You can map the territory of a songbird quite easily: the cock sings loudly from selected points inside the territory, and, in theory, he never strays outside it during the breeding season. Avocets don't make things as easy for the censor. Some nest close together on a shingle island: they will defend their own nestspace vigorously, but their feeding territories will inevitably overlap. Some birds prefer to nest away from the crowd, and will defend their entire feeding area as vigorously as the communal nesters will defend a nestspace. There is, it seems, a clear advantage to the early nesters. The older, and necessarily more experienced birds were hard at it in March, and there were chicks visible in April. Experience is clearly useful, for these are long-lived birds, who will often carry on into their mid and late teens. But as Ian and I watched, there were still some birds sitting on eggs: these were mostly younger birds, slower on the uptake, less certain of the way the world works. Others were birds whose early nest had failed and had been abandoned for some reason or other, perhaps because a predator had taken the eggs or the chicks. Another advantage for an early nester is the possibility of a second chance.

Ian's eyes were constantly flickering from bird to bird, and from bird to water. Waterlevel becomes a complete obsession with Minsmere people, for the Scrape is a phenomenally ticklish environment. You want a small amount of water, and you need it to last through the summer, while the chicks are growing into viable subadult, free-flying birds. Too much water would be as great a disaster as too little: salinity is a crucial factor. 'We got an inch of rain over the past three days, and that has made a lot of difference. It really is a difficult business. We need the water shallow, so the baby avocets can feed, but once the mud gets exposed, it gets cracked and hard and is totally useless. There's always a lot of messing about. A lot of conflicts. You want to keep the algae down, algae levels get high because the water gets de-oxygenated. You eliminate that by keeping the waterlevels up – and that conflicts with the optimum conditions for the chicks. We're always getting complaints about the waterlevels from the punters.'

Birdwatchers always want plenty of exposed mud because they want to see waders, though sometimes they insist on plenty of open water, so they will see wildfowl, or whatever. Perhaps they think the Scrape operates with tapwater and a plughole. The point is that every form of management works on priorities. The priority in managing the Scrape is avocets, *breeding* avocets. Everything else is a bonus. 'We've had too much salinity, so we've let water from North Marsh onto the Scrape,' Ian said. 'And it's not pleasant to do that. We know that it is to the disadvantage of the birds on North Marsh. The bitterns and the other birds in there will suffer. But it is a matter of complex hydrology, complex ecological juggling. In a sense we are robbing the bittern to pay the avocets. That is the reserve strategy. I wish it were not necessary. There is simply not enough water to allow us to flood the marsh *and* soak the Scrape.' Jeremy had spoken cheerily in February about juggling the sluices to provide optimum conditions for both bittern and avocet. But dry year had followed dry year, and just when it needed a decent soaking, Minsmere had had a devastatingly dry spring. You can't juggle your hydrology to the best purposes if you are short on hydro. No one, of course, could say whether the succession of dry years was the result of a climatic shift, or of a routine meteorological blip in the pattern, or of man's lack of control of his technology, like global warming. It was the same with the profusion of gales in recent years: there were a dozen theories, and no facts. But you can only run a nature reserve by pragmatic acceptance of what has actually happened. Wild and gloomy speculation is no good to man nor bird.

All of this meant that things were not looking good for bitterns. The last census had revealed four booming males. No one was seriously happy about that total. It was not high enough, and it was very likely wrong as well. It was probably too high. The notional total had varied throughout the spring: reactions had ranged from 'there can't be only two', and 'there must be more than three', to 'I know we were hoping for more than four, but are there really as many as that?' This weird, invisible ventriloquial bird is a censor's nightmare: counting bitterns makes a task like assessing the confusion of the Scrape seem almost an easy option.

Why favour avocets over bitterns? An impossible question. The traditions of Minsmere management have been built around avocets for forty years. In that time, the reedbeds have also prospered: as recently as 1988, they had nine booming male bitterns. But since then, there has been a falling off: and the portents this year looked poor. A blip in the pattern? Or a long-term decline? Already Jeremy was wondering if a change of policy would help bitterns. How could they be encouraged without troubling the avocets? Was this possible at all if the present succession of dry years continued? Should bitterns be made the number one management priority if the decline continued? The conundrum seemed unanswerable in May.

An avocet paced virtually to our feet, as Ian and I sat in the hide. It swept its bill through the water, taking something at almost every swish. These delicate-looking birds often seem to be insatiably greedy feeders. On an island, one of the chicks was standing at the edge of the water, a bundle of fluff with an absurd uptilted little stump of a bill. It was trying the same thing with

Black-headed Gull

great concentration, with no success whatsoever, quite unaware how daft it looked. 'The trouble with Minsmere,' Ian said suddenly, 'is that there are too many habitats and you want to have them all in peak condition all the time. And you can't. Like the marsh and the bitterns. And then I wonder how many more breeding birds we could get here if the reserve was totally closed to visitors. But I know that's not really worth thinking about. Members and visitors pay for what we are doing. Minsmere wouldn't exist without them.' Minsmere's first function is as a breeding ground for birds. Its secondary function is to show people conservation in action. It reinforces the conservational zeal of many people who come, and it converts a good few as well.

'But then you get ardent birdwatchers screaming at you because they want low water on the Scrape for the waders. You try to explain, you say that if you took all the water off in the spring there'd be nowhere for the breeding birds to feed in the summer. And they don't always listen. It's hard to keep sane sometimes. But you know how important the people are, all the same.' Ian is no longer the bushed refugee from Abernethy, but sometimes the effort shows.

A little tern shot arrowlike in front of us: a wonderful streamlined vision. Ian had been censusing the little terns as well. They were a little down on previous years. 'Funny birds,' he said. 'One year, they find a place, decide it's perfect, rear lots of young. Next year, they won't look at the place. They have to find somewhere else. They used to nest on the beach: now they're nesting here on the Scrape. That's got to be safer for them. I hope they stay put. I've counted twenty to twenty-five nests: they're very hard to count accurately, in fact. You keep losing them among the dock plants. Around thirty have hatched.' I was cheered by this, because of my special fondness for little terns. I hoped it was to be a bumper year for little tern.

'The balance of species and numbers out here on the Scrape is about right this year,' Ian said. 'Everything can get on with the job and breed without bothering anything else.' A lesser black-backed gull passed overhead: such a sight does not cause the mass panic you get from a sudden falcon. The avocets and the black-heads just watched it warily, as it shifted a little on the air, and settled into a flightpath for an island full of nesting birds.

Flying in the Face of Nature

'Sometimes the avocets are so stupid you want to shout at them,' Ian said. 'They leave the nest alone and unguarded, to go hurtling after the lesser blackback. So the lesser blackback just twists a wing and drops straight down onto the unguarded nest. Bang. Thanks very much. They don't seem to have a lot of common sense. They leave their chicks alone just so they can have a good scream at a bird.'

One avocet, no doubt overhearing, decided to act exactly as Ian suggested. It launched itself skyward, beak first and kluuting like a maniac. 'Ground to gull missile,' Ian said. The gull twisted away – and carried on, overflying the Scrape. It would be back. 'All right this time,' Ian said. 'Bloody crazy kluuts. They're supposed to have a survival mechanism. Not a self-destruct mechanism.'

WHITETHROAT

I VISITED an area of wasteland at Minsmere: not wilderness, just a lonely and scruffy place littered with the detritus of departed humans. There were bits of old iron: the remains of a dead sawmill. Old shooting butts were scattered across the landscape, little pens of iron, their camouflaging straw bales long since removed. At either end of a field full of bramble stood a sad pair of goalposts. There were no people around here any more and the land had simply been abandoned. The Scrape seemed a million miles away: that lagoon, product of man's ingenuity, and subject to daily inspection, might as well be on another planet. So too might the other much-managed Minsmere habitats: the reedbeds, Island Mere, the rides and clearings in the deciduous woodland. This place was a mess.

It had been left to itself about ten years ago, and the succession was in its early stages. It was an unattractive thigh-high jungle of bramble, a bit of gorse and broom, and that was about it.

Rubbish like this? On a bird reserve? At *Minsmere*? There was an excuse for it. The place was teeming with birds. Rob Macklin, Jeremy's number two, was spending a fine May morning taking a census of this, the least frequented and apparently the least exciting place on the entire reserve. But with the right kind of eyes – and with the right kind of ears – the place was lovely.

People had been playing football on the pitch just twelve years previously. The territorial games played across its length were far more important now. The echoing birdsong across the ruins of the football pitch really was a matter of life and death – and more important than that, the immortality of genes. Every singing cock, every hen on the nest, wanted the same thing: to leave thriving progeny; to leave their genes on earth in living birds.

'We've never done anything to this place,' Rob said. 'Just let it go. You can see how the succession works, just looking across here. It's all come back, heather and gorse, probably too much gorse, and of course, bramble. If we let it go, the scrub would come in, and then the trees. But we'll probably take some of the gorse away later, later this year, maybe. After the breeding season is over, and when we've got some extra labour.'

Rob looks and even sounds like a nature reserve warden straight out of Central Casting. He is burly, copiously bearded, and his voice has a burr of Hampshire. He is a phenomenal allround field naturalist. With every step you walk alongside Rob, more and more wonders are brought to your attention: birds overhead, flowers at your feet, insects all around you. He will be happy to explain precisely which species of bee is coming in to sting you. Most RSPB wardens have a profound knowledge of birds and a working knowledge of the invertebrate and plant life that affects the birds. Rob is a cricketer, and he is also an allrounder in the Ian Botham class when it comes to fieldwork. 'Spotted brown here, lovely . . . super carpet of ground ivy here. Silver studded blue colony here, not a big one. This general mosaic of heather and gorse seems to suit everything. We have natterjack toad further up. I tend to look for green hairsteaks around here, it's the commonest hairsteak in Suffolk, but it's not that common.' If you press him, Rob will admit that he is pretty poor when it comes to knowledge of the fieldmarks of spiders. 'Not a great spiderman, I'm afraid.' Never mind, he can baffle you completely by calling the name – in Latin – of every dragonfly you see when you walk along a decent dragonfly ditch.

Rob's knowledge seems inexhaustible, but, of course, it is not. It is his curiosity that is inexhaustible: and his love of it all. He seems to get a kick from every living thing he sets eyes on. This is wonderfully infectious. We were treading a public footpath along the edge of the football pitch, but it was a footpath seldom walked. Minsmere's staffers and volunteers pass that way, mostly in the spring for censusing, but that is about it. An occasional fine weekend would bring out the walkers. But mostly, this was a sad, forgotten place. Most of Minsmere has been managed to within an inch of its life, but here the place had been left to do with itself what it would. Given a run of decades, a century, it would, in the end, tumble down to woodland. But more likely, a management scheme would cut in. Right now, there was no need: the air was thick with song. 'They love it down here. Really love it,' Rob said.

He was carrying a clipboard to which a series of frenziedly detailed maps was attached: monstrous things drawn to a six-inch scale. Rob and I would have shown up on the map ourselves had we sat down for long enough. But Rob is not a great one for hanging about: there is always another living thing around the next corner, and he is agog to record it. You could certainly record every single bramblebrake on that map. The idea was to map every singing bird. In this stretch of wasteland, the birds were mainly warblers: birds about four inches long. It sounds impossible, but in fact, recording them precisely on a map is perfectly feasible. All you need are good observation skills and a tidy mind. A willow warbler goes on the map as an open circle ○; a chiffchaff is a filled-in blob ●.

Rob was mapping every place from which a bird was singing. There is nothing random about birdsong. A song is designed to proclaim territory *from* the territory. The area where the cock sings is the area in which it will stay, feed, roost, court, raise a brood and have its being over the brief course of a breeding season. May is the absolute peak of the year: that is why the entire reserve was echoing with song from one end to the other. When Rob found two cockbirds singing close together, he drew a dotted line between them, to indicate two separate territories. 'You know it's a territorial male, simply because it is singing. And if you come back in a week's time, and there it is, still singing – then you know you have a definite, established territory.'

Song, even from a human perspective, is more than a pleasure, and it is more than a useful aid to birdwatchers. It is also a crucial tool in ornithological research. The patterns of birds and their breeding is largely done by ear. And the gathering of information is vital: for science, for reserve strategy, for conservation. You cannot tell what areas need attention without accurate facts. And you cannot impress people, developers, local councils, public enquiries, or anyone else with sincere statements alone. What people believe are figures. The government's white paper on the environment was published later that year, and amid a lot of platitudes, it stressed the need for accurate research. This can be seen as a narroweyed 'prove it' mentality. Facts are central to conservation. They are weapons.

A song burst from a bramblebrake: loud and insistent. It sounded a little like Donald Duck doing an impersonation of a songbird. Rob drew a circle on the map, and wrote in the centre a neat W. Whitethroat. 'Scratchy song, you see,' he said. Everyone always tells you that a whitethroat song is 'scratchy'. You need daft mnemonics to help with learning song: whitethroat/sorethroat, I thought.

A few years ago, in the early '80s, there were no more than eight whitethroat breeding on the reserve. The previous year, 1989, there were seventy-six. Facts, yes, but how do you interpret them? Partly, this enormous increase shows, or could show, how much more attractive the reserve has become for whitethroat, as the gorse and the bramble has grown up across the football pitch, providing with each passing year better cover and better food sources. Secondly, it can and does show that there are simply more whitethroat about. Figures gathered across the entire country and collated by the British Trust for Ornithology show that the species took a hammering in recent years. This was because of the series of droughts in the Sahel, the area south of the Sahara where whitethroat overwinter. This is the same drought that caused the Ethiopian famine and which prompted Bob Geldof to such heroics. Now the whitethroat are making a recovery: a fact loudly demonstrated in this sawnoff jungle of bramble.

Rob stepped down into a little hollow: a dell, more sheltered than its surrounds. Another whitethroat, another, another, another: it seemed that we were in whitethroat heaven. These are rather drab little birds, scraps of nothing, olivey-grey on top, and greyish-olive underneath, with a little patch of white at the throat – for once we have a bird name that is reasonably accurate. Whitethroat spend most of their lives poking about in dense cover, eating insects and berries in season. Their survival plan is based on secrecy: skulking about, keeping out of harm's way in their olive-drab camouflage. It is the ambition of every whitethroat to be overlooked, because an overlooked whitethroat is a survivor.

But every spring, they turn their entire world upside-down, reverse all their customary patterns of behaviour and forget all they ever knew about survival through secrecy. When a cock whitethroat claims a territory, he perches on the top of the bramblebrake, in full view of the watching world, and he proclaims his existence to everyone within range. Look at me, look at me: I'm *here*. And to rub the point home, he will suddenly fly into the air in a brief, bouncing songflight: here I am. Look at me. This is an invitation that any passing sparrowhawk will certainly take up. But far, far stronger than the usual urge for discretion is this annual passion for self-advertisement. Outside May and early June, you scarcely ever see a whitethroat, scarcely know they are about. But here, in the height of the breeding season, Rob and I were standing in a cauldron of whitethroat competition: a dell filled from end to end with whitethroat, each one showing off with every fibre of his being. The Donald Duck song, the whitethroat anthem, was being sung on every gorse and bramble you could see.

Territory: that is what this is all about. People have misunderstood the urge to hold territory ever since the phenomenon was first identified in the eighteenth century. People confuse territory with property, with real estate, with nation and with warfare. But territory is nothing to do with the acquisitive urge. Birds do not seek ever bigger, ever more glorious territories. The cockbirds seek the best place to which they can attract a hen, mate and raise young. If whitethroat nested too close together, none of the pairs would be able to find enough food to raise young. So they take a territory and hold it. They will defend it against other cocks of their own species, but this is not warfare: this is survival – survival of the immortal genes.

Flying in the Face of Nature

Nor does every male whitethroat alive seize a territory, sing his head off and raise a brood. The numbers of breeding birds are regulated by the number of breeding territories available – by the carrying capacity of the land. Whitethroat Dell was filled to capacity. W, wrote Rob. And again, W. 'Five pairs in just this little bowl,' he said, filled with pleasure at the thought. 'Amazing. Really amazing. This is courtship and territory, that is what song is about. The edges of the territories may overlap, and then you can get conflict between rival males. Even a bit of a fight, sometimes. But singing is usually enough.' Would that all the world's disputes about ownership could be sorted out by a singing competition – though come to think of it, that would disqualify me as a territory holder from birth. But then, not all birds' songs are musical, so perhaps I would qualify after all. The song of the water rail is a kind of clucking squeal. It is called 'song' because its function is courtship and territory. It is less musical than the lovesong of the domestic cat, but it carries the same glorious message as the song of the nightingale: here I am.

Rob and I walked on through the paths and lanes, with Rob's pencil recording birds and butterflies at almost every stride. 'Cinnibar, yes, more of them around than there used to be. Tiger beetle. This bit here, you see the gale damage from '87? I'm planning to do nothing with that, and it should grow into a nice big thick tangle. Good for blackcap and whitethroat. Heard about North Warren?'

'No.'

'The Society has had a reserve there for years, not done much with it of late. It's been run from here, it's just a few miles down the coast, the other side of Sizewell. We've just bought a whole lot of grazing marsh – that's really something. There is some potential there all right. That could be turned into a really super reserve.'

We walked on through a stretch of wooded lane and hedgerow: ideal country for ○ and ●: willow warbler and chiffchaff. Willow warbler seemed to be singing out their lovely lisping cadence from every branch. As we walked and censused on, Rob kept repeating the willow warbler song to himself in a thin, whispering breathy whistle. He didn't know he was doing it. ○, he wrote, and again ○.

We came upon one of the longterm volunteers, a long-haired lad named Robin (R?). He was wielding a shovel in an extraordinarily purposeful way. No doubt he had heard our approach. We stopped to exchange pleasantries. About six feet away, in its unashamedly Minsmere way, yet another bird burst into song: *twit twit twit jug jug jug.* 'N,' said Robin helpfully. Rob wrote N and we walked on, taking a shortcut through the woods to the cottage where he lives in Sheepwash Lane.

'Stop!'

Rob's call of alarm was a fraction too late. My bootheel came down an inch behind his own. Even as he called, I saw a tiny brown bird whizz away from him, ankle-high, hugging the ground. Rob was on his knees at once: 'Let's see. Let's see.' He was going through the bramblebrake prickle by prickle. 'Here it is. And it's all right, too. We both managed to miss it. That's a bonus, you don't see many of them. This is the first I've seen for twenty years. Not seen one since I was a boy nester. No, not a nest robber, but I used to spend my time looking for nests. Well – just take a look at this.'

It was worth looking at. A tiny purse of grass, containing five impossibly minute white eggs. 'A willowchiff nest,' Rob said. Impossible to say whether this was willow warbler or chiffchaff, ○ or ●. They are almost impossible to tell apart. Unless they sing.

But here, in Rob's hand – now carefully letting it go and replacing the brambles, leaving everything as it should be for the returning bird – was the reason for all the excitement, all the noise, all the song that echoes the length and breadth of Minsmere in May – and for that matter, the length and breadth of Britain, anywhere that a bird can find a foothold and a life free from disturbance: eggs, breeding, young, the survival of immortal genes.

KESTREL

PICTURE the nature reserve warden: rifle in hand, he gazes hawklike across the Scrape, the sound of kluuting avocets ringing in his ears as his finger itches for the trigger. On 8 May, Jeremy opened fire. There is something wonderfully insane about the picture this conjures up: one imagines Jeremy suddenly driven mad by a lifetime of conservation, running amok and blasting away at the avocets in a black Basil Fawlty rage: 'Right, you vicious bastards! You've asked for this!'

But Jeremy was plugging at foxes. It was a black night. Jeremy was in North Hide, trying to stare the enigmatic black shapes into self-revelation, knowing that a dog fox had just got onto the Scrape and was looking to polish off as many nests as he could. Not avocet nests in particular, any nests would do. But Minsmere does not have any avocet chicks it can spare. Accordingly, when a fox – or the shadow of a fox – came into sight, running up the fence supports and back to cover, Jeremy fired without compunction.

These were not ideal Bisley conditions for target shooting. The distance was 180 yards. The weapon was a .22 Hornet rifle with a telescopic sight. It was too dark to see both crosshairs: this does not make for perfect accuracy. 'I don't know if I got it,' Jeremy said. 'But I worried it. It certainly *looked* worried.'

'I think he may have worried permanently,' Ian said. But guns aren't the half of it. Guns are only for the foxes you have failed to electrify. Jeremy had built an electric fence around the entire seventeen hectares of the Scrape, and this was the first breeding season it had been in use. He was quite enraptured with it. Every time I walked around the Scrape with him, he was unable to resist the temptation: he would take a piece of grass and touch it to the live fence. 'Ow! Yes, that's working all right.' And Jeremy would chuckle with satisfaction. 'You try it.'

'No.'

Guns and electric fences are more the stuff of a concentration camp than of sweet, innocent nature, but it gets far more complicated than that. A foxproof fence is all very well, but it won't do much to stop the stoats. Stoats, long and sinuous little predators, can squeeze through impossibly small gaps. So the bottom third of the seven-foot fence had an additional layer of fine mesh; a broad mesh was used for the fence above waist height. Three electrified strands ran through it, and the fence was liberally covered in notices warning punters not to electrocute themselves.

It is clear that we are a long way away from the natural world. The avocets continue to thrive, but they do so with the help of bullets and electricity. The previous year, a fox had got onto the Scrape in May when the hides were crammed with birdwatchers. That did not stop Jeremy. Though he didn't scandalise them by trying to blow the fox out of the water with a snapshot from the hip, he certainly made something of a splash. He leapt onto the Scrape and belted across at full speed. The fox watched, bemused as Jeremy, by then shoeless, having had both sucked off by the mud, charged towards him waving and shouting. Finally, the fox made the sensible decision, dropped the gosling he had just taken and took to his heels and ran, with Sorensen still in helterskelter pursuit. Again, this is not quite in the natural order of things: a bird that needs a mad, wild-eyed, hand-clapping warden in order to breed in safety is asking serious questions of its environment.

But these are by no means the oddest facts about the environment in which the Minsmere avocets breed. Their lagoon was scraped out by a bulldozer; that is why it is called the Scrape. The avocets saw the Second World War flooding, liked the look of it at once and moved in. The Scrape was dug out to make things still better for them in 1962. The sluices give control of the waterlevels, so long as there is enough water available. You have to have the rainfall before you have water to control. Too much water and the avocets will be unable to feed, too little and the mud will get exposed and, again, make feeding impossible. Even the islands on the lagoon are manmade.

The plants that grow on these islands are also managed. If you let them do as they wished, the Scrape would become overgrown, the succession would march onwards towards its distant dream of oakwood, and the open-ground nest sites that avocets love would vanish. But you cannot take the simplest route towards exerting control over the plants, which would be total eradication. Many important inverts breed around the plants and their roots. The Scrape involves a colossal amount of work. Every autumn, when the breeding season is over and the avocets have scattered, Jeremy runs a couple of days when volunteers are asked to 'Bring a Rake to the Scrape'. This is a jolly day of backbreaking labour in which goodhearted people from all over the place clear away the buildup of plants across the lagoon. Were this not done, the lagoon would start becoming a reedbed, dreaming of oaks. All in all, the Scrape required 500 manhours of labour in a single year. If this is a wilderness, it is a very singular one.

I went to Minsmere seeking a wilderness and found instead a kind of genetic casino: a place in which every living thing gambles, but the house always wins. The house manipulates the odds: the house always has an edge.

'Ow!' said Jeremy. 'I felt that from eight inches away. I didn't even touch it.'

'Lord knows what it does to the damn stoats,' I said.

The situation is very complex in terms of management, and more problematic still if you start to worry about the ethics. What is the point of wild places that are not truly wild? What is the point of encouraging a rare creature to breed, if you must deal out electric shocks and bullets to other creatures? Practical conservationists can get a little macho about this, talking about omelettes and eggs, hefting the chainsaw purposefully, and telling you that conservation is all about mashing up habitats and shooting foxes. No point in being sentimental, is there?

Conservationists over the age of twenty-five take a slightly more thoughtful attitude. Where does management stop and interference begin? 'I hate to shoot foxes,' Jeremy said. 'I'll do it, but I don't want to do it, I hate the idea that it is necessary. That is why I have gone for the strategy of the electric fence: I hope that was the last fox I ever have to shoot at. There'll always be foxes on the reserve, but I want them to stop thinking of the Scrape as a useful food source. It would be nice to think I have killed off the foxes' tradition of going onto the Scrape with that last shot. But if you want avocets, you have no choice but to control the foxes somehow or other.'

Where does control stop? In 1983, sixty-nine pairs of avocet reared 111 chicks, the best year ever. The following year, there were fifty-two pairs. They did not raise a single chick among them. There were no little terns raised either. Virtually all the chicks were wiped out by a single kestrel, a bird that became known in Society legend as The Kestrel with the Schedule One Diet. Schedule One birds are the rarest breeding birds in Britain, as classified by the Wildlife and Countryside Act. 'There had to be a reason for it,' Jeremy said. 'Kestrels don't eat avocets in the normal course of things. They don't eat many birds at all. So why had they turned to avocets and little terns?'

The kestrels' staple is the short-tailed vole. These rather agreeable, plump little animals come and go in cycles: you can get a short-tailed vole glut, and then a precipitate crash. Numbers build up slowly, the pace of increase gets faster and faster, then crash, down they go again. Jeremy's explanation – more than that, a 'gut feeling' – was that the short-tailed vole population was in a desperately deep trough year. This was totally contradicted by national findings. Later research revealed that there was, indeed, a strictly local crash in vole numbers, in defiance of the national trend. This was not a matter in which Jeremy took much satisfaction.

'There were plenty of people who thought I ought to kill the kestrel. I fundamentally disagreed. I am opposed to control. I have always held to the basic notion that it is the prey population that controls the predators. I will control foxes, and I have done, but

Flying in the Face of Nature

there are better ways to run a nature reserve than that. The electric fence being one. You can see it is working.'

Controlling kestrels was out of the question. Controlling foxes is done with reluctance. Controlling mink, controlling coypu: that is done with alacrity. They got rid of the invasive mink and coypu at Minsmere, they 'controlled' them – or to be more accurate, they trapped them and killed them. Both animals were introduced to this country by fur farmers, and they inevitably got out and set up feral populations. Coypu are hard-digging, beaverlike planteaters; mink are fierce weasel-like predators. Both can wreak havoc in their different ways: both can have a dramatic effect on a habitat, one by eating vegetation and digging holes, the other by direct predation. The last mink was killed in 1986; the last coypu was taken out a few years earlier.

These aliens have been kept at bay to allow the traditional breeders to keep going. That seems fair enough. But there is so *much* management required to let the avocets and the rest breed: have we created a totally artificial environment for avocets?

The answer to that is yes, why the hell not? Virtually all of this country is an artificial environment: grazing land, hedgerow, arable land, coppice woodland, heath. What is not artificial? Avocets traditionally bred on the coast of the wet country in England. The sea would march in and march out, the coastline was not a firm line on a map, but a thing in a constant state of flux. Just a few miles north of Minsmere lies Dunwich. Dunwich was once the busiest port in medieval East Anglia, but now it is under the sea. The Suffolk coastline was traditionally full of coastal lagoons. One might get overwhelmed by the advancing sea one year; another might be created elsewhere by the same advancing tide. And if the sea kept out for a season or so, the reeds would invade the lagoon, and the scrub would follow, and the succession would continue on its normal march towards woodland. The sea, washing in and washing out, kept all the wet country in a state of flux. The avocets nested where they could find their lagoons and where they could hunt for their ostracods.

That time is long since passed. Mankind has taken control of the land and the sea. The sea is now kept in the same place, year after year. Minsmere river once ended in an estuary, and was no doubt surrounded by a sea of reeds booming with bittern, on a coastline dotted with changing, shifting lagoons, which would have been full of kluuting avocets. Who stole the wet country from the avocets and the bitterns? Mankind did. Vast tracts of East Anglia are now open-air food factories: green deserts. We have lost our wet wilderness: we owe it to ourselves, and we owe it to the avocets, to make good. Having destroyed so much, it is time for mankind to put things into reverse. We have lost enough: the idea of losing more to an ethical argument about whether or not avocets should be able to fend for themselves is a nonsense. The avocets are not *fed*, this is not a *zoo*. But we have stolen their lagoons, so we should do something about putting them back.

The entire dichotomy between interference and non-interference, it becomes clear, is another nonsense. Mankind is already involved. We have created the environment, sculpting the landscape according to our whims and for our own purposes. We are 2,000 years too late to consider *laissez-faire*. The question is no longer whether we *should* manage and control our wild areas, but how we can do so for the best. We lost our wilderness, along with our innocence, a long time ago.

We need wild places for our own sanity: we need wild places because we owe a debt to our fellow animals. The debt can never be repaid: but at least we still have some places – albeit places touched by the hand of man – where wild creatures can still live. To keep these places for these creatures is a matter of unceasing labour. Much of conservation is like the Red Queen in *Alice*: it takes all the running you can do to stay in the same place. The 500 manhours expended annually on the Scrape make sure that it is the same as it was last year.

'It was here that I took that shot at that fox,' said Jeremy, as we entered North Hide. 'And the fox was over there, by that fencepost.'

'Not a bad shot. Not bad at all.'

'If I got him.'

'Bloody good shot just worrying him from here, in the dark.'

The kluuting of the avocets reached a sudden frenzy. I was beginning to see what Jeremy meant by the change in tone, the alarm note that invariably wakes him in his bed half a mile away, whenever a fox gets onto the Scrape. But this time we had yet another lesser black-backed gull, flying overhead and wondering about a mouthful of avocet chick. In a dramatic climax of kluuts, an avocet sprang into the air, trailing its silly legs, flying directly at the gull in a whirl of aggression. The gull lazily dropped a wing, slipping by easy stages down towards the great honeypot of the Scrape. Never think that being a Minsmere avocet is one of life's easier options.

ORTOLAN BUNTING

ON 3 May, Jeremy rang Birdline and told them that there was an ortolan bunting at Minsmere. That meant that within hours every twitcher in the country knew about it, for this is nothing less than a rare bird, and Birdline is how the hot news travels from one end of the country to the other. Some of these rarity hunters would drop everything and travel to Minsmere as fast as they could to see the bird and tick it the following morning. Others would shrug, mutter that an ortolan was 'a tart's tick' or a 'trash bird', and anyway, they didn't *need* it. That's twitchers for you.

I ring Birdline every week, as it happens. I speak to one of the organisers, Richard Millington. I pass the information on, in a spirit of reader service, in my weekly column in *The Times*: in response to my time-honoured query of 'what's about?', Richard will pass on such delights as the report of a Ross's goose. 'Possible first for Britain. But it's of unknown origin. That means it might be an escape.' And that, of course, means that it can't be ticked. Richard's information comes from observers all over the country; sometimes it even comes from bird reserve wardens.

But wardens have a bad reputation with twitchers. Many

believe, as I say, that a warden is a man who spends his entire day birdwatching, and who keeps all the rare birds to himself. He does this out of simple malice: so that he can, in twitcherspeak, 'grip them off'. To grip someone off is to see a bird someone else has missed (or 'dipped out on'), and this is a great teasing delight to twitching folk. The nature of the wardens' job will, I trust, become clear through these pages, so I will not rush to their defence here: suffice it to say that they do not actually have the time to spend all day, or often any part of the day, hunting for rarities.

But it is quite true that wardens will often keep rarities to themselves. This is not for the delights of gripping off, but because reserves are, by definition, pretty fragile places. To suffer a sudden influx of several hundred twitchers – more if there is a major rarity, more still if it is a first for Britain – is to create huge logistical problems. Carparking and overcrowding are the first of these, and yet they are the least of a warden's worries. The major problem is the possibility, even the likelihood, of disturbance to the birds. Disturbance of the rarity is not the problem: a warden is concerned about disturbance of the more humdrum birds, birds that some twitchers may regard with contempt, birds that are no more than tart's ticks, but which might be trying to breed and raise young. Minsmere in May is the last place and the last time you want a major disruption to the birds.

Jeremy has suppressed many a bird himself, but he told Birdline about the ortolan bunting because it was Thursday. There was a logic behind that, in Jeremy-fashion. Had he kept quiet about the bird, it would almost certainly have reached Birdline by Friday evening – bringing in a seething horde of twitchers on Saturday. And that was the first day of a Bank Holiday weekend. Even without twitchers, the place would be packed to the gunwales. Far better to have the twitchers through on Friday.

I was there the day before the twitchers, and Jeremy and I walked over to the spot where the ortolan 'was last seen': another great twitching phrase, that. We walked to the northern, inland corner of the Scrape, facing away from the Scrape itself. Oh! The thrill of the ortolan hunt. Twitchers are called twitchers because of the state of almost ungovernable excitement that seizes them when a rare bird is about and they have yet to clap binoculars on it. I wasn't exactly twitching with anticipation myself. For a start, an ortolan bunting is not actually the world's most exciting bird. It is not quite your classic LBJ – Little Brown Job – but it is pretty close. A yellowhammer (yellow bunting if you prefer) is far more colourful. Your ortolan, says the field guide, is remarkable for its buffish-pink underparts and yellow throat. Hm. That sounded like an LBJ with a little splash of yellow. Buffish-pink sounds like brownish-grey to me. Right, any LBJ out there with a little bit of yellow? Hallo? Hallo? Couldn't see it. Nope. Not there. Hiding. Dipped out: how ghastly. Would I ever have the chance to see one again? How was I going to cope with such a disappointment?

I turned and looked back across the Scrape. A little tern stopped, hung briefly in the air, and hit the water like a winged dagger. The sound of avocets kluuted over the water towards us. Bugger the ortolan.

On Friday, the twitchers arrived. It made a hard day for everyone working on the reserve. The carpark at Minsmere had been planned years ago with Sorensenian thoroughness, but the twitchers, overexcited and desperately eager to see their bird, refused to abide by the system and parked all over the place, abandoning their cars in Sheepwash Lane in their frantic need to see and tick the magic LBJ. 'Not much discipline,' Rob said crossly afterwards. It takes a lot to make Rob cross. Everyone was pleased when the twitchers went away: everyone was fairly pleased when the ortolan went away too.

Just about everyone you meet on the birding side of conservation – or on the conservation side of birding, come to that – wants to establish good and early that he or she is not a twitcher. What matters most are breeding birds, and the important numbers of overwintering birds. The Minsmere Big Five – avocet, nightjar, marsh harrier, bittern and little tern – are all far more important than any ortolan, more important than any lost, wandering stray. To think that birding is something to do with rare birds is a serious error of judgement. Most of the mega-rarities are freaks: wanderers blown across the ocean by weird weather conditions or drastically faulty navigation. I have seen a good few of Britain's mega-rarities myself, but never actually in Britain. It has always been on the other side of the Atlantic, or in Asia. The pursuit of lost souls does not excite me, and many of the rarities are common birds that have simply got hopelessly lost. They are interesting, but they do not matter, in the sense that breeding avocets matter.

Twitching is a branch of collection mania. It is a more civilised pursuit than shooting the birds and having them stuffed, which was the hobby of countless Victorians, and still is a passion over much of the Mediterranean, but twitchers are driven by the same raw acquisitive urge: they don't see birds, they *have* them. There is something trainspotterish about them, at their worst. Some of them are hopeless birders, relying on others to find the birds for them.

Others are superb field naturalists, and some are experts on bird movements and shifting populations, all fascinating aspects of avian ecology. Some twitchers are also very good people indeed. Everyone likes to see a nice bird: everyone likes an unusual bird, too. But the obsessive keeping of a list, the notion of charging the length and breadth of the country in pursuit of a tick – well, as Miss Jean Brodie said, for those that like that sort of thing, that is the sort of thing they like. There are more important things in birding than writing a list.

Oddly enough, the king of the twitchers is one of the least maniacal people you could wish to meet – at least, that is how he comes across. This is Ron Johns, and he works in senior management for the gas board. He could not tell you exactly how long his list is, in fact he rather prides himself on his vagueness on that score. When I met him in 1990, his total was reckoned at 482 by Lee Evans, and he is a fanatic if ever there was one, and a fanatic who keeps a list of other people's lists. He provides a regularly updated list of lists for the 400 Club, an informal group of twitchers who have passed that stunning total. 'The list phenomenon is something I have some misgivings about,' Ron said. 'There are people who don't want to see or listen to a bird if it isn't a major rarity. Redstarts, they'll say, are "trash birds". Unless it's a bluethroat they're not interested.'

Twitching has changed dramatically in recent years. At one stage, a list of 300 was regarded as a major achievement, and 400 was a crazy, mythical idea. Ron was the first to reach 400 and he now has 500 in his sights. There are two reasons for the dramatic changes: both are connected with the availability of information. These days, all major bookshops stock books packed with information on American birds and Siberian birds and many others that might stray to Britain. Before, even where such books existed, no bookshop would see the point in stocking them. But twitching is a growth market, and so is foreign birding travel. Secondly, the information flow about individual birds has changed out of all recognition. Before, birders relied on an informal grapevine to tell them when and where a rarity turned up, and also when it had vanished. Now there are two services that offer taped messages of the latest birding information, for a specific area or for rarities nationwide. Birdline is the market leader.

'If you had asked fifteen years ago if any would ever reach 500, I would have said definitely not,' Ron said. 'But now I am quite close. It would be nice to reach 500, and – God and finances willing – I hope to do so.' The expenses of twitching can be fierce, often involving the chartering of planes to places like the Scillies and Fair Isle. 'Chartering is much cheaper than paying a standard passenger fare, for a start,' Ron said. 'But I wouldn't seek to justify anyone travelling hundreds of miles to see a bird. All the same, people are entitled to do it. One can't say it's worthwhile – but it's a way of enjoying your birding.'

Ron is a very easygoing and affable man, and one wonders how a man with such a temperament could have led the field in a competitive business for so long. He said: 'I think deep down I am competitive. The very fact that I am still actively in pursuit of new birds after forty years of birding, that I will still travel across the country to see yellow warblers and other firsts for Britain in strange places – obviously I am competitive to an extent. But it's not the be-all and end-all of my life. I have other interests, I am passionate about Liverpool Football Club, I travel abroad a lot, and have even travelled in October, which is the peak month for rarities in Britain. And when there is no rarity to go and see, I am happy just to go to my cottage in north Norfolk and enjoy whatever birds happen to be about. There have been many times when I have been happy birding in one particular spot, most often north Norfolk ... and I have heard of a rarity and thought, I would much rather stay here. And sometimes I have stayed.' He smiled self-deprecatingly. 'But more often than not, I will go.'

Ron is a birder through and through. He is not a birder *because* he loves collecting, he is a birder *and* he loves collecting. He gives out a feeling of great contentment, of great enjoyment of life. I have met a good number of pro birders who know him, and all say he is a top-flight field naturalist.

All the same, the idea that birding is the task of finding rare birds is a nonsense. Shortly after the ortolan incident, Ian and I went to the Eel's Foot. Ian was still feeling a little bruised after that hectic ortolan Friday that preceded the usual hectic Bank Holiday weekend. He sighed heavily into his pint of Murphy's and said, 'People seem to have the idea that chasing rare birds is what it's all *about*. I've seen grannies sprinting across the reserve because they have heard there is a rare bird to see. They think that this is what they are supposed to do.' There is, in truth, something of the twitcher in Ian – but he is a lapsed twitcher, rather than a practitioner of the faith. One of the very good things about the sport of twitching is that it brings people in to birding and to conservation. That was something of the case with Ian. He had a Damascus Road conversion to a different faith when he was doing his first spell at Minsmere; still, as it were, doing his apprenticeship. 'I was with a bloke in North Hide, and he said, have you seen the teal? And I thought, *teal?* Where's the rare birds then? And then it hit me. What the hell's wrong with teal? So I spent the next half-hour watching teal, and it was amazing. It turned the tide for me. And after that, I was at Abernethy, in Scotland, where there just aren't any rare birds. There are a lot of *unusual* birds that are specific to the region – but that's your lot: a very small range of species. It was a case of enjoying them, or going mad. No, looking at common birds is great.'

Many twitchers had a similar Damascus Road experience at Tesco's carpark in Maidstone. This was the famous incident of the golden-winged warbler of 1989: a devastatingly rare bird in a ludicrously accessible place. Just about every twitcher in the country rolled up to see it: the bird attracted 3,000 people in a day. It was, veterans of that day tell me, a real horror show: desperate people with telescopes and binoculars charging about, pushing and shoving furiously and asking eternally 'Where was it last seen?' The futility, the frustration and the pettiness of it all rather got to some people, who resolved never to take part in a mass twitch again. The bubbles had gone out of it. Go to some lonely bit of water and look for teal instead.

There are all kinds of daft twitching stories, as you would expect, because the whole subject is fundamentally daft. There was the grey-cheeked thrush that arrived on the Scillies and was eaten by a ginger tom. There was another grey-cheeked thrush that arrived, exhausted from the windblown folly of its journey across the Atlantic, perched on the first rock it came to on the Scillies, was ticked by a handful of alert twitchers – and was then washed straight back into the sea and drowned.

'Well, I ticked it before it drowned,' said Rob mockingly. 'I mean there's got to be something wrong with that, hasn't there?'

There are also plenty of horror stories about twitchers. Jeremy is apt to recall a Montagu's harrier, one of Britain's rarest breeding birds. A lone male turned up at the reserve one year, and despite the absence of a female, it started building a nest in the reeds. One of the odd things about birds of prey, the fiercest birds in creation, is their readiness to abandon a nest. At the least sign of trouble, they are off, leaving their eggs, and sometimes even their chicks behind them.

Jeremy saw a pair of twitchers watch the Montagu's go down into the reeds, clearly onto a nest. They stood for a while convincing each other that this could not have been a marsh harrier, and arguing whether or not it could possibly have been a Monty. Meanwhile, the bird showed no sign of leaving the nest – *so the twitchers marched into the reedbed and flushed it out.* Jeremy is the kindest and most charitable man you could wish to meet. 'Is it surprising,' he said, 'that wardens are sometimes reluctant to inform twitchers about a rare bird?'

I asked Ron about this. He hadn't heard the story and was appalled. Twitchers, he said, had been a pretty ill-disciplined lot a few years back, but had made so much trouble for themselves among such people as Scilly farmers, that they had become very much a self-disciplining body. There are stories about pushy twitchers getting out of line and trespassing or disturbing birds, and receiving disciplinary measures from other twitchers. Some are said to have been so thoroughly disciplined that they have required hospital treatment.

However, you can't say that twitchers don't care about birds.

Flying in the Face of Nature

They care very much. They just have a funny way of showing it. 'All twitchers are conservationists at heart,' Ron said. Sir Peter Scott said: 'The first thing to do is to enjoy birds. And the second is to give up any idea that you can't do anything to help save them.' Twitchers are people who enjoy their birds, so good luck to them.

But all the same, bugger, as I believe I said before, the ortolan. After Ian and I had finished our pints, I walked over to Island Mere. A marsh harrier crossed the reedbed: a supreme master of laziness, wings carried in that indolent vee as it quartered the marsh, turned – flinging one ragged-rimmed wing skywards, dramatically dipping the other, revealing its stunning tricoloured markings – and crossed back again. It was a male, with that tricolour wing: Ian had told me in the Eel's Foot about one male that was not bigamous, as is the occasional custom among marsh harriers, but trigamous. I wondered if this outrageously handsome devil was that most famous of Minsmere harriers.

If I had been a twitcher, it would have been my sacred duty to say bugger the marsh harrier, I don't *need* marsh harrier. Trash bird. I must have that ortolan: where was it last seen? But I wasn't and I didn't. The trigamist dropped like a shuttlecock into the reeds.

SPARROWHAWK

IRDS eat birds. There is no getting away from it. It does not need the extreme example of the Kestrel with the Schedule One Diet to tell us that. Even in a normal year, without the exceptional conditions that produced that particular falcon of destruction, a number of rare birds, in which great numbers of manhours, not to mention money, have been invested, are going to get scoffed. A pair of sparrowhawks will kill around 500 birds in a breeding season. What do you do about this? Jeremy will, with reluctance, shoot the odd fox. But he will not shoot at a kestrel, no matter how rarified its diet: he will not even take a pot at that great hate of a thousand birdtable owners, the magpie. As for the marsh harriers and sparrowhawks, there is no question of controlling them. It would be, quite apart from anything else, illegal. And so birds, both common and rare, will continue to be killed and eaten, even – or especially – in the Eden of Minsmere. This is not a simple business.

One May afternoon – so much of the significant action in Minsmere takes place in this month – I was marching through the woods with Rob. It was back to the clipboard: the everpresent tool of Maytime. He was checking out 160 nestboxes. Nestboxes provide sites for birds that normally nest in holes in trees. If there are no holes in trees, a nestbox provides a chance for holenesters to move in and fill their ecological niche. Even if there are holes, the accessibility of nestboxes gives you a chance to keep an eye on the birds: a pleasure for people with gardens, and a useful research tool for conservationists. Rob was checking how many of the nestboxes had been taken up, by which species, and what stages they had reached in the task of raising a brood.

None of the nestbox birds is rare. Mostly, they were blue tits and great tits, with a few coal tits thrown in: familiar birdtable birds. The nestboxes do not give any degree of control of the environment, but they help to understand it. Any change in the pattern would be worth investigating: a drastic drop in the population would be cause for worry; a dramatic rise would have you scratching your head wondering what you, or the climate, was doing right. The idea was to gather facts: though of course, no fact, especially not in conservation, is unambiguous. Everything needs to be evaluated in terms of everything else. But the more facts you have, the more likely you are to come to a proper understanding of your habitat, and that is why throughout May everyone I saw at Minsmere was marching about with a clipboard. Every ecological and conservational strategy starts with the fact-gatherers in muddy boots.

The data about nestboxes are used for Minsmere's own records, and also go to the British Trust for Ornithology. The BTO builds up a huge and ever more complex mosaic of facts and figures: local and national trends can be understood by anyone capable of interpreting this vast complex of information. Conservationists may start out with good, caring sentiments, but that is nothing without hard facts. Facts are used to improve and understand the environment: they are also weapons against destruction. 'I think it's *vital* to contribute to that sort of research,' Rob said.

Rob moved through the woods with a great air of bustle, as always. 'Redstart, hear it? No, I really like to contribute to this research, it is a very satisfying business. Holly blue. Let's see if it's a common blue. No, holly blue. Grey underneath, black dots on a grey background with a blue suffusion. A common blue has red spots all the way down the back of the hindwing. Corsican pine this one. Not a Scots. Scots have a reddish, tawny bark.' There is a great, galloping content in all of Rob's busyness. And all his massive cheerfulness comes from three or four hours' sleep a night: in this, the peak time of the year, there is so much going on the length and breadth of Minsmere that sleep must be taken in odd snatches, and lucky you are to get that. The thirty-hour shift is by no means uncommon. 'He slept namoore than dooth a nyghtyngale,' wrote Chaucer of the squire. The same is true of everyone at Minsmere in jugjug season.

'All these facts go into the reserve monitoring programme,' Rob said. 'You want to try to monitor the effect management is having on the place. It also goes to the Suffolk Ornithological Group. It is important to get an idea of the general trend.' We approached the next nestbox and Rob lifted the lid. A bird flew up almost into his face. Rob peered in, unperturbed, muttering, 'Seven . . . eggs. Great tit *on*. Number 14. Right. That's enough. Don't need anything more.'

I was beginning to get accustomed to Rob's casual way with nesting birds. At the next stop, the hen refused to move at all. 'Come on, dear,' Rob said. 'Out you go.' No response. So he slid a hand into the box and goosed the bird off the nest. She flew off a few feet, perched on a branch above our heads and cursed us with every obscene cheep she knew. Again, Rob counted the eggs. I looked in and saw the exquisite cup of moss with its eleven tiny masterpieces. 'They always go straight back on,' Rob said airily. Should it need saying, this is not recommended behaviour for any amateur, and with many species it is not only potentially disastrous, it is also illegal. 'If there was any chance of disrupting them, I wouldn't dream of doing this,' Rob said. 'Raptors, they are very susceptible to disturbance, and if you just get close to a nest, they are likely to abandon. But I've never known tits do anything other than pop straight back on.'

We marched on, passing from nestbox to nestbox: some of them empty, but a gratifying number of them full of tiny, perfect eggs. Some of the boxes carried great scars: it looked as if someone had been attacking them with a chisel. And in fact, someone had: a great spotted woodpecker. Within the limits of their treetop environment, the great spots are opportunistic birds, and will take nestlings as well as invertebrates. Some of the boxes had been protected with a facing of metal around the hole, making it beakproof. But these are smart birds: they are quite capable of battering their way in through the unprotected sides. It is a big job, but woodpeckers are gluttons for work: and besides, getting on for a dozen fledglings makes a meal worth working for.

Several times, Rob opened a nestbox and found only a few scraps of moss in the bottom, nothing more. A nest had been started, and would never be finished. Why? There were a number of possible reasons, but the most likely was that the bird has been killed: like as not, by sparrowhawk. As Jeremy had pointed out, with such delight, there were three pairs of sparrowhawk nesting on the reserve: that adds up to an awful lot of songbirds. And blue tits are special favourites: for a blue tit, a sparrowhawk is a purpose-built engine of destruction. A male sparrowhawk especially: the females are bigger and will take blackbirds and even bigger birds. Stock dove, jay, lapwing, partridge, even pheasant have been recorded. Their taking of bigger stuff tends to happen by chance, often when an injured bird comes their way. They cannot carry such birds off. When they kill to feed their young, particularly early in their breeding season, it is the small birds that get hammered. The male does all the hunting from egg-laying until the young are half-grown, and he is a small bird specialist. The female then assists him, and she takes bigger birds.

Sparrowhawks kill birds in enormous numbers. And they are definitely on the increase: to have three pairs, a record number of birdkillers on the finest bird reserve in the country, looks on the face of it to be a recipe for total disaster. Sparrowhawks are in the process of recovering from the drastic effects of pesticide poisoning. They have been fighting back gradually since the mid-'60s, but it is only recently that they have made much show in the arable counties of eastern England. Sparrowhawks went virtually extinct over the green desert countryside, but now you see them all over the place: a sudden, dashing flight as a bird disappears into a wood, a leisurely glide over the trees. The silhouette is quite unmistakable, if you have a moment or two to see it clearly. People confuse them with kestrels, but kestrels are falcons, with slim, pointed wings. Sparrowhawk wings are short and round, designed for rapid charges in narrow spaces, between trees: a bird

Sparrowhawk

designed to strike from cover. And across Minsmere, again and again through the spring you hear that sudden, wild catyowl: a song of triumph for the returning killers.

It is a strange anomaly: that the fiercest animals, those at the very top of the food chain, are the most vulnerable. For a start, there are far fewer of them. A moment's thought makes this clear. You need an enormous number of caterpillars to service one blue tit family, so there are far fewer blue tits than there are caterpillars. The same holds true for blue tits and sparrowhawks. This makes the top birds of prey extremely sensitive to direct persecution. You can shoot blue tits and have very little effect on the local population. But if you shoot sparrowhawks, you can wipe them out remarkably quickly. To make things more difficult still, even without the DDT, a top predator's breeding strategy is not designed to cope with predation on itself – and that is roughly what direct persecution, at the hands of gamekeepers, amounts to. Gamekeepering, in the traditional sense of blasting away at every raptor that dares show its head, has very little effect on the gamebirds you are trying to protect – for after all, prey species are designed to cope with predation, and anyway, sparrowhawks seldom take anything as big as partridge, let alone pheasant. Traditional gamekeepering gives a little help to gamebirds, but it is catastrophic for raptors. Call that Gamekeepers' Error.

Thus sparrowhawks have struggled for years against persecution, and the effect of DDT poisoning was close to disaster. In the north and west, the population was halved: in the south and east, they were virtually wiped out. But now it seems that, in the course of half-a-dozen seasons, they have gone from unusual to almost common in these areas. Minsmere had never known nesting sparrowhawk before 1983. A single pair bred most years after that. There were two pairs in 1988, and the three pairs in 1990 were a total delight to all.

The reappearance looks dramatic and sudden – and it is. Exponential growth is a fundamental principle of ecology. Once a certain level has been reached, numbers start to increase very rapidly. Wherever a sparrowhawk could make a living, it seemed there was one ready to move in. The population was doubling and trebling before our eyes. Exactly the same thing is happening with the human population of the world – and that is probably the major ecological problem facing the world today. Exponential growth can be as frightening as it is gratifying.

But it is worth cheering the exponential growth of the sparrowhawk population. True, it is a tough person who can laugh off those pathetic little scraps of moss in the abandoned nestboxes. I got a shoal of distressed letters when I wrote a piece in praise of the returning sparrowhawk in *The Times*, a piece for which the subs wrote the provocative headline 'Hurrah! The killer is back'. The letters ranged from the indignant to the mildly distraught. Well, if you are a nice person and you enjoy the birds in your garden, it is sad to see a sparrowhawk grabbing one of your birdtable favourites out of the air and plucking it alive before the kitchen window. Several readers said they wanted to interfere, to take sides, to chase the sparrowhawk off.

And I sympathise. When I see the pair of mistle thrush in my garden trying to commit assault and battery on magpies five times their size, I cannot help but cheer for the thrush ('Go on! See the bugger off!'). I know intellectually that my concern is ill-founded, but birding is an emotional business as well as an intellectual one. The RSPB gets more letters on magpies than it does on anything else. Letters range from the distressed and bewildered to the downright abusive: these horrible city slickers, with their correspondent plumage and their mirthless giggles, are eating *all* the eggs and *all* the babies of *all* the lovely songbirds. And there is something particularly horrible about nestrobbing. It seems so stunningly unfair: worse, the sin of cannibalism, a banquet of infants. The RSPB had always replied to these letters by stating that it is a truism of ecology that the prey population controls the number of predators, and not vice versa. But there are so many magpie letters that they wondered if this long-established truth were really, in this case, still a truth. Perhaps magpies really were cutting a savage swathe through the songbird population.

However, all the facts and figures are on the magpies' side. The mass of data gathered by professionals like Rob, and by top amateurs across the country, seemed to prove that magpie fear was unnecessary. The Common Bird Census stated unambiguously that year after year, the same numbers of songbirds were breeding. Magpies and sparrowhawks have increased, unquestionably – but not at the expense of the songbird population. In fact, further research demonstrated that where magpies had increased most rapidly, songbirds had also increased.

It seems hard to believe, does it not? You would think that the breeding sparrowhawk pair's annual 500 would take an awful lot of making up. But the figures do not lie. If you examine them, they do, indeed, indicate that certain small birds are losing ground, declining in numbers. There are fewer and fewer tree sparrows, corn buntings and linnets, but this is nothing to do with sparrowhawks and magpies. These are birds associated with traditional agriculture, and changes in farming techniques have affected them. They suffer from a combination of things: the loss of hedgerow weeds, and the increasing use of pesticides. But classic sparrowhawk fodder, like tits and starlings and thrushes, is going great guns.

What does regulate populations? There was a hideous experiment carried out by a group of ecologists now known as the Maine Gunners. They were researching ecological relationships in a wood in Maine and their experimental method involved the shooting of all the songbirds in their wood. First they censused the singing males, found 148, and then they shot them to bits. They shot a total of 302 – and *still* the woods were full of song. This indicates that there was a huge surplus population of males just waiting for the chance to breed. The number of breeding birds, it would seem, does not necessarily indicate the total population of birds, but the number of breeding slots available: the number of territories.

There was a rather less horrific experiment carried out in Oxfordshire on great tits. The researchers relied on very close and very accurate observation, rather than shotguns. Their findings indicated that in areas where there is a decent sparrowhawk population, then yes, a good number of great tits get eaten. Young birds, in particular, were taken by the sparrowhawks. In areas without sparrowhawks, a lot more young birds survived – until the autumn. Then the scarcity of food began to put pressure on the population. Young birds, inexperienced at coping with meagre resources, suffered particularly. With or without sparrowhawks, about the same number of birds survived to the following spring. If the sparrowhawks don't get their annual tithe of 500, the cold does the job instead. The number of birds that survives is controlled by the amount of food available over the winter – not by the presence or absence of predators.

Sparrowhawks or no sparrowhawks, every great tit breeding-ground suffers the same enormous losses. And with or without sparrowhawks, the areas sustain a roughly similar breeding population year after year. The tits fill the breeding slots that are available, and thus they propagate their immortal genes. Sparrow-hawks kill day after day, but the songbirds sing on.

And every spring, they produce new birds in quite prodigious quantities. Time and again, Rob and I found ourselves gazing into a nestbox with a little moss cup that contained a dozen eggs. A familiar corner of the woods can be transformed in an instant when a clutch of blue tits all leave the nest at once and take the place over: a sight of great confusion and delight. There seem sometimes to be hundreds of them: brave little bundles preparing to face the sparrowhawks and winters of outrageous fortune. How many will survive to breed? One? Two? As many as that? But the answer is always the same: enough. At least, there have always been enough so far; but the problem is not the way in which sparrowhawks control the conditions under which breeding will take place. Mankind does that.

It is as certain as anything in life that more offspring are born than can possibly survive and breed. This is true of blue tits and of man: it is, if you like, yet another aspect of the meaning of life. This understanding is central to Darwinism. The conventional notion is that Charles Darwin had a Eureka experience on the Galapagos Islands. He saw the finches and the tortoises, and bingo! he wrote *The Origin of Species*.

Darwin did, indeed, have a Eureka experience, but it came some years after his visit to Galapagos. It came from his reading of Thomas Malthus, and his work on the dynamics of human popula-tions. Malthus wrote that more children are born than possibly survive to breed. And Darwin saw that this must be true of the populations of all other animals on the planet: in that moment all his research and his travels came into clear focus. Those animals that manage to produce surviving offspring are likely to do so because of some advantage they possess over the failures, and this advantageous variation will be passed on to the next generation.

Sparrowhawk

If increasingly long necks provide successive advantages to those who inherit them, then necks will get longer, until you reach the limits of usefulness of a long neck as a survival aid – and you have a giraffe, or a heron.

I have referred to both blue tits and sparrowhawks as masterpieces. This is true enough: but in one sense, it is quite irrelevant. Evolution is not about the pursuit of perfection: it is about survival. To be more precise, it is about the production of surviving, breeding offspring. If a design can bring about the successful rearing of young, then it is good *enough*. Evolution does not pursue perfection for its own sake. There are, indeed, designs that look like perfection, but there are other constructions that look quite absurdly jerryrigged. No one could call a Canada goose a master of digestive economy, or a triumph of design. Canada geese exist by grazing, but they have a slight problem. They cannot digest grass, not properly: not as a horse or a cow or even a rabbit can.

The four-footed grazers can digest the cellulose in grass, but geese cannot. Horses carry a huge bag of a stomach about with them, and brew the grass in a great bacteria-laden soup. Cows have a complexus of stomachs that allows them to chew the stuff twice. Rabbits get the most out of the grass they eat by eating it twice: they eat their own dung. But these options are not available for geese. Lugging heavy bags around does not go well with flying, so Canada geese have evolved a thoroughly inefficient means of dealing with grass, one that makes poor sense in time and motion terms. They eat enormous quantities of grass, and pass it through their systems very quickly, extracting what small amounts of goodness they can. The expression 'loose as a goose' does not exist for the rhyme alone. In a pure engineering sense, Canada geese are a dreadful piece of design. But that does not matter: the design is good *enough*. It works. That is good enough for any goose, any gosling, any bird or any other living creature.

Perfection is not the point, but all the same, evolution can produce something pretty close. You would find it hard to beat the design of a sparrowhawk: the combination of speed, stealth and manoeuvrability in that short, broad wing and agile brain is one of evolution's great achievements. To see a sparrowhawk barrelling through a wood and jinking at breakneck speed through the treetrunks, is one of the finest sights in British birding. Sparrow-hawks can even fly inverted for brief moments: those wonder-fully lethal grappling irons they have for feet can strike from just about any angle. Sparrowhawks are killers, and they are superbly designed for the task, but they do not control the destiny of their prey populations. That is controlled by the number of breeding slots available, by the carrying capacity of the land. And the land is controlled not by sparrowhawks and magpies, but by mankind. The sparrowhawks and magpies, accused of countless crimes against conservation, emerge without a stain on their characters.

Rob and I had checked out 160 nestboxes, and just over 100 of them were occupied. The average number of eggs was nine: a lot of birds would soon be emerging. This was not the total population of the wood, nor even of that section of the wood: this was a mere representative sample, those birds that had chosen custom-built nestboxes instead of traditional holes. The occupants of the very last box had already hatched. 'Eight young,' Rob muttered. 'Naked and blind.'

I looked in when he had finished. How absurdly, how unbeliev-ably small they all were: tiny, ugly little bags of flesh, a pulse beating visibly in each one. They seemed to be nothing but a horrid pink beak and a sightless bootbutton of an eye. You could pick the lot up with two fingers and a thumb: little scraps of life. We left them to the sparrowhawks and the winters. Would even one survive? But sure as eggs are eggs, the woods were going to be full of song and songbirds next spring. And, I hoped, sparrowhawks.

CARRION CROW

THE last train of the day gets in to Saxmundham station at half past ten in the evening. Eric was there to meet me, and he was very amused when I told him I was to spend the night birdracing. It seemed to him a preposterous way to spend one's time. I had no quarrel with that assessment at all. It seemed completely daft to me as well. The daftness was, in a way, the point.

We drove to the reserve, and along Sheepwash Lane, beneath the trees. A great white shape materialised in front of us, and then vanished. For an instant, I thought I had seen my great rogue bird of Britain: barn owl. It is confession time: I had never seen barn owl in Britain. Damn it, they are not rare, and I had been in the right place at the right time often enough. But there it was: everyone has some rogue bird or other, some really pretty common bird he has somehow never got around to seeing. A tart's tick, in twitcherspeak. A friend of mine, a lifelong birder, was thirty-six years old before he saw a dipper. I remember seeing a barn owl in Africa: the ghostly white shape in the middle of the road, taking wing like a gigantic and fearsome moth. But an English barn owl – the same species, as it happens – had, infuriatingly, always eluded me.

And it was still eluding me, for this was a tawny owl. Tawnies look pale in the headlights, and are often mistaken for barn owls. A real barn owl is not pale but sheet white, and quite unmistakable. No one who has seen a real barn owl is ever in any doubt about it. Well, pleasant enough to see the tawny, and besides, perhaps the birdrace would be the night on which I would break my duck, if such an expression is permissible on a bird reserve.

Eric stopped outside Jeremy's bungalow. I opened the door, and filled the car with sound: a Minsmere cacophony. 'That bird's working late tonight,' Eric said.

'Nightingale,' I said shamelessly, and swaggered off to knock on Jeremy's door.

'Ullo,' he said. 'Hear that nightingale! Coffee?'

The others, he said, would be along a little after midnight. They were going to check a barn owl site on the way to Minsmere. Huh, I thought. 'The others' were a band of four birders from the Suffolk Wildlife Trust, and they were taking part in a birdrace to raise money for the Trust. They had managed to borrow a Saab from a kindly sponsoring local garage, and planned to race around Suffolk with it. The race, sometimes known as 'a sponsored twitch', is a deeply nonsensical way of spending an entire day. The idea is to stay awake for twenty-four hours and, in that time, to see as many different species of bird as possible. You get sponsored for every species you record: the point is the nonsense, the fun and the lolly. It is also, incidentally, a first-class test of birding skills. Jeremy had agreed to escort the group for the first eight hours of their twitch. A birdracing team could have no better start than eight hours at Minsmere with Jeremy Sorensen.

Jeremy is a veteran birdracer. For some years, he was involved in an annual competition, in which a team from *Country Life* magazine would take on a team from the Fauna and Flora Preservation Society. The latter, which included Bill Oddie, was emphatically a team of twitchers. Jeremy was never on a losing side. The game is about organisation as much as birding.

Jeremy was involved in establishing the rules and conventions of birdracing. The crucial one is that you don't have to see a bird: hearing it will do just as well. That way, there is no temptation to charge into the bushes to flush the bird into sight. A further rule is that all three members of the team must see or hear the bird, while a fourth keeps the score.

It is a pleasant excuse to be completely frivolous about birds and birding, and to test out your fieldcraft. And it turned out that the night was a virtuoso performance of the superlative birding skills of J. Sorensen, the man with radar tracker ears: it was a privilege, an education and an inspiration to observe him in action.

We sat in the bungalow, drinking coffee and listening to Rachmaninov. Jeremy has a good collection of CDs, and a decided weakness for late nineteenth-century piano music. But there was a lot of competition that night, even for the boy Serge: *twit twit twit jug jug jug*. The music came to an end, and we allowed the nightingale to take over centre stage. We sat, chatting quietly and enjoying the flamboyant cadences of the only bird that makes Rachmaninov sound shy and retiring. Fabulous noise.

The birding team arrived at twenty past midnight. They were Dudley Shepherd, a builder, Reg Etheridge, who worked in building supplies, Roy Green, a welder, and the recorder, Graham Peck, who worked in pest control. And they had missed their barn owl. 'Well,' said Jeremy. 'There's bird number one singing away outside.' Graham put pencil to clipboard for the first time that night and wrote '00.21 Nightingale'. The twitch was on. Jeremy led us out into the night. He had a clear plan of action in his head. The secret of birdracing is to visit as many different habitats as possible. After all, you are not going to get a moorhen in deep woodland nor a nightingale on a saline lagoon. Minsmere, with its wide range of habitats, all closely packed together and managed intensively for birds, is the best place in Britain for this arcane pursuit. Is the money-raising the reason or the excuse for this night of madness? I wondered, as we turned towards the carpark and the Scrape. Don't even try to answer. The night's second bird spoke to us: '*Peewit*,' it said. 'Lapwing,' said everyone else. We had just reached the edge of the Scrape when we heard bird number three: that surprisingly soft, far-carrying sound drifted towards us from the reedbed. '*Om*,' said the bittern, sending his timeless mantraic grunt outwards. '*Om*.'

Jeremy wanted both to find as many birds as possible for the men of Suffolk and to give himself some wholesome amusement.

Accordingly, he led us to the Scrape. He had never birdraced the Scrape in pitch darkness and was curious as to how this would work out. Sedge warblers sedgewarbled all round the reedbed as we headed to a hide: nightingales are not the only songbirds that sing at night. A ringed plover gave its sweet disyllabic call: no, I wouldn't have got that one without Jeremy. Two minutes later, a redshank, an incurably jumpy bird, sounded its triple-note alarm. That set off an avocet: *kluut!* Seven birds, two of them Schedule One. Not bad for a start: that is Minsmere for you. The place doesn't let you down.

We entered the East Hide, and opened the shutters. The Scrape, a sight I had gazed at for hours that year already, looked strange and distinctly spooky. Not that it was dark: far from it. It was eerily lit up, for Sizewell never sleeps. The lights of the power station construction site were so bright, it was hard to look at them directly. Surrounded by darkness, it looked like the closing scene in *Close Encounters*. The work continued on Sizewell B, and the air, even at one in the morning, was filled with clanking and groaning. Sound carries better at night, which is why bitterns boom in the dark. The sounds of Sizewell fill your ears, sinister and spooky. No one goes to Minsmere to make good bird recordings any more: there is too much background noise.

But at least the birder has his ears, and with them a brain that can try to filter out the noise of Sizewell. A short, angry cry from a coot. Then a rather nasal quack: Jeremy called a gadwall at once. Oh, really? The others all took his word for it. They were all good birders: good enough to know that they were in the presence of a master. What was there to do but lie back and enjoy it? A black-headed gull quarked: then a honk from a greylag goose. Jeremy was calling it while the rest of us were working through the possibilities. But the next scream was too much: not a black-headed gull scream, said Jeremy, but a common tern scream. I began to feel like Butch Cassidy. He wonders how the trackers could possibly follow him in the dark. He turns to Sundance and says: 'How can they do that? I couldn't do that, could you do that?'

A bird roost at night is not the most sleepful place in the world. There is constant wariness, constant shifting of position, constant little niggles and arguments. A mallard quacked, and amid yet another volley of screams, Jeremy distinguished sandwich tern and little tern. I couldn't do that. *Ah-honk! Ah-honk!* Canada goose: yes, I *could* do that. That made it sixteen species in the first hour, but in birdracing, the early scores are illusory. Many will be birds that you are likely to see or hear a dozen times over in the course of twenty-four hours. Successful birdracing depends on picking up all the common birds. After all, this is the one day of the year on which a house sparrow counts the same as a bittern. An oystercatcher gave his sharp whistle, and then, wonder of wonders, and for the first time that night, we actually clapped eyes on a bird. A pair of shelduck flew over on whistling wings.

We left the hide and marched on around the Scrape. Jeremy called the whistle of a teal drake, and distinguished effortlessly between reed and sedge warbler. He claimed a shoveler from some enigmatic grunt: nobody argued. Then the endless reel of a grasshopper warbler: now that was a really good one to get. Jeremy, of course, knew where it ought to have been, that was why he led us to that corner. 'Now we'll go along to the rhododendron tunnel and get a Cetti,' he said.

On the way, we heard the sharp *kee-vit* call of a tawny owl. This was another revelation: I confess that I had always thought tawnies restricted themselves to that Hammer horror film sound: *oo-oo-oo*. But tawnies, though they never say '*tu-whit, tu-whoo*', do say both '*tu-whit*' *and* '*tu-whoo*'. The second is their territorial acclamation: the first is a contact call, and is normally transcribed as '*kee-vit*' rather than '*tu-whit*'. I had once been informed that this was the sound made by a rabbit. It is rather an odd noise for an owl to make, I agree, but how I swallowed the rabbit story I will never know. Still, foolish though I felt, at least Minsmere continued to open my eyes and my ears.

We walked to Cetti's Alley by way of a moorhen, cormorant and mute swan: mute swans are not mute after all. The Cetti's warblers were in full cry exactly where Jeremy said they would be. He suggested a mnemonic for the song was '*je suis Cetti*'. We listened to the simple, immensely vigorous song for a few minutes, and then recollected that we were not in Minsmere to enjoy ourselves. It was two o'clock, and we had twenty-seven species on our list, as Jeremy led us up, away from the Scrape and onto the heath.

There was one principal reason for visiting the heath at night,

Flying in the Face of Nature

and that was nightjar. But as we walked on, the nightingales sang all around us, each striving to outdo the other for volume and for glory. If females really choose their mates by the beauty of the song, what problems they must face in making the choice. But as we reached the fringes of the heath, the sounds of the nightingales following us still, we heard the eeriest sound of them all: one of the strangest and least birdlike sounds made by any bird anywhere in the world.

Nightjar. It was a moment that transfixed you. There we were, six loonies wandering around the heath in the dark, and the air was filled with seven voices: the very essence of a May nighttime. We were supposed to be dashing about all over the place collecting birds, but no one could walk away from this. Four nightingales, two of them unbelievably close, and three nightjars: an unearthly concert of jarring, stirring sounds. The time had just passed half-past two; in another sense it was standing still. The nightingales jugjugged to each other in their most competitive way, while the nightjars churred unceasingly. Were they, too, competing? Certainly they seemed to be vying with each other in the length, volume and pitch of that weird and penetrating trill.

I remember someone once asking me which bird sounded like a computer. That is an odd, rather inaccurate comparison. My wordprocessor just makes impatient bleeps to tell me I am behaving like a moron. But no other bird makes a sound weird enough to bring the thought of computers to mind. My mother tells me she used to hear nightjars in Kings Heath Park, a place that was once on the edge of Birmingham, and is now close to the middle. Will they ever go back there, I wonder? Some of the London commons look perfectly suitable: surely nightjars churred their nights away in London before the city grew so large and obstreperous. But they have gone from those places; they are declining across the country. To hear them, it is best to go out into the wilds in the pitch black with a bunch of loonies – you must, in truth, be something of a loony yourself. I have no problem there. Maybe the real loonies are those who have never tramped a heath at half-past two in the morning, and stood transfixed by that chorus of seven voices: voices that sound like a breath of sanity.

Jeremy wanted the men of Suffolk to find a long-eared owl, which would be a very useful tick indeed. He led us to a spot just forty yards from a known nest, and we stopped, sat and listened. We needed just the faintest murmur of a long-eared owlish voice, a voice described as more cooing than hooting. We sat there, silently, ears straining. Way across the heath, a fox was baying, a truly atavistic sound. Perhaps 200 years ago everyone in Britain would have been familiar with that sound. Now, hearing that strange, surprisingly undoglike voice carrying across the heathland, I felt a terrible townee for finding the sound so unfamiliar. Yet this, like the tawny owl, was just a matter of learning and listening: now I regularly hear foxes from my bedroom window. In my pre-Minsmere days, I would have written this off as a dog (or a rabbit for all I know) or, more likely still, not have heard it at all.

The mammals were surprisingly vocal that night: perhaps I mean surprisingly vocal every spring night. We heard the barking of red deer, and the weird jaylike screaming of muntjac. The song of the rabbit was about the only thing missing. If you spend a night relying almost totally on your ears, strange sounds in wild places will never pass your ears unheeded again.

There was, however, not a coo to be heard from the long-ear. It would have been rather a coup to tick it, but there you go. We gave it every opportunity, waiting, getting surprisingly cold at this, the lowest ebb of the night, the time the Gestapo knock on the door. But, ridiculously enough, it would soon be getting light. The birds of the night would soon be packing up, and the long, relentless hours of the daytime birds would be beginning: eighteen hours of non-stop singing to be got through before the late May dusk. And so we headed down to the deciduous woodland. Jeremy had performed a series of aural conjuring tricks: now as we waited for the dawn chorus to begin, we prepared ourselves for his masterpiece.

At quarter-past three a pheasant gave his shattering peacocklike crow. Moments later, the first songbird of the day began: faint, distant, almost inaudible: a distant snatch of a lovely song. *Chirrup*: redstart. The day was gathering pace again. Jeremy had chosen this particular patch of woodland as part of his great plan, and, as if pre-arranged, a woodcock rose out of the pale grey morning and began a roding flight, beating the bounds of his territory while uttering a series of squeaks, grunts and groans. He was indefatigable. Every five minutes, he would make a metronomic reappearance, fooling us – or me, at any rate – into thinking we had a new species, before croaking mockingly and vanishing again. Dawn was breaking, four o'clock was approaching.

Cuckoo! I had no problem with diagnosis here. Then a robin, greeting the day with his pleasantly gentle territorial acclamation. The first robin immediately started every other robin within earshot: as we have seen, these are not birds that like to get left behind in the race for territorial announcements. We were racing for fun: they were racing as a matter of life and death. Within minutes, the woods were full of that sweet and gentle song. No other bird was awake: it was a single species chorus of robin. A hard job, being a robin. The hours are terrible.

A woodpigeon cooed, not a great coup, true, but all the same, on this day a woodie is worth the same as a long-eared owl. And then at last, a song thrush, clearly feeling that the robins had held centre stage for quite long enough. And things started to quicken again: a wren's song exploded from a brake of bramble, a blackbird fluted from overhead. Jeremy picked out the rambling cadences of garden warbler. Chiffchaff: an easy one. Then a mistle thrush, giving us a long football-rattle alarm call. Jeremy then picked out blackcap: whose song, some say, is as glorious as a nightingale's. I'd place it as a thoroughly acceptable second myself, but who is competing? Apart from the robins? Apart from every single male in the wood? Apart from the six loonies listening to all in their pursuit of the elusive goals of birdracing?

Jeremy then claimed a treecreeper. I had learnt their contact call: a high, unbelievably thin whistle, something I had been hearing all my life without ever noticing it. But their song was beyond me: I could not prise it from the background of static, robins and chiffchaffs and song thrushes all round. The men of Suffolk swore they could hear it, and ticked it. A jackdaw called 'jack', and then a great tit began to shower the woods with its ringing double-note. It is the easiest song of them all to recognise. Great tits have, it seems, several million different variations of song and call, but this basic version, the 'teacher' song, ('*teacher, teacher*', calls the bird) does not need the Sorensens of the world as interpreters.

Then lesser whitethroat: this was a tricky one. The song is like a yellowhammer's, but not quite, a little bit of bread, but no ventilation of the cheese question at all. A chaffinch chimed in, and then the cheery whistle of starling. Then a real yellow-hammer, singing '*a little bit of bread and no cheeeese*', just as it is supposed to. Then a spotted flycatcher, another Sorensen special. I neither saw nor heard it myself.

At last, we turned and walked back in the direction of the carpark. A party of stock doves flew overhead and were ticked without worry. 'Listen!' said Jeremy, for about the 300th time in the past five hours. This time, it was a nuthatch. An alleged nuthatch, anyway.

'I don't believe it,' I said. 'You're just teasing now.'

Jeremy chuckled: 'Listen. Piercing whistle, way off. Now. And now.'

It was months before I got that bird sorted out, for I never heard Jeremy's. It happened the following February, when I heard a clear, sumptuous whistle from the top of a tree in the heart of a snow-covered wood. The sound filled the white spaces and in deep winter, it filled me with thoughts of May and Minsmere. And a few weeks later, a pair nested in a treehole at the bottom of my garden, and filled every morning with a wonderful range of whistled phrases. The other birders decided they could hear Jeremy's nuthatch – I mean no vulgar cynicism here, merely that I found the bird impossible. Still, the whistling in the snow might have seemed less sweet had I managed to hear it that morning in May.

Then a goldcrest: the highest, tiniest, squeakiest song of them all. It is so high that some people cannot hear it all: it is close to the upper limits of human hearing. Goldcrests must be the most overlooked birds in Britain. In some woods, they are as common as robins, but they are tiny, they sing a tiny song, and they live in the canopy, out of sight and mind. Once Jeremy had taught me the song, it was as if he had performed a conjuring trick that affected every wood I walked in: like a rabbit from a hat, scores of goldcrest appeared from the leaves, squeaking and chattering, and occasionally flashing into sight with that bright little Mohican haircut. Perhaps that is one of the most appealing things of all about song: to understand a call is almost to be a magician, calling the birds into being.

Flying in the Face of Nature

But these thoughts came to me later, for after this long night in Minsmere, no walk would ever be quite the same again. My curiosity about songs and calls and barking and baying became a fact of daily life, whether I was walking to the train station listening for willow warbler, or walking in the African bush with my ears open for the wild cry of the fish eagle. We marched on across Minsmere, bagging a feral pigeon, a sordid but useful tick, and then the sharp ratatat of a woodpecker. Great spotted, Jeremy said, differentiating it from the lesser by the nature of its ratatat-ting. We swung seawards, collecting herring gull and lesser black-backed gull. A dunnock sang its quiet and pretty song from a bush. A crow flew by, and Dudley the builder somehow managed to miss it. That meant it was untickable, but it is not the worst bird in the world to miss. No one dared to miss some of Jeremy's more esoteric snatches of song, but carrion crow – it was socially acceptable to miss a crow. A great crested grebe was visible and unmistakable far below us on Island Mere, and then a marsh harrier (counting the same as the feral pigeon) glided away from us over the reedbeds.

It was not until 5.12 that we had the first willow warbler: I had not realised that they were such slugabeds. A linnet followed, and a heron flew overhead in its relentlessly purposeful manner. And then Jeremy performed another conjuring trick, calling a lesser spotted woodpecker: a totally different drumming to the greater, he insisted. Oh really? 'It's easy when you get used to it,' Jeremy insisted, laughing at my cynicism. I don't know about easy, but there is a difference right enough, as I learnt from listening, first to recordings and later to real birds. The sound of the lesser is softer and more sustained: the great is rapid and staccato. There has to be a difference: there is *supposed* to be a difference, because both birds drum to proclaim territory. There is absolutely no point at all in territorial acclamation unless it is clearly distinguishable from the acclamations of all other species. Woodpeckers make spaced-out, single thwocks when they are feeding or making nestholes. They only perform a drum solo for territorial reasons. It is a more martial sound than the gentle song of a robin, but the meaning is exactly the same: a personal bugle call. A whitethroat/sorethroat gave its own scratchy bugle call from the depths of a scratchy thicket of bramble.

Carrion Crow

This was prime ticking time, and the birds were coming at us thick and fast, rather as they did at Tippi Hedren in the Hitchcock movie: swallow, blue tit, coal tit, the first magpie, a swift overhead. We looped back towards Sheepwash Lane, aiming to make a pass across the Scrape, and now I must record my sole contribution to the night's birdcollecting. Jeremy paused, looking a touch puzzled. 'There *ought* to be long-tailed tit here,' he said, mildly peeved that the birds were not acting exactly as per programme.

'There!' I said. Well, not even I could fail to recognise that flying stick-and-ball shape, which passed just where my eyes happened to be resting. The others swivelled their own eyes rapidly, and all saw it disappearing. Tick. Three more followed in quick succession: turtle dove, greenfinch, bullfinch. The last one was a particularly good bird to get: a relatively common bird that is infuriatingly difficult to see. Many a birdracing team has cursed its misfortune at missing bullfinch. The first sand martin cruised by, and minutes later, the air was full of them.

It was six o'clock, and the list was bulging. Any more birds to tick before breakfast? We went to inspect the Scrape. How absurd Minsmere is: a spoonbill, of all things, was there to welcome us. Did he know that on this one day of the year, he counted the same as the carrion crow, or would do if Dudley managed to see one? Rapidly, we scanned the Scrape to see if anything else had turned up – really, birdracing is a daft game. Ticking birds in this rushed way at Minsmere is like going to the Sistine Chapel, adding up the number of figures (God, tick, Jesus, tick, Adam, tick) and running off again. Dunlin, tick, snipe, tick. Look out, Dudley, carrion crow! Got it, got it that time. Turnstone. A party of bearded tits pinged away in the reeds. Reed bunting, the worst singer of them all, gave his feeble little burble from cover. Meadow pipit. Great black-backed gull. Graham's pencil was flying, but soon it would be slowing down: that was inevitable as the list grew. The rest of the day was going to be a scramble for odd birds. Skylark, sanderling.

We walked a rapid circuit of the Scrape, picking up a stonechat in the gorse along the beach. Wheatear: a useful bird to pick up. A kestrel, a hovering speck miles away: another easy one. We gathered a quick black-tailed godwit on the Scrape before heading back to Jeremy's bungalow and coffee. A wigeon gave his kettle whistle call. We passed on into the trees, and were greeted by the yaffle of a green woodpecker and the scream of a jay.

We had sandwiches and coffee at Jeremy's bungalow, heroically doing so outside in case we should pick up an addition to the list. If a thing is worth doing, it is worth doing maniacally. In fact, we got nothing, but the Suffolk birders were very happy with things, and Jeremy was pleased to have given them so many birds. I drank my coffee, and decided to leave them to it. The team went on, and I had another cup of coffee with Jeremy as I waited for Eric the taxi. The night was over.

It was, I suppose, inevitable that the birders saw a barn owl almost as soon as I left them. They also picked up pied wagtail, house martin and common sandpiper before heading off into the depths of Suffolk. Minsmere had given them ninety-eight species in eight hours.

They managed a further seventeen as they charged about the county in their borrowed Saab. The ten hours away from Minsmere brought them rook, curlew, red-legged partridge, collared dove, goldfinch, black redstart, shag, tufted duck, kingfisher, little ringed plover, pochard, little grebe, hobby, whinchat, stone curlew, grey partridge, tree pipit, ruddy shelduck and Egyptian goose. They then raced back to Minsmere in the Saab, and picked up common gull and ruff, which brought the grand total to 119, of which Minsmere's share was an exact century. They raised lots of money for the Suffolk Wildlife Trust, and from their own pockets, rather than these profits, they very properly bought Jeremy two bottles of rather good Rioja.

Later, I asked Dudley what he had enjoyed most about the twenty-four hours of nonsense. He laughed, and said it was missing the carrion crow. He then added more seriously that the barn owl sighting was one of the best he had ever had. I gnashed my teeth unobtrusively. But after more thought, Dudley said that the best thing about it was the fact that you were doing something you would never get around to doing without the lunatic notion of birdracing. It was sitting in the dark, all night, just listening. The nightjars, the nightingales, and the baying of the foxes drifting up towards us across the heathland – unforgettable.

CANARY

A FEW days after the great twitch, riding the rattler to Saxmundham and reading *Birdwatching* magazine in a spirit of research, I began absentmindedly to answer a questionnaire. But I gave up when I got to the question: 'How often do you go birdwatching?' *Go?* I don't go birdwatching. Birdwatching is not to be dismissed as something you *do*. With every visit I made to Minsmere it became more and more clear that birding is actually the way you face life. It is not a dilettante pursuit, a mere hobby, a divertissement, a distraction from real life. It is real life.

By that, I do not mean that birding is merely all-consuming: I do not mean that it is necessary to be obsessed with ticks or subspecies or identification conundrums or population shifts or behaviour or censusing, fascinating and absorbing as these things may be. The point is that birding should become the central part of a person's moral, philosophical, political and spiritual outlook. Birding is not about telling a water pipit from a rock pipit and an ortolan bunting from the back row of a hundred twitchers. Birding is about mankind's place in nature.

Birding asks how far our responsibilities extend. This is the central issue of all kinds of political systems: Marxism and democracy for a start. It is the question at the heart of many systems of ethical philosophy. Birding does not, or at least, does not seem to me to ask questions about mankind's role in eternity – I leave that to theologians and metaphysicians. But it asks questions that are relevant for as long as *homo sapiens* survives. I once visited a conservation project in New Zealand, where they were working for the regeneration of a kauri forest. It takes 2,000 years for a kauri tree to reach its full strength: as timespans go, that seems to me a good place from which to start.

But this sort of long-term thinking runs against the nature of a democracy. Newspapers express the belief that the most serious subject in life is politics, and career politicians must, of necessity, think in terms of short-term expedient. In a democracy, seriousness tends to work on a timescale from one election to the next. Conservation looks beyond such trivial matters, and is concerned with the larger issues of living and dying, and passing on a bearable world in which our grandchildren and our great-grandchildren can live. This has never been a traditional priority for political life: but it has never before been necessary for politics to adopt such priorities.

There are two arguments that support the importance of conservation as a long-term major priority. I shall refer to these as the Katie Pratt Argument, and the Bill Shankly Argument. Katie Pratt is a delightful lady, now twenty-one, and a former neighbour of mine. Bill Shankly is the former manager of Liverpool Football Club, a man whose memory is much beloved by Ron Johns, the king of the twitchers.

Katie is intelligent and uninhibitedly raucous in the expression of her beliefs. I recall discussing the coming 1987 election with her in the Two Brewers pub. She laughed in my face when I talked about 'responsibilities'. 'God, what a stupid idea – you've got to be *selfish*, haven't you?' When girls of sixteen believe that selfishness is a worthy moral code, then God help all of us, I thought.

But then I wondered if she might not have a point. The most profound selfishness concerns not the comfort of your mortal body, but the survival of your genes. And if you pass on your genes but leave behind a ruined world, you have not merely destroyed your own posterity, you have, in effect, destroyed yourself. If you truly believe that 'you've got to be selfish' then you, more than anyone else, should be a conservationist: your priority must be a world that will sustain your genes from generation to generation. I read Richard Dawkins's *The Selfish Gene*, thought of Katie Pratt, and laughed. Logically, Katie should have voted for the Green Party.

It happens that birds are particularly useful to people who accept the pure Katie Pratt Argument. Coal miners didn't take canaries down the pit for the pleasure of hearing them sing: the birds, infinitely more fragile than the miners, gave them early warning that things had gone badly wrong: that the environment of the coal mine was being poisoned.

Wild birds – always visible, always audible, an inescapable part of our own environment in cities and in wild places – are our canaries now. In the '50s and '60s, birds of prey suddenly grew scarce, and went extinct in many parts of the country. It was discovered that this was because we had filled the land with poison. Insecticide had entered the food chain, and it was the creatures right at the top that felt it first. DDT was the most dangerous. It is a poison that stays in the system, and slowly builds up. We were, in fact, slowly poisoning ourselves: but birds like sparrowhawks felt it first. It was when the plight of the sparrowhawks and the inescapable links with DDT became clear that we were able to see what was going wrong and, eventually, to stop it – not just for the good of sparrowhawks, but with our own long-term good in mind as well.

DDT and related pesticides were subject to increasing restrictions and were finally made illegal in this country in 1986. But the stuff is still used all over the Third World: it is very cheap, and very good at killing insects. Lessons must be learnt and learnt again: but if we monitor our wildlife and work as good conservationists to maintain the numbers, the ranges and the diversity of our species, then we will know that our world is still a safe place in which to live and breed. We can be assured that birds, as visible as they are fragile, will be the first to tell us whenever anything befouls the planet.

All the same, I prefer the Bill Shankly Argument. Shankly said famously: 'There are people who think football is a matter of

life and death. They're fools. It's much more important than that.'
For football, substitute conservation. For we have, I believe,
responsibilities that go beyond our own species. Mankind has, in
the past, interpreted the role of Steward of Creation to mean that
we have *carte blanche* to exploit anything we need and kill anything
we fancy. I have read a terrifying first-person account of a
Victorian hunter who shot a rhinoceros because he fancied rhino
liver for breakfast. He was a hero once, but times change. Genera-
tions ago, it would have been far-fetched to suggest that a person
had moral duties beyond his tribe, or later, beyond his nation.
Even today, the notion that we have responsibilities beyond our
own race are not favoured everywhere: but racism is under siege.
To explain yourself as a racist is to expose yourself as a fool.

The area of moral responsibility grows wider as mankind's
power over life and the world grows greater. It becomes clear that
we do, indeed, have responsibilities and duties towards animals of
species other than our own. Certainly, this is a view that is
increasingly taking hold and winning acceptance. The extent and
nature of these responsibilities are debated by people who work on
the cutting edge of ethical philosophy. Peter Singer, an ethical
philosopher himself, coined the inelegant and hissing term of
speciesism. A speciesist is someone who denies all rights to animals
other than humans, and believes that people have a right to inflict
pain on them at will, for whatever purposes they like. There is
nothing intrinsically wrong with torturing rabbits or shooting
avocets. Oh, really?

Thus I seasoned my reading on evolution with a spot of ethics,
as the rattler rattled on. It is a poor person who refuses the moral
claims of an avocet. Conservation is not something that one
undertakes from the goodness of one's heart. Conservation is not
a good thing because birdies are jolly pretty and I like the way
they go cheepcheep in the spring. Conservation is, ultimately, a
moral obligation. Speciesism is more than folly. It is a crime
against life.

Birds are a part of life, and *that* is what conservation is about. If
we destroy life, if we destroy birds or their places of resort, then
we destroy something in ourselves.

Nightjar

OMETIMES Minsmere felt like a city under siege. It was an odd, upside-down feeling. With most of the great sieges in history, it was civilisation that was under threat, and the forces of wildness and anarchy that threatened it.

That was how the British felt at Lucknow and Mafeking: a civilised place under dire threat from some terrible untamed force. But at Minsmere it was the other way round. The untamed forces were about to go under, squashed by the ravening hordes of civilisation.

The road to Minsmere takes you through square after square of flat green fields: a land of ploughed-up footpaths, massively fertilised soil and energetically growing crops of money. This is a place where no one can walk and where no one wants to walk. This is the countryside as industrial site: a place where people are not welcomed. And this impression is, as ever, reinforced by the great siege engine of Sizewell, looming up over the Scrape and Island Mere, clanking and groaning. It seems that Minsmere is fighting a desperate rearguard action, and one that it is doomed to lose. As conservationists make their long-term plans, like kauri planters and the papacy, so the short-term thinkers continue to dominate British life. The countryside around Minsmere is a great factory that produces cash crops, which are grown at the expense of massive amounts of energy: and over at Sizewell the production of energy is at the price of providing a sword of Damocles that hangs over the entire biosphere.

If global despair seems sometimes the only rational response to an irrational situation, the best antidote available is local action. And at Minsmere, they are actually expanding the boundaries: pushing back the siege. To expand Minsmere's boundaries is to push back the frontiers of sanity in the shadow of the madness at Sizewell.

I remember causing a burst of unbelieving laughter when I mentioned this expansion when I was in Africa, visiting Hwange Game Park in Zimbabwe. Hwange – previously called, believe it or not, Wankie – is a park the size of Wales. That, in fact, seems to be the standard size of every game park in Africa – 'elephant roam free in a park the size of Wales' – but the point is that they have a different idea of big in Africa. We were talking about conservation, which is a matter as pressing in Africa as it is in Suffolk, and everywhere else in the world for that matter. I was talking about Minsmere's latest and most exciting new project. It involved the purchase of 400 acres of land. '400 *acres?*' The safari-types laughed unbelievingly. To them, 400 square miles is a fleabite. But in England, under the shadow of Sizewell, 400 acres was a major advance.

The land was purchased from the farmer who owns a good deal of land surrounding the reserve, and the deal was made public early in the year. Minsmere grew at a jump to 1,968 acres ('1,968 *acres?*') with the purchase of this land: 400 acres of green desert. This was arable land: a product of biochemical knowhow. Rob and I had walked along some of its boundaries, censusing willow warbler and yellowhammer in the hedgerows. The hedges were still there, praise the Lord, but the rest of the arable land held more or less nothing. Exactly what you would expect from a desert. But Minsmere had the outrageous plan of reclaiming the desert, destroying progress, and turning the land back into its own past, to recreate what is now seen as the most endangered habitat in Britain: heathland.

Heathland has suffered from neglect. It is the forgotten habitat.

Nightjar

It lacks the emotional appeal of woodland. It doesn't attract wildlife in great hordes, as wetland does. Heathland is just – well, sort of scruffy and overlooked. You would walk your dog on it, but you wouldn't stop and gaze at it with great soul-filling raptures, like Wordsworth in the Lake District. You probably wouldn't even choose to go birding there, because there is not all that much to see. But the priority of conservation is birds, not birders. Heathland looks useless to man and beast. Vast tracts of it have been built on; many seaside cottages along the south coast stand on land that was once heathland. Heathland doesn't look much: so it has largely been wiped out.

Yet heathland is a living part of human as well as natural history, for it is emphatically a manmade habitat. It has depended for its existence on management for two thousand years and more. Heaths are low-lying, and characteristic of dry areas: quite different to moorland, which comes in wet areas and is a climax community of vegetation in its own right, like an oakwood. Heathland is not. Left to its own devices, it will be invaded by trees from the edge, which will march inexorably to the middle until the whole thing has 'tumbled down to woodland'. This expressive phrase, one I have already quoted in these pages, comes from Oliver Rackham. Rackham's book *The History of the Countryside* is a vital work on social and natural history, and it should be compulsory reading for both historians and conservationists.

Heathland was a vital resource for the human population. It was exploited, or managed, for and by cutting and grazing. Much of it was common land, and it provided rough grazing for the commoners' livestock. The main heathland plants, furze and ling, were cut for fuel: furze 'produces a quick, hot blaze, suitable for heating ovens, getting up a fire in the morning, or burning heretics,' said Rackham. Bracken was cut for livestock litter and for thatch. Heather was cut for bedding. In the early Middle Ages, rabbits were introduced to England: on heathland they were regarded as the property of the landowner and they shared the grazing with the sheep and cattle of the commoners.

Heathland, then, is a part of ancient England. Rackham said: 'Almost every rural change since 1945 has extended what is already commonplace at the expense of what is wonderful, or rare, or has meaning.' I particularly like the notion that land has *meaning*: heathland has a meaning, and it would be a crime, in merely human terms, to allow our remaining heathlands to be abolished. But it has been vanishing fast. Dorset once had 23,000 hectares of heathland: now it has fewer than 2,000. The traditional management practices have fallen into disuse, and without them, heathland stops being heathland. Its meaning is grown over, the unique community of wildlife can no longer make a living there, and it has nowhere else to go. Heaths tumble down to woodland, or are converted to arable land at the usual high energy costs, with a massive introduction of nitrates. Or they are simply built on. Heathland is getting rarer and rarer. We are in danger of losing part of our history, and something more elusive and intriguing than that – nightjar.

The enduring memory of the night of the Great Bird Hunt was the nightjar, churring across the heathland. The spooky birds of darkness have acquired perhaps the finest mixture of traditional names of any bird in Britain: fern owl, jar owl, churr-owl, goat owl, goatsucker, nighthawk, dorhawk, moth hawk, wheel bird, eve-chur, eve jar, puckeridge bird, puck bird, litch fowl. I have kept the best for last: gabble-ratch. This means corpse-hound. Nightjars are neither hawks nor owls, and certainly not hounds. They are related to swifts. But even their scientific name is odd: *caprimulgus*, or goatmilkers. People believed they stole milk from goats in the night as they flew in their ghostly patterns across the ancient heathland of Britain. In fact, they were hawking for insects, in honest swiftlike fashion, and insects are attracted to a goatish presence and disturbed by goatish passage.

But as the heathland vanishes, so the nightjars vanish with them. Habitat destruction is the key to the falling numbers of many a bird. Minsmere's heathland had long held a stable population of summer nightjars: until the early 1970s, there were around twenty pairs every year. But by the end of the decade, and on into the '80s, this had been halved. In 1977 the RSPB began an important piece of research into nightjars. The aim was not just to investigate the private life of the birds out of scientific curiosity, but also to find out what a nightjar wants from his habitat. From there, the next step was to set about providing it: to custom-build habitats for nightjars. The results demonstrate the effectiveness of the research, and the effectiveness of one of the men who put the research into practice, this last being, of course, a certain J. Sorensen. In 1989, there were forty churring males censused at Minsmere.

'It's a question of containing the natural succession in a way that nightjars like,' Jeremy said. This is, of course, the answer in just about every aspect of practical management for wildlife. Nightjar, the researchers concluded, like open heathland that is studded with trees and bushes: low, spreading bushes in particular. They nest on the ground, beneath these overhanging bushes, and there they feel safe, and rear their young successfully. The nightjar is a declining species across the country but at Minsmere this decline has been put into reverse. The new acreage will all but double Minsmere's heathland: we must wait and see what this does for Minsmere's nightjars. If all goes well, Minsmere would become the nightjar capital of Britain. But it will be a slow business, even if we are not talking about the 2,000 years of the kauri tree cycle.

The existing Minsmere heathland has been stable as far back as anyone knows. Early photographs show that it was a sea of heather, with hardly any grass. But at the end of the nineteenth century, the heaths were grazed more extensively: the people at Scotts Hall kept 500 sheep on the estate. This had the effect of cutting back the heather and letting the grass invade. Sheep were kept on the heath until the 1930s. The grass was still less than dominant, even after this, because there was a large rabbit population. The myxomatosis epidemic of 1953 put paid to that, and allowed the grass to establish itself as never before, which changed the character of the heath. On a heath, you want heather. Management practices have mostly involved burning, which encourages the heather at the expense of grass. But of late, Jeremy has been able to manage a heather-clad heath without needing to set fire to it all the time. Many people will tell you that a heath *must* be burned. With some people the notion of obvious human control is always the most seductive option. Rackham's research reveals that burning was nowhere near as common a practice as was thought. The cutting of heather and ling was all the management a heath needed: that and a little light grazing. Burning obviously affects the invertebrates and the plant communities.

The pattern of wholesale destruction has left us with small islands of heath, instead of noble expanses: that makes burning an increasingly heavy-handed form of management. Anything that puts heathland out of action for a period, when this can be avoided, is clearly counterproductive.

The task facing Jeremy and the rest was to turn a green desert into an ancestral heath. A green desert is absolutely bulging with fertilisers, so the first thing to do was to get rid of them. This was to be done by continuing to farm it in the same way. In this, the first year in the process of regeneration, the fields looked just the same as they ever did: three swaying fields of barley. But there was a difference, though it was completely invisible in this first year. The barley was growing without any additional fertilisers. The usual massive dose of nitrates had been withheld. It would still get a decent crop, which would raise money for the farmer who had leased the field subject to these novel conditions. The plan was to grow successive crops of barley, year after year, all without nitrates. Each crop would be poorer than the last. Each crop would take with it a measure of the surplus, artificial fecundity of the soil.

What then? One option was to do absolutely nothing, and let the natural succession take hold. But this would, like as not, bring in bramble and scrub, and that would eventually tumble down to woodland. The point is that heathland has always been a manmade, or at least, a man-maintained environment. So the preliminary notion was to give the heath an artificial kickstart by seeding it with heather and ling. This would be done by forage harvesting an area of existing heath, at a time when there was seed on the growing plants. In this process, you keep everything you cut. The next step would be to spread this stuff on the nutrient-poor former green desert. Once again, in short, to light the green touchpaper.

There are, it is fairly obvious, a number of variables in all this. How best to prepare the ground? Should it be fenced? Should it be rabbitproofed? The researchers at Sandy had a number of ideas, and were keen to set up an experiment to see which form of preparation would work the best. How long would all this take? Perhaps forty years. Perhaps it would be a little longer before the new heath was full of the sound of churring male nightjars. But compared to the kauri tree project, it was likely to happen in no time at all.

Perhaps all this, the deliberate creation of an unnatural habitat, seems an odd goal for conservation. But heathland has existed for 2,000 years, and in that time the nightjars have adapted their lives in this country to suit such a habitat. Lord knows what they did before heathland was invented and managed by cutting and grazing: no one can help us there. The point is that people created what turned out to be the perfect place for nightjars: now they are destroying it. What people are doing, then, is moving the goalposts in the survival game. The nightjars can't adapt fast enough. If you take away their British heaths, they will go extinct in this country. If you feel that life would be poorer without nightjars, or that nightjars have a right to their ancestral habitat, then Minsmere's philosophy of flying in the face of progress makes the most obvious good sense. Sometimes flying in the face of progress is, in the long term, the most progressive move of all. 'Funny, innit?' said Jeremy. 'When they say "development" you know they mean something nasty. And when they say "waste ground", you know they mean something beautiful. And that they're going to destroy it.'

Sizewell continued to clank and groan, but at Minsmere they were pushing back the boundaries. This is a good place to be a nightjar. Nightjars need open ground teeming with insects: exactly what a heath is. Why open country? I learnt the reason for this from personal experience on the night of the Great Bird Hunt. In the woods, it was very dark indeed, and in the rhododendron tunnel, hunting for Cetti's warbler, it was almost pitch black. We tried to do without torches, in order to keep our night vision, and this made for several Laurel-and-Hardy moments of collision and laughing apology. But out on the heath, with our eyes attuned to the night, we could walk about in perfect comfort. In open country, the ambient light, even on a moonless night, is far brighter than it is under the closed canopy of a summer woodland. Nightjars need their sight. They do not have a supersense: they do not have eyes that are miraculously better than our own.

There are seventy species of nightjars across the world, all of them living exclusively on insects (I am excepting their fruit-eating near-relatives, the oil birds of South America). They use two methods for catching them. The principal one is trawling: flying about with open beak through insect-heavy air. Nightjars have a specialised skull structure which allows them to produce a massive, out-of-proportion, almost circular gape. They also have bristles that surround this and which nudge near-misses towards the black pit of the nightjar gape. As a further adaptation to their eccentric lifestyle, they have specially sensitised bills. The lining of most birds' bills is tough, horny and insensitive. Nightjars lack this lining, which means they can feel the touch of every insect they come up against. Every time, they can react by slamming shut the gape and devouring the insect. The second technique involves the deliberate chase and capture of a clearly seen insect: that seems only to be worthwhile with something pretty big. They have adapted to fill the ecological niche of the eater of nocturnal insects, a niche that is, in the day, filled by swallows, martins and swifts. But the nightjars are still performing relatively complex flying manoeuvres, and they do not have the radar sense of bats. Bats can operate in pitch darkness: nightjars cannot. Thus, across the world, you find nightjars on heathland, grassland, open savannah, sometimes over lakes and rivers, in broad woodland rides, and in tree plantations before grown-up trees have established themselves. They cannot hunt below the canopy. It is too dark.

It is not clear how good nightjars' eyes are: more research must be done here. They are the only birds whose eyes shine in the dark, like a cat or a dog, for they are the only birds that have a tapetum: the reflective bit at the back of the retina that effectively doubles the night vision of animals that possess it. All in all, they are very special birds: not only fabulous birds, but unique birds. Well worth 400 acres that cost the RSPB £500,000. And well worth the many manhours it will take to return the green desert to nightjar-friendly heath. Jeremy was as delighted about this as he was about any other development in the course of the year, and wondered if, in forty years' time, there would be sixty – seventy – eighty nightjars churring away on what he had taken over as green desert.

'Some of the heather will come back naturally,' he said, as we walked the barley fields one morning. 'Natural regeneration. And I expect some natural regeneration of birch and pine: what I am looking for is islands, if you like, in a sea of heather. There used to be 40,000 acres of heathland on the Suffolk coast. Now there's about 4,000. To pull in another 400 – well, it's the right direction to go, isn't it?'

'Damn right,' I said.

A few weeks after this conversation, I was in Africa, once again risking bankruptcy for the sake of a return to the lion-coloured land. I was sitting on the deck of a houseboat moored on the edge of Lake Kariba in Zimbabwe. There was nothing to see but bush and open water: perhaps it was the finest view in the world. And rather a lot of insects: as dusk fell, it seemed every night that a million insects appeared out of nowhere. At this time, the dayshift was clocking off and the nightshift was clocking on: the shorebirds were flying off to roost, and the bats were beginning to appear. I was doing one of my favourite things in the world: drinking beer and listening to the sounds of the African bush. It is a rigorous business, chasing wildlife across the face of Africa, but someone has to do it. Beside me was Graeme Lemon, a game guide, and an excellent field naturalist. He was drinking a beer also. It had been a day of great adventures, like all other days in the bush. Graeme had taken me within a cricket pitch or so of an elephant herd: since we were on foot, this was not a small experience. Time after time, Graeme had amazed me with his relaxed familiarity with the ways of the bush: knowing exactly what liberties could be taken, and what could not. As the night fell with tropical suddenness, a new sound broke on our ears.

'Ah,' said Graeme. 'Tree frogs starting up.'

'Never!' I said. I think this was probably the cheekiest thing I have ever done in my life. Contradicting a game guide on his own patch: it's like swearing at the Queen – just not done.

'What do you think it is, then?'

'Nightjar.'

'Could be.'

'I'll bet every beer on the boat that it's nightjar.'

'Well, you could be – there!'

I followed his finger: a dark, spooky swiftlike shape flying low over the surface of the water, trawling for the insects that thronged, it seemed, in every cubic inch of air. Nightjar. I raised my Lion beer bottle in triumph. Graeme laughed.

The first instant of churring had taken me straight back to

Minsmere and the heathland: the long, electronic trill. Soon the dark, ghostly shapes, with the patches of white on wings and tail, were flitting about all around us. We were in nightjar heaven: exactly the place that I hoped the green desert of Minsmere would one day become. This was a different species, the Mozambique nightjar, but the sound it made was almost identical to the European nightjar. Later on, in Hwange Park, the one that is the size of Wales, I heard the voice of the fiery-necked nightjar, which is completely different. This one chirrups, making a sound that is always transcribed as 'Good Lord deliver us'. Its nickname is litany bird.

The nightjar churring on the Suffolk coast, repeated so surprisingly on the shore of Lake Kariba, provided one of those delightful links, or coincidences, one of those formal patterns of life that are so satisfying. No matter whether you are in a Third World country, where every walk requires a gun to keep you safe, or whether you are in a country that has been industrialised and agriculturalised up to its ears and beyond, you still come back to the same thing: conservation. For the sake of human sanity, for the sake of the creatures and the wild places themselves, conservation is all-important. 400 acres? In the bush that is little or nothing: at least, that is the case today. But in the heart of the green desert, those 400 acres represent a major victory. Then we turn our eyes towards Sizewell again, and think of progress. In the immortal words of the fiery-necked nightjar, good Lord deliver us.

ARCHAEOPTERYX

A LITTLE tern dropped into the water in front of me, inevitably lifting my heart as it did so. Ah, what a sight, I thought, as I always did whenever I saw a little tern: a shape of primeval simplicity, as modern as a jetfighter. The deep past, and the most pressing demands of the contemporary world were summed up simultaneously in that slim, arrowlike bird: evolution; the struggle to survive and to raise young, to pass on the immortal genes; the survival of the fittest. All this meaning of life business was summed up in the perfection of this little bird.

Its headlong dives reminded me of the way they drew pterodactyls in the books I had as a child, for I was not only a boy birder, I was also a boy fossilhunter. When asked, I would naturally explain that I was an ornithologist and a palaeontologist. Fine words. I had a collection of fossils to prove my palaeontological street-cred. Some of them were unquestionably genuine, though I can admit now that the trilobite I found in the back garden was a little iffy. I could boldly mispronounce the names of every geological era; and most importantly, I knew which periods comprised the Age of Dinosaurs. The words Jurassic, Triassic and

Cretaceous have thrilled children for years. Every Saturday, I used to make a pilgrimage to the Natural History Museum to gaze at dinosaurs. Would a child's pocket money now run to the paying of the admission charge that this wonderful place, this Aladdin's Cave, now scandalously insists on? But the Saturday afternoons of a London childhood filled my head with the mysteries and wonders of evolution.

Practically all children have a period of fascination with dinosaurs. I remember Daniel Boyden, when aged four a few years ago, roaming around a cricket ground pointing at everything he saw and shouting clearly and tellingly: 'Dinosaur!' Later that afternoon, Princess Anne arrived to be presented to the teams. Sitting on his father's shoulders, the better to witness this great event, he saw the princess and, choosing his moment to perfection, pointed his finger at her and called: 'Dinosaur.'

In the resulting hush his father said clearly: 'Only in the political sense, Daniel.'

It is good to learn about such fascinating things as evolution when one is a child, but the trouble is that the subject suffers the same fate as religion. Both subjects are taught to children, often in a rather perfunctory fashion, and then, as often as not, dropped. One is left with a rather vague notion that the world was once full of fabulous and dangerous monsters, which were eventually and thankfully replaced by the crown of creation, the allegedly sapient ape. In the same way, children learn about baby Jesus, the animals in the stable, turn the other cheek and that's it. Both approaches leave a vacuum in adulthood. Evolution and religion tend to get relegated to uncluttered, unvisited corners of the mind, along with other childish things. Odd, really, for both subjects offer answers to the questions that plague us through adolescence and for the rest of our lives: What is it all about? What *is* the meaning of life?

Religion is as childish as Søren Kierkegaard, and I speak with real, if completely vicarious authority here. My wife is working on a study of that gentleman a few yards from my wordprocessor as I write these lines. And evolution, inheritance, genetics: these are the hottest topics in science, now as ever. The topic absorbed me throughout my Minsmere year: long before it and long after it too. My train journeys to Saxmundham were wonderful opportunities to read. I became more and more amazed at the incomprehension surrounding evolution, and more, the resistance to the basic truth. This is not that we are descended from animals – it is that we *are* animals.

Sigmund Freud once said that each major science had made a contribution to human thought, each one of which had progressively shattered man's self-esteem and his cosmic complacency. The first came when it was realised that the earth was not, in fact, the centre of the universe, but instead, a freakish speck whirling around in chaos. The second came when Charles Darwin demonstrated that man was not specially created, but was a part of the animal world. Freud's third hero of science was himself. Before Freud, mankind could say that he may indeed be descended from an ape, but he had the priceless gift of perfect rationality. Oh no, he hasn't, said Freud.

I have always found it disconcerting to realise the amount of resistance people are still prepared to put up to these shocking truths. Despite the current habit of sprinkling the word 'subconsciously' around conversations, people are deeply resistant to any suggestion that their own behaviour could spring from something other than fully conscious motives. And as for evolution – you cannot write about the subject without getting a weird postbag. I wrote a piece about evolution in my 'Feather Report' column in *The Times*, and was thoroughly disconcerted at the tone of the letters I received in response. I was a 'propagandist' for the 'discredited' theory of evolution, apparently. It's only a theory, people say. That's also what Ronald Reagan said, when in electioneering mode and addressing an evangelical group in Dallas. 'Well, it's a theory. It's scientific theory only, and it has in recent years been challenged in the world of science – that is, not believed in the scientific community to be as infallible as it once was.'

On a point of information, this is piffle. Mere babble from the sickbed, as Bertie Wooster would say. Evolution is a fact, and the theory of natural selection explains how it works. The mechanics of evolution have been discussed and researched endlessly. That is what science is supposed to do. But the fact that evolution occurred and is occurring is not an area of scientific doubt: any more than it is discredited by the amount of scientific debate it has involved. Quite the reverse. Gravity is not in doubt because

Newton's theory gave way to Einstein's. No matter which way you explain it, you will not make apples fall upwards.

However, I got my regulation wodge of mail from the creationists, those who insist on the Bible's literal truth. I dealt with these as politely as I could, showing heroic self-restraint in my decision not to close each letter by expressing the hope that the writer did not fall off the edge of the world after reading my reply. Surely belief in a flat earth is required by biblical literalism as well? This was all rather on my mind, after I had admired the fighter-plane-like little terns and then adjourned to the Eel's Foot with Jeremy to partake of the Slimmer's Lunch. 'How can people write these letters?' I asked, gesturing with the chip butty. 'I mean, all you have to do is to go to Minsmere, and you can see that the air is full of flying dinosaurs, and the woods are full of dinosaur song.' I had been rehearsing such phrases in my mind ever since the creationist mail had arrived.

'Is it?' said Jeremy. 'Is it?'

'I mean, birds being descendants of dinosaurs, direct descendants. Right?'

'Are they?' asked Jeremy. 'Are they? What was it you wrote in this piece of yours, then?'

So I talked him through it as we drank our pints of Murphy's: three standard demonstrations of evolution. I started with the peppered moth: a British insect. It is called 'peppered' because it has speckled wings, though occasionally people have found aberrant peppered moths which have been all black. Speckles are an advantage to the moth. They are camouflage, and when the peppered moth lands on a treetrunk, it is very hard to spot against the lichen-covered bark. But things have changed. In the industrialised parts of Britain, peppered moths are no longer speckled. Almost all of them are black. The trees have also changed: they too are black. Air pollution kills lichen: lichen simply cannot tolerate any serious level of pollution. Soot blackens the treetrunks. And a conventionally speckled peppered moth would stand out on a black treetrunk like a bar of soap in a coal scuttle.

It is not the industrial pollution *itself* that has coloured the moths black. This is evolution in action. Obviously, the moths that stood out from their backgrounds like cakes of soap would be the ones most likely to be taken by predators. Far more speckly insects than black ones would be eaten. So more aberrant black moths would have a greater chance of surviving and breeding and passing on their immortal genes, including, of course, the genes for blackness. This is, in short, the survival of the animals most suited to their environment. The survival of the fittest means the survival of the most appropriate – not the strongest, or the butchest.

If the goalposts are moved, the whole game is changed. The Ice Ages were a spectacular example of goalpost-shifting. The rules of the game changed, animals that could disperse heat rapidly were no longer favoured. Huge size and immense hairiness were favoured by the new conditions. But the problem with recent extinctions has been the speed with which the goalposts have been shifted. These have not been geological processes that take place over a geological timescale, but manmade changes happening in a geological microsecond. The longer the breeding cycle, the more time an animal takes to adapt. In this short lifespan of an insect, we can see natural selection favouring this new colouring: industrial melanism.

Jeremy listened to the peppered moth story: no doubt it was familiar enough to him. 'I see the point you're making,' he said. 'But when all's said and done, it's still a peppered moth, isn't it? Still the same species. That example doesn't actually show that one species can turn into another.'

All right, I said, here is the second argument: the argument from common ancestry: the argument, if you like, from imperfection. I said earlier that I enjoyed the little tern's perfection: well, so I do. But all the same, evolution is not about the pursuit of perfection, as we have seen with the Canada geese and their profligate feeding habits and their need to spend hours a day gobbling grass and whizzing it through their inefficient digestive systems. For animals do not keep on changing and adapting until some elusive Platonic ideal has been attained. As children, we are often presented with a 'Ladder of Evolution'. This starts off with unicellular animals, climbs through insects to squids and then to fish, then to birds, upward again to mammals, and at last, on the top, we find a sapient biped that is capable of causing industrial pollution.

This ladder is a nonsense. Evolution is not the quest for perfection: it is the quest for survival, survival and breeding: passing on the genes. Any ad hoc device will do, if it works well enough to see a creature through to the raising of young: this brings us back to Darwin's leap of understanding through the work of Malthus.

The extension of this process of jerryrigging is that different creatures, evolved for totally different lifestyles, share common structures. This is because they share a common ancestor. To quote Stephen Jay Gould, Harvard professor of palaeontology and a masterly writer: 'Why should a rat run, a bat fly, a porpoise swim and I type this essay with structures built of the same bones unless we all inherited them from a common ancestor? An engineer starting from scratch could design better limbs in each case.'

Again, I passed this on to Jeremy. Again he pursed his lips. 'Isn't this just evidence of a certain style? The handiwork of a craftsman? The way all Chippendale chairs were clearly designed by the same hand?'

I was not a little taken aback by this. But manfully, I played my trump: a bird. Archaeopteryx. This was a favourite of mine when I was a boy palaeontologist: many people consider it the most important fossil ever discovered. Archaeopteryx is a bird, yet not a bird. It is almost as much a reptile as it is a bird, but it has something that no reptile, and every bird possesses – feathers. Feathers are clearly and unmistakably etched in the stone that bears the fossil.

Darwin's big book, *The Origin of Species*, was published in 1859. Throughout it, there is a tone of gentle stubbornness interwoven with mild sheepishness. Time and again, he points out the weaknesses in his own argument: time and again, he comes back to the same weakness, which is the poverty of the fossil record. There just wasn't the hard evidence in stone to demonstrate that the boundaries between species were fluid, that different species could be descended from a common ancestor. If Darwin was right, where were the transitional species, where were the in-betweens, where were the missing links?

Two years later, the most famous missing link in history was discovered at a quarry in Germany: 'It seemed,' said one writer, 'an unparalleled act of cosmic goodwill towards science.' Archaeopteryx looks, even to the least scientific person in the world, like a cross between a dinosaur and a bird. It is an upsetting subject for many people, and creationists cannot deal with it at all. It has been suggested several times that archaeopteryx is a forgery, like the Piltdown Man. But there are half-a-dozen archaeopteryx in existence now, and the Piltdown objection really will not wash. It is beyond rational argument to deny that this creature existed, and flew – perhaps merely glided, who can tell? – among the vegetation of the late Triassic.

Jeremy was polite about archaeopteryx. All right, he said, perhaps archaeopteryx existed. That didn't prove it was the grandparent of all birds, did it? It didn't actually prove that all birds were descended from dinosaurs, that there really were, in fact, fluid and mutable boundaries between species. Did it?

Well, I don't see how much more evidence you could want, myself, but I saw the point that Jeremy was making. And I was, naturally, aware of the subtext. I had guessed that Jeremy was a religious man, more from his way of facing life than from anything he let slip. But this apparent acceptance of creationism, of the literal truth of the Bible, smacked of a rather specialised scion of religion. It transpired that he was, in fact, a Jehovah's Witness. He had been converted by one of those trying people who knock on doors. This intrepid person had made the journey down Sheepwash Lane, and knocked on the door of Jeremy's bungalow. Instead of getting the dusty response he was no doubt used to, the proselytiser found a man who was – perhaps 'subconsciously', who is to say? – looking for religion. Jeremy was taken on board by the Witnesses: and thus he took on board the notion of creationism. Not pure literalism, he explained. We are currently still in the seventh 'creative day'. 'Hm,' I replied.

Jeremy and I finished our pints, and then got up to return to the reserve. 'There was something unusual about that conversation,' he said suddenly.

There certainly was, I thought, but all I said was 'What?'

'We didn't lose our tempers. It's very hard for people to talk about evolution without losing their tempers.' It is very hard to be a creationist without being an objectionable fanatic, but Jeremy is, as I have said before, an unusual man. I am sure the Witnesses find him so as well.

All the same, I was pretty well gobsmacked. The man who

runs the finest nature reserve in the country, who lives on the front line of conservation, whose job is to fight the natural succession, who is dedicated to providing the perfect conditions to suit the different needs of creatures so differently and so wondrously adapted to such different habitats and such different ecological niches, who has a head full of ornithological data, of censusing and territory, a man who has for years performed all these tasks with notable success – that he should find the central reason for it all – evolution, genes, life – unacceptable . . . well, I found it baffling.

I have far too much affection for Jeremy to mock, or to pour scorn, or in any way to try to discredit what he believes. Jeremy has done more for wildlife and for conservation than a million people with more orthodox ideas about the operation of life. You get people as a package, after all: you must take Jeremy's beliefs along with his infinitely agreeable nature, his commitment to conservation and his massive talent for problemsolving. I recalled talking to Robin, the ponytailed volunteer. 'You know,' he said, 'I think Jeremy is probably the most brilliant man I have ever met in my life. I know he has his religious beliefs, but he never tries to preach to us. All he tries to teach us is the job. And I have learnt so much from him, it's quite amazing.'

I had many wonderful days at Minsmere, but the day when Jeremy and I discussed evolution over the Slimmer's Lunch was without question the weirdest. We returned to the reserve after the lunch, Jeremy to the wordprocessor and I to the Scrape. The shallow waters were full of avocets, the islands with avocet chicks. Sandwich and common terns stood on the shingle. The air was full of the sound of the blackheads: *Quark! Quark!* The occasional kluut rang out. I sat in my hide and drank it all in with delight. Just sitting there, watching the dinosaurs.

BITTERN

DAWN in the reedbeds. A magical time. A watery sun rose, giving no heat. Pale watercolour colours. The rising clamour of kluuts and screams from the Scrape. Over on the North Marsh, there was very little birdsound nearby: the wind was soughing in the reeds, a very Minsmere sound. And then it began. To quote the prophet Zephaniah: 'And flocks shall lie down in the midst of her, all the beasts of the nations: both the cormorant and the bittern shall lodge in the upper lintels of it; their voices shall sing in the windows; desolation shall be in the thresholds; for he shall uncover the cedar-work.' The bitterns far-carrying mantra whispered across the reeds: *Om!*

I was spending the vigil with Doug Ireland, who had just joined the Minsmere staff. He is another blackbelt expert on birdsound, and he did pioneering work with Cetti's warbler at his previous post at Radipole reserve in Dorset. He could tell each and every male Cetti's on his patch from the idiosyncrasies of his song. At Minsmere, he was recording bittern booming, trying to resolve the question of how many bitterns there were on the reserve. The situation seemed to be deteriorating. The RSPB had been getting increasingly worried about bittern for some time. That year, they were taking important steps towards putting that right. As the investigations into nightjars had allowed Jeremy and other wardens to manage the habitat to suit them, with such dramatic results, so an investigation into bitterns was put into operation. The person at the sharp end of this project was a ponytailed eccentric named Glenn Tyler.

There is something very beautiful about the notion of spending a great deal of money, thousands of manhours and devoting considerable tracts of land for the conservation of a bird that nobody ever sees. Saving the Avocet is wonderful PR stuff. Avocet must be the easiest rare bird anyone could ever see: five minutes from the carpark, into the first hide, you can't miss 'em. But bittern – how many people clap eyes on a bittern?

I didn't have a single bittern sighting all year. I heard them often enough: that melancholy boom. I spent hours in places where bitterns roam, with eyes ever open for a chance glimpse, but no. I have only ever seen one once, in England, and that was at Minsmere, a few springs ago. It flew the length of Island Mere in its leisurely, purposeful way, looking more like a giant owl than a heron.

But bitterns are the most exasperatingly difficult birds to see. They live in reedbeds: habitats don't come more opaque. The birds are not just wary of humans: they are wary of each other: secretive, solitary, skulking. They loathe company and they are completely intolerant of disturbance and invasion. They are grouchy and difficult creatures, and they seem to be dying out. They have already been extinct in Britain once: they are in serious danger of being so again.

Minsmere has always had a fairly solid, if fluctuating population of bitterns. There were between four and eight booming males every year until 1976. Then they started to fall away. There were just three in 1987, which was reckoned to be close to disastrous. Then in 1988, there were nine: wonderful. But conservationists know all about wonderful years, so often the prelude to a new disaster. In conservation, nine times out of ten the light at the end of the tunnel is an oncoming train. After that freak year, the numbers resumed their pattern of falling.

Things were bad. Before you find out why, you must find out

how bad the situation is. You cannot do anything without accurate information. But, of course, censusing bitterns is a horribly tricky business. It sounds easy. The males boom: so count the booms, and bingo! that's your male population. But the bitterns wander about the reedbeds and hold large territories, and these tend to overlap at the edges. One boom sounds much like another. You can never be *quite* sure how many times you have counted any one bittern.

This was the perplexing situation that Glenn was faced with when the RSPB invited him to spend two solid years crashing about in the reedbeds. It is an unusual assignment, but Glenn is an unusual man. Before the bittern assignment, he had spent two years researching stone curlews: these are birds nearly as antisocial as bitterns, and nocturnal to boot. What's more, they turned out to be even less common than people thought. The apparently insuperable problems posed by the bitterns were always going to stimulate rather than overwhelm him.

The work with stone curlew had been a great success. Farmers with nesting stone curlews on their land had been approached, asked to manage land in sympathy with Glenn's findings, and almost all of them had been enthusiastic and helpful, proud to have such a rarity on their patch. 'Brilliant, to see something work like that,' Glenn said. 'And if we could do the same with bitterns . . . we've got to take a very *critical* look at bitterns. We must be sure that we can prove that what we believe has happened *has* happened. Then we can get the wardens involved – and they'll be keen to do everything they can. Well, you know what Jeremy's like. When people like him and Ian take something on, you know it's going to get done.'

The same thing is emphatically true of Glenn in his own sphere. His gameplan was simple enough: to spend two years in the reeds. He would learn the intimate family secrets of the bittern. This is the sort of life that gives you a completely new perspective on the world. Just as I found five minutes in a Minsmere hide boring, half-an-hour enthralling and an hour quite mesmerising, so the longer Glenn spent in the reeds, the more time he wanted to spend there. All Bittern Life is Here. All night, all day, in the reeds. Once you are below the level of the reedtops, you are cut off: in another world, on Planet Bittern.

Flying in the Face of Nature

Glenn divided his time between Britain's two best bittern sites: Leighton Moss reserve in Lancashire, and Minsmere. Minsmere had three, or maybe four booming males. That does not sound like a centre of bittern civilisation, but there were probably no more than twenty booming males in the entire country. The bird is in deep trouble. So, first the accurate information. Glenn set out to solve the conundrum of Minsmere's bittern population by recording the voices of booming males, and then comparing the voiceprints. Each bird has an individual voice that can be distinguished by those skilful enough to read the weird inky splodges of a sonagram. The eventual answer to the Minsmere conundrum was three. Three out of maybe twenty males, and falling. There were around seventy booming males in the '60s. There are more bitterns in Holland, but there, too, numbers are falling.

But they were once common enough. Back in the eighteenth century, before the draining of the wet and reedy country had really got going, the voice of the bittern was heard all over East Anglia. But as the draining projects gathered pace, the reeds began to vanish. And all this time, bitterns were shot regularly. Like just about every other species, bitterns were considered legitimate gamebirds. And so they went extinct. The last bittern nest in Britain was found in 1856. Not a boom was heard for forty years.

But they lived on elsewhere, notably in Holland: a land flatter and reedier even than East Anglia. And presumably it was from Holland that they advanced again. In 1901, booming was heard in a wild, desolate, seldom-visited part of the country called the Norfolk Broads. In 1911, the first nest of the recolonisation was found in Britain: this, too, was in the wet wilderness of the Broads. And by then, times had changed. There was much less wild wetland than ever before. However, there was now in existence a body called the RSPB. And there was also a major change of attitude to wildlife and the countryside. The bitterns were back. In the 1950s, the Broadlands population of bittern peaked at sixty booming males. But once again, the light at the end of the tunnel was an oncoming train. The population in the Broads, and across the country, has crashed. Glenn came in to investigate the crisis.

If you want to find out why bitterns are dying out, you must first investigate the way they are living. Since it is a fact of life that no matter how expensive your binoculars are, they will never see through the reeds, an alternative to sustained visual observation had to be found. The obvious answer was the animal behaviour student's tried and tested tool: radio tracking. That only leads you to your next problem: first catch your bittern.

Glenn managed to catch two, both of them at Leighton Moss. He had discussed and researched various methods of catching them. The consensus was that the best method was to lure them with bait into a cage trap. But bitterns are birds of low density and high shyness. If you leave out a tempting bait, it is a hundred to one that some other bird will nick it. Glenn found that the most effective method was the rugby tackle: to take advantage of a chance encounter with a bittern, and then to fling yourself at it. Bitterns believe in confrontation. Fight comes before flight: if they meet a marsh harrier in the reeds, they will switch at once into their threat posture. They spread their wings and look as enormous and as fearsome as possible. Two of them tried the same thing when they met Glenn Tyler. 'If you're lucky, you get a hand around the neck before it stabs you in the eye. They go for the eye: there are a lot of records of people being stabbed in the eye. It's a tempting target, because it shines, I suppose. They use the beak like a spear. When they are hunting, they use it as a grabber, rather than a stabbing device, but when they defend themselves – well, it really comes at you. It's got more reach than you'd believe possible.'

It says much for Glenn's scientific objectivity, not to mention his affection for the birds, that he was quite enthralled to discover, as one of his captives responded by vomiting all over him, that its recent diet had included five eels, a water vole, a moorhen and rather a lot of caddis-fly larvae. This was useful evidence in squashing the notion that bitterns were heronlike in diet and habits. Bitterns are not fish specialists, but opportunists who will grab anything that comes along.

Both captives were released after Glenn had attached a radio tag to the birds' legs, using a leather strap. The radio sends out a pulse every 3.5 seconds, and it allowed Glenn to keep track of a bittern's daily movements for eight months. After that, the battery runs down. Some time after that, the leather strap rots away, and the bittern is rid of the device. All this was vital for the long-term conservation of the bittern, but it was a very tough, undignified business for the birds involved. Glenn had to carry each poor beast away from the reeds, tag him up, and then release him. 'That vomiting bird,' Glenn said, 'it must have been such a terrible day for him. Percy, I called him. Captured and tagged and released and losing his dinner. But within twenty minutes of capture, he was back in the reeds, and booming away again. That was great; great relief too. It will be interesting to see how long he lasts: I'll know from the voiceprints. You know, these are endlessly fascinating birds. I think you could go on studying them forever.'

The first thing Percy made clear, as he marched through his reedbed domain sending his position Glennward every 3.5 seconds, is that bitterns need an enormous amount of land: far more than was thought. Each male holds around forty hectares. 'They spend their time moving about that territory. They spend a few days at a time at favoured locations inside it, and then move on to the next favourite spot. The territories overlap, but the overlapping bit will only be used when the other bird is at the opposite end of his territory. They won't overlap when they are booming. They are really careful about avoiding each other, because when they do come together, they must fight, and the fights are really vicious. There's a lot of literature on birds killing each other, bodies found full of puncture wounds. Their life seems to be based on the principle of keeping out of each other's way.'

Fighting to the death is, for all that some people love to stress the redness of tooth and beak, pretty unusual behaviour. Most encounters between males of the same species take place along lines that have evolved to avoid violence. Birdsong is not a reckless challenge to all-comers: it is a proclamation that says it would be advisable to keep clear. In any species, the survivors, the successful breeders, will tend, on the whole, to be the animals that avoid lethal combat. Social interactions are based on the principle of backing down gracefully, or at least hurriedly. I have watched one elephant surrender the best drinking place to another at the merest flick of the ears: the most perfunctory token threat. But bitterns are not social birds. They live alone. When they come together, they are likely only to mate or to fight. They do not have the habit of ritual confrontation and graceful backing down that more social creatures possess. Therefore, the best bet for long-term survival is for every male to keep out of every other male's way.

'When they are booming, they all know where the other males are,' Glenn said. 'So they can avoid each other easily. In July, when breeding is over, the territories expand. That's when they are most likely to overlap. I don't think the birds are particularly long-lived – but that's not something I can really find out in two years. It will need more research. People have asked whether or not the birds are monogamous, a lot of people have said that they are. But, in fact, they are not. There is a case in Germany of a male with five females, and I've found one male with two in Britain. The females do all the incubation and rearing.'

Glenn found the bitterns endlessly exciting, but they are exciting in a slow and silent way. They do not provide birding fireworks. They like to stay in the same spot for hours. Often, Glenn would take a bearing on one of his radio-tagged birds, and three hours on, take his routine second reading, and find the bird had not moved an inch. And three hours on again, the bird will have moved, perhaps 100 yards along the reedbed. The birds make their living in daylight. People had wondered how much they worked at night, but Glenn's findings were that they did nothing. The males *boom* at night, but that's the extent of it. The sound carries better at night, but they boom more or less from the same spot. They hunt by sight, and need daylight to do so. Nocturnal booming gives the male most of the day to go fishing.

Booming proclaims territory and summons the females. The males boom and wait. 'When they come together to mate, the female indulges in spring flights, quite high up over the reeds. She makes a certain call, one I've only heard at that time of the year. She goes up, generally at dusk, and passes over the reedbeds, calling away. The male responds by upping his boom rate, and the female drops lower, till she is circling over the male, who's still down in the reeds. Sometimes the male will then get up and chase the female until she crashes down into the reeds, or sometimes he will wait until the female comes down of her own accord. The male does nothing but mate and then forget about it. He carries on booming after the mating. And the female, she might go her own way after a couple of successful copulations. She may not

Flying in the Face of Nature

even lay her eggs in the male's territory, and she might mate with more than one male. Certainly there are cases of rape as well.'

There are so many factors that can affect a bird. Ecology is a vast subject: the study of the interconnectedness of everything. For example, Glenn recorded all the plantlife he found in a bittern's favoured habitat: what species, their numbers, their ages. He measured water purity. He measured the levels of PCB in eels: eels are fatty and long-lived, and so are well-designed as a living storage jar for these residual poisons. These affect their predators, just as DDT poisoning affected the birds of prey. Very high PCB levels have been found in bitterns, herons and otters: all great devourers of eels. It is possible that this affects breeding performances, just as DDT did with sparrowhawks. It is one of the many avenues Glenn was exploring.

But as the first year continued, Glenn was beginning to feel that he was on the track of something. This was a crisis in the reedbeds themselves. Reeds are a fragile habitat: fragile and impermanent. Every reedbed wants to turn into an oakwood, given a decent run of a few centuries: it is the job of a nature warden to make the succession mark time, and to keep the reedbed as reedbed. At Minsmere, staff and volunteers spend hours and hours every year trying to do this: hacking away at the invading scrub: keeping the succession at bay. But in a sense, this is fighting the symptoms, rather than the disease. Scrub comes in because the reeds grow and die, and put down humus as they do so. That gives the scrub a toehold, and allows it to invade. You can combat this by taking out the scrub, but the humus is still being deposited. Taking out scrub is a postponement of the inevitable. The reedbeds are ageing before our eyes. The Minsmere reedbeds, formed by those coastal defences of the 1940s, are at the end of their tether. And of course, no new reedbeds are being formed anywhere else. Modern land management and farming practices have seen to that. The few reedbeds we have left are maintained as little islands, run by conservation bodies. And these islands are past their sell-by date.

What bitterns like best, Glenn believes, is *wet* reedbed; that is, young reedbed. The older a reedbed gets, the more humus it puts down, and the drier it gets. Bitterns are not birds that fish on the edge of the reeds: Glenn's radio tracking showed that they do most of their hunting deep in the impenetrable heart of the reeds, roaming their territories and eating anything they come across. It is a way of life that has evolved to suit reedbeds that are wet and teeming with life: water voles, moorhens, caddis larvae, eels – all these need plenty of water, and so does their sneaking, secretive predator. 'Fresh, encroaching reed,' said Glenn. 'That's the stuff. But there is less and less of it. There are two ways of working on this. You can raise the waterlevel in the reedbed. Or you can take drastic measures – and that means scraping the reeds down, removing all the top of the reedbed, and letting it regrow. You must remove the old reeds, and most of the acid peat underneath, leaving behind just enough to put the water onto. You need plenty of nice shallow pools throughout, not so deep the reeds won't go into them, not so shallow you get plants like thistles coming in. And to do all that, you need a huge amount of work, and heavy machinery as well. It's a massive project. Massive.'

Conservationists can sound like miseries, gloom'n'doomers, despair mongers. But all practical conservation is the study of solutions. And though the plight of the bitterns was dramatic, Glenn was cautiously pleased as his first year continued. He had a better idea of the problem, a better idea about its possible solution. 'We must convince people that what we want to do with the reedbeds is necessary and will work. Once that has happened, I am sure things will get done, and that in ten years' time, bitterns will be on the way up again. Even in the Broads. They are into the idea of tackling the problem. Of course, it will be a few years before things can improve there. The first thing to do is to close a few more broads to boat traffic, because conditions are pretty terrible in the summer. Apart from disturbance, the reeds get damaged: all the up and down movement from the wash breaks off the rhizomes – the roots, as it were. That has changed the vegetation on the Broads: you used to get a lot of hover reed, but that can't grow now. So it's practically all ground-based, and that's the stuff that dries out fastest. So there are a lot of problems. But it's great to know that in the current environmental climate, they are very keen to tackle them.'

It is also great to know that in the current environmental climate there are people like Glenn who are keen to tackle just about anything, including enraged bitterns vomiting moorhens at them, forty-eight-hour solitary shifts on reedbeds, established scientific thinking on bitterns and just about anything else. In this sort of work, you must be prepared to work from scratch. There is no percentage in looking back, bemused and saying, 'I assumed . . .' You must observe, and record what you observed, not what you think you ought to have observed. You need great mental clarity, and the capacity for unending amounts of work. The job is like assembling a vast pointillist painting, and doing so a dot at a time: one dot in the middle, then another in the top left corner, then a third halfway up on the right. It makes no sense at the time: only when you stand back does the ghost of a picture begin to appear, slowly filling up and becoming substantial as you work on, dot by dot by dot. Bitterns are birds of myth, and Glenn loves all the bittern myths. But he was in the business of sorting out the business of real bitterns in the real world.

The stuff from the prophet Zephaniah delighted him. There are also a couple of bitterns in Isaiah. 'I will make it a possession for the bittern, and pools of water: and I will sweep it with the besom of destruction, saith the Lord of hosts.' And later: 'But the cormorant and the bittern shall possess it; the owl also and the raven shall dwell in it: and he shall stretch out upon it the line of confusion, and the stones of emptiness.' These are, of course, from the Authorised Version: in later translations, the bittern becomes a 'porcupine' and a 'hedgehog'. This baffles me: the question of what the hedgehog is doing in the company of owls and ravens is confusing enough, but how the porcupine 'lodged in the upper lintels', as he does in Zephaniah, is something quite beyond me. Typically, Jeremy pointed out that, since Babylon was in ruins, the upper lintels were probably on the floor. But I am still unsure what the hedgehog's voice will sound like when it 'shall sing in the window'. One thing is clear enough: bitterns are as confusing philologically as they are ornithologically.

In the Bible, bitterns are always birds of woe and ill-omen. They must have seemed so, for they like the bleakest and most desolate of places: the horizonless expanses of reeds to which men only resort in times of persecution, like Hereward the Wake. The voice of the bittern is as spooky as that of the nightjar. The fens of old, I thought at dawn in the Minsmere reedbed, must have been a fearsome place, in the chill of half-light, even in what passed for warm months, as May now turned toward June. Damp and bleak was the place, even then, even at dawn, the most hopeful time of day. The mournful, far-carrying voice of these birds must have seemed like the voice of the wilderness itself: the very sound of desolation.

But these mournful places have almost all gone. We have taken them from the bitterns: those we have left are growing old beneath the bitterns' feet. The only hope for the bittern is that we put time in reverse. This is true of more birds and more animals than the bittern, but with the bittern it is dramatic: twenty males and falling. Glenn has devoted himself to finding an answer, and has set about his task with unquenchable optimism. The voice of the bittern is no longer one of desolation and despair. Conservationists can look at what wilderness we have left, and think: 'I will make it a possession for the bittern, and pools of water.' The ancient words of woe have been stood on their head: today they mean hope, and the doleful voice of the bittern is the voice of optimism.

SAND MARTIN

H OW those sand martins worked. You arrive in the carpark and the air is thick with them: whizzing round and round quite tirelessly, hawking for insects, feeding the brood that squeaks from the depths of the hole-riddled sandbank, behind its electrified stoatproof fence. Spring of hope was over: this was summer of achievement. Broods were being raised, and some of them were already fledging. The Scrape was full of avocet chicks, and there were also a good few fledged subadults, emerging apologetically into semi-maturity in their sepia and white version of adult plumage.

Round and round went the sand martins, whizzing over the Scrape and Island Mere, and back to the carpark: over such important Minsmere places as the shop, the storeroom, the weather station, the volunteers' hut, the poisons shed, the tractorpark, and Jeremy Sorensen's hitech workstation. It is the time of year when every bird must work flat out if it is to raise a brood: the time of year when the staff on a bird reserve must shift from the congenial if exhausting task of censusing, and return to the humdrum, backbreaking tasks of practical management. Neither martins nor reserve staff have taken an easy option in life.

Sand Martin

I left the carpark and set out to look for conservationists. I found them easily: I simply followed the sound of destruction. The voice of the chainsaw was heard in the land. There, straddling one of the lovely woodland rides that run through Minsmere, were three figures, each wearing an exotic costume unsuited to the warmth of the day: reinforced kneeboots, protective trousers, hardhat fitted with ear-defenders. The whine of the saw, a sound that generally means wanton destruction of a fine tree when you hear it in the suburbs, fell courteously silent as I arrived and greeted the three figures that stood there in the wood. They looked more like American footballers than people on the side of saving the universe.

Under the helmets, they were Jeremy, with the contract warden Neil and Robin, the longhaired volunteer. Greetings over, Jeremy continued his lecture: he was teaching the others how to use a chainsaw. 'Now, I need my hinge *here*,' he said, drawing a line on the trunk with his finger. 'Now I know that the tree is not going to fall that way' – jerk of the thumb in the appropriate direction – 'so I can move away knowing it won't fall on me. *Never* cut through the hinge. Sometimes a tree won't go: there are various things you can do then, and we'll get onto them later in the week. It might be hung up, and you have to bring in a winch before you can get it out. So you get a winch. The one thing you never do is to cut through your hinge. If you do that, you lose control of your tree.'

Neil and Robin listened with great solemnity, like children listening to a priest. There is something about the brutal simplicities of controlling a full-grown tree that commands the attention. Jeremy then put the principles into action by bringing the tree down, with gentle, precise gestures with the chainsaw. In less than a minute he had removed a piece of trunk like a slice of melon and, with a sigh and a thump, the tree came down, right across the ride: exactly where it should have done. Now to get the tree out of the road, Jeremy began to explain the techniques for carving a tree into luggable chunks.

Chainsawing is one of the essential skills of wardening on any reserve with trees. It is not a desperately complicated business, but there are principles that you need to get right. 'What we have now,' Jeremy continued, 'is a tree under tension and compression.'

A horizontal tree places different stresses on the branches in contact with the ground. Some are trying to spring up, others to sink down. The knack of stripping the branches off a fallen tree is all in the reading of these forces. Get it right and the branches simply fall away: get it wrong, and tensions will cause the tree to lock like a clam around the saw. Then you need a second saw to cut it free.

They are fearsome things, these chainsaws. The Society insists on all the protective equipment every time you switch a saw on: the trousers contain a spaghettilike mass of threads that is supposed to jam the saw if you start accidentally cutting your legs off. You must get over the natural desire to hold the things as far away from you as possible: at arm's length, you have only tenuous control. You must cuddle up to the machine, rest it against your thigh, and take the weight on your shoulders, rather than your wrists. It was fascinating to watch the way the two students made their first attempts to come to terms with the machine. Robin is a big lad, extroverted, noisy and jokey. Neil is a good bit slighter, a quiet man with a taste for being marooned on islands, counting seabirds. And inevitably, it was Neil who got the hang of the chainsaw first. He took to the thing like a duck to water, or like an avocet to the Scrape. Almost at once, he was straddling the trunk, and swiping off branches as if it were the most natural thing in the world. Robin was shy with the machine, constantly hefting it in his hands, staring each branch into submission before making his decision and daring to cut. Jeremy let him take his time and work through the self-doubt.

'Don't try and do an Ian,' he said. 'Take it at your own pace.' After the hurricane of 1987, Ian and Jeremy had enough chainsawing to last them the rest of their lives. The fall of several hundred trees cut Minsmere off from the world. Sheepwash Lane was impassable: a mile of fallen trees barricaded them all inside the reserve. Jeremy had to cut his way out, and he set about it with frenzied energy. In three days of working flat out through every scrap of daylight, he had cleared the approaches and allowed Minsmere to return to the world again. He had also ripped the ligaments from the bones in both his arms, needed intensive physiotherapy, and, four years on, still feels it. The chair in which he was accustomed to relax and listen to Rachmaninov had the

Sand Martin

uncharacteristically sybaritic addition of a pair of cushions: these allow him to rest his arms without the usual discomfort.

Ian had something like six months of chainsawing after the gale, but fortunately at a less demented pace. Once Minsmere was back in the world, there was no need to go at it so extravagantly: besides, Ian has younger arms. The days and weeks of sawing gave Ian the sort of skill and nonchalance you find in a forester with years of experience behind him. He can strip a fallen giant into kindling within minutes. Jeremy is happy to delegate the serious lumberjacking to Ian: in those three days, Jeremy simply overworked himself. All wardens tend to do this. Jeremy and Ian were constantly telling volunteers to beware of overwork, to find the easiest way to do things, telling me that so-and-so's problem was that he worked too hard, always drove himself a sleepless night too far. And the two of them are compulsive workers. Neither is able to let the sun go down on an unfinished task. That is the nature of the job: or rather, of the jobs.

For, in wardening, there are so many different trades that you must be a jack of. Lumberjacking is one of these. Shooting straight is another. Another nasty essential is the ability to use poisons and pesticides: there are times, even on a nature reserve, when chemicals are an appropriate form of action. There are all kinds of rules and restrictions on their use, and all wardens must go through a course of instruction on poisons, as they do in chainsawing. Running a bird reserve is not all pretty. Accurate recording of climatic conditions is yet another skill that must be acquired. Then you must be able to drive a tractor. Robin was happier with the tractor than the chainsaw. There is a certain, and quite literal rite of passage that a Minsmere tractor driver must go through: this involves taking a tractor and trailer through the narrow and complicated obstacles around the walls and fences of the Sluice, without bending the tractor or needing to reverse. I remember seeing Robin punching the air like a goalscorer the first time he had managed this: the extrovert in full flow. Carpentry is a further skill: Jeremy is rather good at that one, and he was designing – something of a labour of love – a new hide that he intended to build and erect before the next spring.

Wardening also involves an unattractive number of thumpingly mindless tasks: scrub clearance, digging holes, maintaining paths.

They are irritating and uncreative jobs, and they must be done on every reserve, particularly on a showpiece reserve like Minsmere. And on a wet reserve, you have the special delight of chroming the dykes: keeping the ditches clear, preventing them from becoming overgrown. This is done with a tool called a chrome, which is about six feet long, with three spikes at the tip that protrude for a foot before bending at right angles for another foot. You drop it into a ditch and pull out the vegetation. Volunteers agree that this is the worst job of them all. Tones up the stomach muscles a treat.

Many people who love to work outside know that there is a desk waiting to ensnare them. Glenn the bittern man loves his fieldwork above all things, but didn't see any escape in the long run. Many of the most important jobs in conservation are done from windowless rooms. Headquarters at Sandy is a hive of bureaucracy, like any other giant office. The only difference between Sandy and an insurance office is that all the heads jerk upwards when a green woodpecker yaffles in the grounds beyond the office windows. There is a public address system that reaches all over the building, allowing people to be paged. But when a good bird is sighted, someone always announces the information over the paging system, and everyone in the building dashes to windows and doors.

The RSPB is a huge organisation, and everything must be done properly and formally. Wardens are not, by nature, proper and formal people, but they have to put up with these constraints if they are to get anything done. Working to budget is an important skill: planning and control of a budget is crucial. In certain moods, Jeremy would say that his great achievement of the year was in persuading the Society to shell out for a new tractor. Anyone who has worked for a large organisation knows the petty delights of administrative manoeuvring.

The most important bit of administration is the drawing up of the five-year plan, and the annual report. Jeremy had completed his own five-year plan that year, so he was free of its insistent demands for another five years. The annual report is a 100-page document: any experienced warden will have acquired the knack of keeping that on the go throughout the year. The mad panic technique is something you only do once, at the most. Every separate half-hour of anybody's labour must be recorded, every job must be costed. The reports and the management plans go to the Society, come back with a few changes, and then, in the old days, the whole thing needed to be typed out again. Typing is not a warden's favourite job. They took to wordprocessing like a flock of geese to a flooded field. Practically all of them bought Amstrads, and straightaway they found en masse the same affinity with the Amstrad that Neil found with the chainsaw. The wardens tend to be rather cocky about their wordprocessing skills, acquired on an ad hoc basis. Their homegrown systems and self-designed software never have problems, while the supersystem at Sandy is, they claim, *always* giving trouble.

However, the Society was changing the setup that year, and issuing wordprocessing equipment to the reserve wardens, so that the whole business could be standardised. Jeremy went away for a week on a computer course, and as soon as he got back, he set about indoctrinating Ian into its mysteries. I wondered if this was not going to be a tough task for the Dirty Harry of conservation, but not a bit of it. When Ian goes for something, he does not hang back. Wordprocessing is a vital skill, if a rather irritating one. There are many weeks in which Jeremy spends more time staring at the flickering green screen than at birds. But looking at birds isn't what the job is all about.

Minsmere is also part of the world of commerce. There is a shop on the reserve, and it makes a lot of money, and it also recruits a lot of members to the RSPB. A Minsmere warden must know about till-balancing and stock control, and must understand Access and Visa. You can even acquire a Visa card that carries a picture of an avocet on the Scrape: a small percentage of every purchase goes to the RSPB. The shop is operated by two people on a jobshare basis, but it all comes under Jeremy's overall control. The shop turned over £120,000 in the course of the year, and recruited 2,000 members. All of which means more administration jobs for the warden.

'There are wardens who say, "A shop on my reserve, over my dead body",' Jeremy said. 'They're living in cloud cuckoo land. We need people. We need to make the reserve attractive. It needs to be visited. If ever I thought the number of breeding birds was falling because of visitor pressure, I'd do something about it. But though the birds come first, Minsmere is also a place to visit.

And we've got to make these people welcome. It's a vital part of the job.'

It is, arguably, the most vital job of them all, because without public will, conservation cannot happen. And it is unquestionably the toughest job. It is not easy, making nice with people, forever acting the vicar. When you deal with people in their thousands, you know you will get a representative sample of idiots, knowalls and obstructive nitwits. Jeremy had just received a glorious letter from a retired colonel. I was amused by this, since one of the great misapprehensions about the RSPB is that its membership comprises nothing but retired colonels. The colonel had arrived on Tuesday, when the reserve is closed, and had obstreperously demanded admittance. This was refused. So the colonel had written to headquarters to complain about Jeremy on a personal basis: 'I would not wish to have him as a lance-corporal in any batallion I commanded.'

'I don't think much of his staffwork, if he can't plan ahead and find out when a reserve is open,' Jeremy remarked with uncharacteristic tartness. The letter was answered, politely and firmly, by headquarters after Jeremy had been asked about the circumstances that had provoked it: all very tiresome.

There was another letter on Jeremy's desk, this one complaining about the horrors of Minsmere. The hide was packed with people *who didn't even have binoculars*. This, apparently, was all wrong: the hide should be reserved for people who understood what they were watching. What is more, the writer added, the people were disturbing the swifts that had a nest inside the hide. 'For a start, they were swallows,' Jeremy said. 'Oh, people suffer from a kind of selfishness when they come here sometimes. They want the reserve for themselves. They don't realise that we are just as interested in people without binoculars as we are in people with dead flashy binoculars and a 'scope and the latest flashy tripod. We want these new people to learn about birds for the first time, to start to enjoy them . . .'

The other morning, Jeremy had been bearded by an aggressive female birder, who told him that there were too many black-headed gulls on the Scrape. No wonder there weren't any avocet chicks, she said. For a start, there were a decent number of avocet chicks for those who looked, and also, the subadults, birds that had already fledged, were obvious enough. Their sepia livery makes them stand out. And really, do people think that a person such as Jeremy would give his life to wardening, and somehow never consider the little conundrum of the black-headed gulls? 'I started to explain the management policy with regard to the Scrape, and the black-headed gulls, and the kind of balance we are looking for, but she just wasn't listening. I tried to explain about the number of variables in ecology, but she just wasn't interested. All she was interested in was having a go at someone. Some people, they know nothing, and yet they open their yappers and talk . . .'

Jeremy is one of the kindest and most even-tempered men I have ever met. This is, however, a job to test the patience even of the saints of conservation. But there are plenty of compensations: even in the mailbag, between the letters from outraged colonels and elitist birders. 'Dear Jeremy Sorensen,' said one letter. 'I enjoy going to RSPB reserves especially Minsmere. I have a brother called Andrew who is 6 and a sister called Ruth whose aged 2 whose rather a nuisance. One night I made a lego torch and put it in my pocket and got on my bike. The torch fell out of my pocket and broke. Whats a birds skeleton look like? How many birds are in Britain? Yours sincerely, Jonathan Rogers.'

When I started writing this book, I did so in the knowledge that Minsmere is a pretty amazing place. I learnt that the reason Minsmere is amazing is the amazing amount of work that is put into it. I knew the birds were amazing: I had to learn just how amazing you have to be to work as a warden.

The sand martins continue to whirl around over the carpark, relentlessly busy, but come the autumn, they would fly to Africa for their holidays. I planned to take my holiday to Africa that year as well, much to my bank manager's distress, but none of the Minsmere wardens would be going. They should be so lucky. They do far too much work, and do not get paid nearly enough for it – and they regard it as a privilege.

LITTLE TERN

'FABULOUS bird,' said Jeremy. It was not the first time I had heard him make such a remark. '*Fabulous*, innit?' Which bird was it? Well, there have been 327 species recorded at Minsmere, so that narrowed things down from the starting point of 8,000-odd species in the entire world. To narrow the field still further, we were in the garden of the Eel's Foot, partaking of the Slimmer's Lunch. The Eel's Foot list is probably quite a long one, and would include Montagu's harrier as well as marsh harrier, but it is safe to assume that it is below 327. The time of year narrows things down still further: the season was settling down, and June was gathering pace fast. Minsmere was consolidating.

'Come on, mate,' Jeremy said. 'Help yourself.' He tossed a chip to the ground, and the fabulous bird hopped up to it, positively swaggering with confidence. It was a rough-looking cockbird, clearly not in the first flush of youth, but a bird boundlessly enthusiastic in the pursuit of life and chips.

'Ah!' I said, smirking at the chance to demonstrate a little newfound erudition. '*Passer domesticus*. Good morning.' The bird gave me a sideways glance and then continued his harassment of the chip. House sparrow. Fabulous.

Jeremy finds all birds fabulous: who am I to disagree? Birds exist for themselves, but that does not mean you are not allowed to enjoy them. Is it horrifically anthropomorphic to enjoy a bird? If so, every ornithologist and every conservationist that ever lived is guilty of this heinous crime. Birds do not exist so that they can give pleasure to humanity, but people who fail to delight in a bird are less than human. Perhaps if you do not permit yourself to anthropomorphise a little, you are not much of an anthropos. The more time you are able to spend with birds, the more they absorb you: not the sudden sights of fabulous rarities, but the privilege of daily familiarity with their lives.

To have a 'favourite bird' is in one sense quite daft. In another, it is simply an aspect of being human. You can even be quite scientific about it. There is a famous Minsmere person called John Denny, now in his eighties. He rides to and from the reserve almost every day on a motorised tricycle. He has devoted vast tracts of his life to the study of marsh harriers. He is not a man given to whimsy, but these birds absorb him utterly. Other birds scarcely exist for him, save in the manner they relate to his majestic, beloved marsh harriers. Twitchers still talk about an occasion in John's favourite Island Mere hide, when they were all piled in to gaze at particularly stunning views of a rarity. All at once, a marsh harrier arose from the reedbed. One of John's endearing qualities is his willingness to share his birds. Not for him the Minsmere Whisper. John bellows. 'Marsh harrier! Flying right to left! Over the reedbed! Over the P post! Over the purple heron!' To use a fabulously rare bird like a purple heron as a mere marker for a mere Denny's harrier – it was too much, the twitchers felt. But who could fail to admire the absorption of the single-species approach that John Denny represents?

I tend to the Sorensen view of things myself: his pangalactic vision of fabulousness. All of Minsmere's 327 birds are fabulous, and so are the rest of the 8,000-odd birds in the world. Who could deny it? Roseate spoonbill, Buller's mollymawk, rhinoceros hornbill, oilbird, Pel's fishing owl: all fabulous birds I have managed to sneak a glance at myself, here and there. And yet one has one's favourites: not because of their rarity, but perhaps because they seem to express something of oneself, or one's ideals, one's notions of how life should be faced. Amid all the fabulousness of Minsmere, there was *sterna albifrons*: little tern. They are, in my mind, quite *transcendently* fabulous.

Of all the wild birds of Minsmere, these are the wildest. They are wild to the point of utter recklessness. They fling themselves at the surface of the water as if they had abandoned all thought of self-preservation. They dive absolutely vertically: a streamlined, winged dagger, feathered in white and tipped lethally in banana yellow. There is something magical about all terns; perhaps because they look so much like seagulls, and yet quite patently are not. A little tern is what a black-headed gull would look like in heaven, perhaps: a gull made daintier, faster, sleeker, with sharper, cleaner lines, and capable of wild aerial extravagance; a seagull perfected; a seagull angelified.

True, the process of angelification has not reached the voice. A breeding colony of little terns makes an appalling racket. Here are some transliterations of their calls: *krüit-krüit*; *titt-titt-titt*; *tittittittrit-titritt*; *rä-gä-gä-rä-gä-gä* and *gog-gog*. Perhaps it would be boring if everything sang like a nightingale. This is just a sample: the little tern has an enormous range of hideous screams and complicated gobbling noises. The sounds are fabulous enough in their way, but it is in flight that the birds truly express themselves.

They are wonderfully aerobatic. They swerve and cut on wings that slash the air like knives; their ability to change direction is eye-baffling: they can hover with perfect control – and then they perform yet another heart-stopping dive, crashing into the water from twenty feet, always in a perfect vertical. They dive as remorselessly as they do prodigiously: four times as often as a common tern, which is no mean diver itself. And if the common tern dives like a paper aeroplane, the littles dive like little bombs.

More than any of Minsmere's breeding birds, little terns seem born for another age: for a more spacious, less well-trodden age. Their nesting strategy makes no sense at all in twentieth-century England: they like to nest right in the open. A stony scrap of beach, just above highwater mark, is the sort of place a small colony of little terns will find perfect. They are geared for a world with fewer people: for a time more innocent than our own. People have taken up almost every scrap of land in Suffolk, with their towns and their food factories and their holidays. The highwater mark along the Suffolk coast is a favourite walk, summer and winter alike. Frisking dogs love the walk as much as humans: the combination does not give a highwater nesting colony much chance: true, with wild courage utterly characteristic of these birds, they will divebomb intruders and scream *rä-gä-gä* with the utmost bellicosity, but people and dogs have certain size advantages over a scrap of feathers, no matter how daggerlike. They do not seem like birds designed for success in an industrialised nation.

People and dog pressure is bad enough; predation by foxes has made things still worse. The answer to that one is not too hard: Jeremy bunged a fence around their favoured nesting site on the beach just beyond the Scrape, though he did so with the feeling that this was making the best of a bad job. Ideally, he thought, the little terns should nest on the Scrape, where they would be safe from both people and foxes, behind the working electric fence. You cannot electrify the fence on the beach. Naturally Jeremy, with his passion for electricity, has tried, but the salt spray makes this impossible. The Scrape was the ideal place for them: if only you could tell the birds that.

So it was to my particular delight that twenty-nine pairs of little terns decided to nest on the Scrape that spring. One more pair got all huffy and decided to build on Island Mere. There was a brief period when little terns seemed to be everywhere: getting involved in their noisy interactions in front of the hides: greeting and screaming and gobbling and going through hundreds of complex rituals with dead fish. Fish is an essential courtship gift: its offer is part of the pre-copulation ceremony. The ideas of ritual, and for that matter, of foreplay, are often considered essentially human concerns, but the truth is that they satisfy deep avian as well as deep human needs.

It all seemed to be going wonderfully for them, and my heart lifted every time I clapped eyes on one – which was often. Hover. Dive. Splash. *Krüit-krüit*. Fabulous. And then, one morning, there were none.

They had decamped, the whole lot of them. They simply got fed up with the Scrape: the constant harassment from moorhens and black-headed gulls had driven them beyond endurance. One moorhen had gone berserk and smashed four little tern nests: perhaps that was the final straw. The little tern felt hemmed in and oppressed, and they took a group decision to abandon the Scrape.

'It was just hard cheese, really,' Jeremy said. 'It wasn't even that the Scrape was overcrowded. Numbers are about right, overall – but the problem was that the little terns had chosen a particularly crowded part of the Scrape. There was loads of competition for room there. So off they went.'

Their next choice was actually rather a good one, though it doesn't sound it. This was Sizewell Beach, which lies right by the power station, as you would expect: the little terns flew in and nested right along the shoreline. It was not exactly quiet, with all the clanking and groaning, nor was it peaceful, with the eye-dazzling illuminations. But it was private: they had got away from the moorhens and the blackheads, and they had got away from people and dogs. The little terns were on a chunk of private beach, fenced off, and only reachable through gates controlled by power station security. It seemed that, in their fit of pique, the little terns had got it absolutely right.

I missed them at Minsmere, of course, but they were still visible enough. You just had to keep a sharper eye out for them. The Scrape remained a hotbed of activity, the air filled with the snarl of the blackheads and the kluuting of the kluuts. And it was not as if the little terns had failed: all that had been lost was my personal pleasure in seeing them all the time, and I would willingly sacrifice that for a successful little tern breeding season, as anybody would.

So much for my personal nobility. June marched on towards its close, and my next trip to Minsmere brought me plenty of good news: the process of consolidation was continuing. The avocets were in reasonable shape, the nightjars were in fine fettle, and as for the marsh harriers – well, no one, not even John Denny, dared to talk about the marsh harriers. They were going so well it was almost unbelievable. That negligent, floating vee shape was to be seen almost everywhere you looked: wonderful. But it is ever thus in conservation: joy is always mixed with woe. For the little terns at Sizewell had been wiped out. Every single nest had been destroyed.

No, it wasn't some piece of wickedness from the power station people. It was a cockup. Someone had driven onto the beach in a Land Rover. The man on the security gate was supposed to stop people going through, but all he did, for reasons best known to himself, was to take down the registration number. The unknown person then decided to see *exactly* what the machine could do in four-wheel drive. He chucked it round the beach in great style, and no doubt had a lovely time. Certainly he was utterly ignorant of what he was destroying. And what he destroyed was twenty-nine little tern nests. An entire breeding season was smashed into bits for half-an-hour of fun.

Little terns seem birds born out of their time, but conservationists do what they can to roll time backwards. Conservation is not a Canute-like attempt to resist the tide of progress. It is more a question of facing the future in a sane and sensible fashion. Enough progress has been made at a terrible cost of destruction: further advances now need to be made with a wider vision of what is appropriate: appropriate to mankind and to the world. Conservation is as much progressive as regressive: it is, more than any other viewpoint, concerned with the future, safeguarding it, fighting to make sure that we actually have a future to enjoy. Thus conservationists aim to provide safe nesting sites for a bird that is running out of such places. And in these places, quite incidentally, they give great delight, and that is a wonderful bonus for those who visit them.

Turning the tide of destruction is simply part of the conservationists' daily routine, but they are powerless against sheer bloody idiocy. In a way (though only in a way) had this been simple wickedness, egg thieving for example, the loss would have been easier to bear. Wickedness is a known quantity, and something you can rely on and work against. But the sheer unthinking inanity of the adventure of the fool in the Land Rover makes a conservationist's task look quite impossible. It is enough to make you give up – but these people never give up. It was hard cheese. The avocets were still going great guns, and as for the marsh harriers – but no. Don't count your harriers before they've fledged. All the same, it looked as if there was something quite wonderful going on down there in the reedbeds.

BLACK REDSTART

THE irony of it all is that Sizewell is actually rather a good spot for birds. Black redstart, famous for their delight in weird and nasty places, can be seen along the perimeter fence in spring and summer. And out to sea, you can check impressive numbers of gulls and terns for intermingled rarities. The seabirds come to Sizewell because Sizewell A pushes out vast quantities of warm water. The place uses seawater as a coolant, and then returns it, a few degrees warmer, to the sea again. The fish throng in the warmer water, and that brings in the fishing birds. However, this is not quite a strong enough argument to justify the massive expenditure on Sizewell B, or on nuclear fuel throughout Britain.

This is an extraordinary place: a vast construction site, buzzing with activity and purpose. Everything is done on a massive scale. There are 4,200 men working here, 'and that's not counting the blokes skiving off in the pubs of Leiston,' said Eric the taxi. The place reeked of money. I was shown around by a public relations man with the gloriously inappropriate – or as he would say, appropriate – name of Len Green. I liked him enormously: he was moved by the same desire for a better world that motivates a conservationist. Get him out of the suit and into a filthy Barbour, and he would fit in very well at Minsmere. I expect he would love it, too. He was appalled by the story of the mashing of the little terns: not just as a PR person, but I think for the sake of the terns as well. 'Tell the people at Minsmere to talk to me if the birds nest here next year,' he said. 'I'll arrange notices, make sure no one disturbs them. I'll do everything I can.' He meant it, too.

'I was originally involved on the operational side of the nuclear industry,' he said. 'I gave that up after Chernobyl. I thought it was important for someone with working knowledge of the industry to address public concern, rather than someone who just knew what the party line was, and who was pretty shaky on facts once you'd scratched the surface.'

Public relations is pretty important to the industry. There is a nice seagull logo, a little wildlife walk on site where they take schoolchildren, plans for a pond so that children can go 'dipping' and learn about pondlife. There are also displays and flashy interactive videos. 'Sizewell provides an undisturbed habitat for many birds,' murmured a resonant voice with excellent vowels. 'Can you name them?' I could, too. I pressed all the right buttons.

Another video gave us the finest bit of gloom'n'dooming I have ever seen: shamelessly emotional music to a background of global disasters. *Doom dudu doom*, went the music. Conventional sources of energy are drying up! *Doom dudu doom*. Acid rain! *Doom dudu doom*. Flooding in London! *Doom dudu doom*. Then suddenly nuclear power is mentioned, and the music changes, the sun comes out and the world is a happy place again. 'Electricity, like air, is something we all take for granted,' cooed the voice, and added, as a veiled threat: 'Try imagining what life would be like without it!' And as a last image, we have a baby in an incubator, and the music turns in the gloriously uplifting theme from *Chariots of Fire*. Got it? We must have nuclear power, or we will kill babies.

Len was slightly embarrassed by that, as well he might be, but he is a rock-solid apologist for his industry. He agreed that the intrusion of this massive project on such a special piece of coastline was unfortunate, but the location of the place, though horrific, is not the real problem. To oppose the Sizewell project from a

Flying in the Face of Nature

parochial perspective is mere nimbyism: nimby being the acronym for Not In My Back Yard.

There are more serious, not to say devastating, arguments against the development of nuclear power. This is a vast subject, and a confusing one. It is full of claims, counterclaims, figure-fudging, political expediency, and, on the other side, a spot of polarised, kneejerk anti-government reaction. There is an intensely political side to the entire issue, because the Thatcher government invested so much money and so much credibility into nuclear power. But all the same, there are a couple of comprehensible, straightforward nonpolitical arguments that appear to make the promotion of nuclear fuel frighteningly irresponsible. After all, what do short-term politics matter when we consider the future of our grandchildren?

A report, published earlier in the year by Professor Martin Gardner of Southampton University demonstrated a clear statistical link between the exposure of Sellafield workers to radiation and leukaemia in their children. *The Times*, in an editorial, called this 'a calamity of dreadful proportions'.

Nuclear power is hideously dangerous, and disastrous accidents happen time and again. One happened in 1957, at Windscale in Cumbria. The name was then changed to Sellafield. That didn't stop large areas of agricultural land from being contaminated. Millions of gallons of milk were disposed of, and estimates of cancer fatalities range from thirteen to more than 1,000. At Three Mile Island in the United States, a core meltdown took place in 1979, and by 1986 the costs of the clean-up operations were put at over $1 billion. And in 1986, we had Chernobyl. Casualties were enormous, and the figures are still contested. Certainly hundreds died at the scene of the accident, and estimates of subsequent radiation-induced casualties are somewhere between 24,000 and half a million. Do we really want even the *possibility* of a similar disaster in Suffolk?

'The chance of a major accident is once in a million years,' Len said, despite these three major accidents in the past thirty-odd years. 'I know people don't want to hear that. They couldn't care less, if it happens just once, they feel that's too often. We have got to show people that we understand those concerns. Nuclear waste concerns people: well, this is the only large-scale industry that takes its waste out of the biosphere. I want people to get things into perspective, to understand the importance of nuclear fuel as the end to our supply of fossil fuel comes into sight, and I want them to understand the margins of safety we work to, and the safe way we dispose of the waste. People say, "Chernobyl and Three Mile Island did happen." We have to redress the fears these disasters have given rise to.'

But if the safety record of nuclear power stations does not frighten you, the costs will. Such organisations as Greenpeace and Friends of the Earth, committed anti-nuclear campaigners, have changed tactics. Having stressed the dangers inherent in any nukes programme, they have turned to the economic argument. To quote Greenpeace's keynote statement, uncompromisingly titled *The Economic Failure of Nuclear Power in Britain*: 'For three decades, public bodies, public officials and politicians, protected by secrecy, have traded upon the gullibility of Parliament, the media and the public to pretend that British nuclear power has saved us money. But there has been no good news from the British nuclear industry – only a staggering succession of cost overruns and performance failures. Nuclear power has cost the British taxpayer and electricity customer about £7 billion (in current prices) in research and development, and some £30-35 billion in capital expenditure, with another £3 billion for Sizewell B. On top of this is a bill for many billions of pounds for decommissioning.'

Heigh-ho. I shall not go on. This is not really the place. But should you ask what nuclear power has to do with avocets, the answer is, well, everything. I intend this book to be life-affirming, after all. And it seems to me that to be pro-avocet, you must inevitably be anti-nuke. This is not because Sizewell is such an unattractive and incongruous backdrop to the glories of the Scrape, but because Sizewell is a blindingly expensive method of placing a loaded pistol against our temples. Sizewell B, when completed, will produce poisonous waste and will pose an unacceptable threat to all of East Anglia.

One wonders why the British government has been so determined, to the point of obsession, to see through its nuclear projects. The government has created a climate in which opposing nukes seems to be an act of major subversiveness. And yet the United States has abandoned its own nuclear programme: no new

Flying in the Face of Nature

nuclear power stations have been commissioned since 1978 – the year *before* Three Mile Island. 'The great dream that many of us had thirty years ago, that nuclear energy would set us free, has been turning to ashes,' said Alvin Weinberg, who was one of the founders of the nuclear energy programme in the States. That dream, thirty years past its sell-by date, continues in Suffolk, and Len is still dreaming it.

So too, as I write, is the British government. Greenpeace suggests: 'The programme has been moulded by four factors: military requirements, national pride, the hope of cheap electricity, and concern about the security of fuel supplies . . . it has been exempt from normal financial considerations because support has been rooted so deeply in national status and prestige, and so much political face has been committed to it that admissions of failure were painful.'

You can make a cheap criticism of the environmentalists' case by calling them Luddites: people who refuse to face facts about the future. Certainly there is an energy crisis, and a continuing one. But nuclear fuel is not an acceptable answer, neither in terms of safety nor costs. Len believes that nuclear power is a fundamental part of planning for the future of the planet, and says so eloquently and fullheartedly. But I disagree, and not because I am rooted in the past. It is the future I am rooted in, as it happens.

Len took me to one of the high points of the construction site, and I looked down at the 4,200 workers all engaged in this amazing project. It reminded me of nothing so much as an anthill. An anthill in which the ants were all busily making insecticide.

BEWICK'S SWAN

I T was a wrench, leaving Minsmere, but Rob was not downhearted. He left Minsmere in the summer, left the glorious product of decades of sympathetic management with its unparalleled breeding success, and moved down the coast to a patch of bare meadow, a place with scarcely a bird upon it. It did not look like an inspiring place, not to me, but there was no doubt about the fact that Rob was a man inspired. To him, this unpromising-looking place was a sheet of blank canvas, and he was a man about to paint his masterpiece. He had swapped the clipboard he had carried during his Minsmere spring of censusing for a cattlestick, but the energy and the sense of purpose were the same – or had they actually doubled? 'Look at this,' he said, gesturing with the cattlestick across his new kingdom. 'Quite a place. Quite a place. It's like Minsmere was at the start. It won't be the same, but it has the potential to be an absolutely super reserve. No doubt about it.'

This was North Warren. It had been in the hands of the Society since 1939, when it was acquired for the red-backed shrike. This is a bird that has been in decline for years. Researchers now tend to agree that the shrike's problems are to do with climate. There is not much you can do about that. The reserve, more or less shrikeless for years, has been waiting for a new lease of life. It has been administered from Minsmere, but it never had been much of a priority.

That all changed that summer when the Society bought the fields that lie between the reserve and the sea: a line of damp grazing meadows that cost £300,000 and which doubled the size of the reserve to 500 acres. That made for a reserve that was, Rob insisted, full of potential, but it took a specialist's eye to see that. I was very much uninspired, myself, as I waited for Rob at the entrance to the caravan park that adjoins the reserve. North Warren lies just north of Aldeburgh, which is a few miles down the coast from Minsmere. Aldeburgh is an odd place, famous for Sir Benjamin Britten, the music festival and for its conserved-up-to-the-hilt architecture. It attracts an odd mixture of MacGill-postcard-buying seaside families and cultural pilgrims; either way it is a tourist town these days.

The North Warren reserve does not look incongruous, just ordinary – and rather poor for birds, too. It was, in short, one of the great challenges of a lifetime: to bring in brilliant birds in brilliant numbers would require brilliant and imaginative management. Minsmere is a going concern: North Warren was inert. Rob's job was to light the green touchpaper.

'Water,' said Rob. 'The stuff of life. That's the key to this place. If I can manage the water right, then we'll get the birds. See there, there's a huge pipe running through to drain the water off. Come winter, I'll get down to it in chest waders and block it off. The water will spread all over, and my word, what will happen next? Winter is the time you find wildfowl in big flocks, in the right places, and I would expect 1,000-odd wigeon. Teal in good numbers. Mallard, of course, and coot will increase massively. Pintail, gadwall. White-fronted geese, bean geese, and, of course, Bewick's swan.' Winter is the season for wildfowl in this country. Any decent patch of water attracts wintering ducks, geese and swans: and perhaps Bewick's swans are the most spectacular of all. They are Siberian emigrés, massively elegant, who drop onto English waters with great triumphant bugle calls, a quite extra-ordinary noise, and then proceed to duff each other up in great family gangs until they have sorted out exactly who gives way to whom. A swanfall of Bewicks is one of the great sights in British birding; in fact, it was the love of Bewicks that prompted Sir Peter Scott to place the headquarters of his Wildfowl and Wetlands Trust at Slimbridge.

I looked across the tufty acres of grazing marsh, and wondered. It was hard to see this as a haven for bugling Bewicks, but Rob could see it. 'And perhaps we'll get a few whooper swans as well. The world's our oyster really. We'll see what happens. Over here, I want to put in a pool for waders. Put a hide over there, so you can look at it. Panoramic view. I can just imagine what we'll get: spotted redshank, black and bar-tailed godwit, little stint, curlew sandpiper. If you provide the right conditions, they'll all come in. That's what it's all about. Providing the right conditions.'

The two essential ingredients in the management of the place were water and cows. The cattlestick was not there just for the look of the thing: it was a working tool. Grazing marsh is, like heathland, a man-maintained habitat. It remains stable only so long as it is grazed. Without cows, and with a straightforward *laissez-faire* policy, the marsh would tumble down to woodland. To maximise the potential of the reserve, the marsh had to be grazed exactly the right amount: like the chainsaw and the chrome, the cows were a conservationist's tool. That day, there were 250 head of cattle dotted over the marsh. They were owned by farmers, who leased the right to graze the meadow from the Society. The marsh itself was under Rob's control. 'It has to be grazed from May to the end of October,' he said. 'It was hayed before we acquired it, and that's not what we want. We won't do that. Haying has left it a bit flat. We want it irregular and tufty; grazing will see to that. If you are a redshank, you come in and say: "this tuft looks rather nice". And you go in, and you pull the rest of the tuft down over you, and you're invisible.'

These newly-acquired 256 acres of grazing marsh will remain a farming operation, but the priorities will shift. The wildlife will no longer be incidental. The cows will be the means to the end. Rob was at home with his cattle, looked the part with his cattlestick. He had worked on a farm in Hampshire, and he had spent two years with the Milk Marketing Board. 'I'm not an expert, but I know a fair bit about cattle.' Most of the graziers are local, and so they can keep an eye on their cows, and Rob also had the services of a stockman, whose job was to check the herd over every day.

As I looked across the meadows, I could see nothing but the immensity of the task Rob was taking on. Walking the marsh I saw the extent of the problems. It took Rob to point out the nature of their solution. The marsh was crisscrossed with dykes and bunds, with ditches and with raised banks. There was one magnificent ditch that went right across the marsh, twelve feet wide and, Rob assured me, fully twenty feet deep. It had been built to stop tanks invading the country in the last war, part of the same defence measures that brought the avocet to Minsmere. There were sluice gates here and there, some of which had not been used for years. This was a manmade habitat, and the waterlevel could be manipulated at will. But this is a highly ticklish business; Rob was planning to bring a hydrologist down from headquarters at Sandy to crack the mysteries of waterlevel and flow, and to give him a dozen different management options.

One option that was clearly visible to the naked, uninformed eye was that the lower field could easily be flooded. That would bring down all the wintering wildfowl that Rob was enthusing about: even the Bewick's swans, perhaps. It was also fairly obvious that such a plan could easily flood the caravan site as well, for that lay still lower. The answer seemed to be to construct dykes and bunds between caravans and marsh: but how high would the bunds have to be? Could you control the water if you got enormous rainfall? Which of the sluices was functional? Which of the dykes were working as proper drainage dykes, and which were useless? All Rob's short-term plans for the marsh, and many of his long-term plans, depended on the answers to such questions.

The northern section looked much safer than the field by the caravan park. It was, as far as Rob could see, completely self-contained. 'It looks as if I'll be able to do what I like here. This winter, I hope. What I want to do is to put water on it as soon as the cattle are off. And then we'll see what wildfowl come down.'

The first step, then, was to take complete command of the waterflow. Rob wanted to keep the waterlevel good and high, the emphasis being on conservation rather than pure stock-keeping. One of the ditches had somehow acquired a dead end, which made it useless for drainage. That would have to be dug out. Many of Rob's plans involved digging: he wanted to establish a series of pools across the field, all freshwater, none of your Minsmere brackish. 'You put saline here, you'll mess up the entire ditch system. And the cattle would die. Got to be fresh.' He wanted a series of pools of varying sizes and depths strung across the marsh. Ponds were once part of English rural life. Horses drank from them; ducks swam on them. But when tractors replaced horses, pools were no longer essential. And as agriculture grew more regimented, with its straight lines and setsquare corners, more and more ponds were filled in and ploughed up. This robbed the countryside of wildlife and also, as Oliver Rackham would say, of meaning. Rob's task was to restore his bit of countryside for wildlife. The addition of meaning would be incidental but inescapable.

The original North Warren reserve, the area for the vanished red-backed shrike, lay on the landward side of the grazing marsh. It was dominated by 170 acres of acid grassland, but it also had thirty acres of scrub, seventeen acres of woodland and fifty acres of reed. The reedbed had not been managed, year by year, like the Minsmere reeds. The succession had taken hold, the place had dried out, was full of scrub, and was, in fact, in mid-tumble towards woodland. 'No good at all,' Rob said. 'Waste of time. Dig it up. My plan is to get in here and hoick out the willow and dig a nice deepwater pool, six or seven feet deep. Get reedbed regenerating, more water on the rest of the reedbed over there – that stuff hasn't gone so far, you see, so that can be saved. And then we should get bearded tit, water rail of course, reed and sedge warbler, grasshopper warbler. And bittern, I would hope.' I could almost see Glenn Tyler's eyes lighting up: the bittern man would be delighted when he heard that someone was planning to take radical measures with a reedbed: a new, wet reedbed for his skulking booming birds. 'You can almost see it, can't you?' said Rob. 'You see how wet it is here. It won't take much doing.'

The marks of neglect were everywhere on the older section of the reserve. With the passing of the red-backed shrike as breeding birds, there was little reason to waste resources on the reserve before the grazing marsh had been bought, but now the forgotten reserve was to become part of Rob's great blank canvas. It was a further management challenge: Rob could transform this mixture of neglected, scrubby land into a fascinating mixture of habitats, all of them teeming with wildlife.

Currently much of the reserve was teeming with bracken and bright yellow flowers. Bracken is so all-pervasive, so inevitable a part of the English landscape that one assumes it must be righteous stuff. But conservationists don't think much of it. Bracken supports very little wildlife, and it is heartbreakingly imperialist in its attitude. It gets everywhere: it takes a place over: it grows everything else into subjection. Nothing can compete with it and nothing will nest in it. And you can cut it and cut it, and it will come back time and again.

The yellow stuff was equally obnoxious in Rob's eyes. This was ragwort: a cheery sight when you see it on a railway embankment, but it provided Rob with a problem. He had a ragwort jungle, and it looked spectacular, with flaming yellow flowerheads blaring to the skies. But like bracken, ragwort seems to exist for itself alone. Rob planned to cut it out, and then, in the following spring, to bring sheep onto the reserve. Sheep will eat the young rosettes of ragwort, but they won't touch the full-grown plants.

Rob had enough on his plate with the natural succession, but there was a little bit of unnatural succession to add to his problems. This was a tree plantation. For the best wildlife results, acid grassland like this should be grazed to support a grassland community of wildlife. The other option would be to afforest it, to hasten the succession onward to woodland. But one corner of the reserve gave neither option. It was an incongruous collection of alien and inappropriate trees planted in an unsympathetic location on unsympathetic soil. There was even a Japanese ornamental flowering cherry among them. This was goodhearted but muddled thinking: 'A classic example of doing the right thing in the wrong place,' Rob said.

It was all a throwback to the 'Plant a tree in '73' business. At that time, the realisation that we had lost so much woodland first began to hit people hard: it was the beginning of public awareness of conservation. Rackham wrote at the time that since the last war 'as much ancient wood has been destroyed in the past twenty years as has been destroyed in the past 400.' This was, and is, a serious area for concern. But the concern has fostered the widespread attitude that all trees are good trees, and that to destroy any tree is a bad, anti-conservationist move.

Rob wanted to flatten this entire arboretum, suburban cherry trees and all. The whole plantation was about as sensible a conservation project as planting a little rose garden in the Scrape. Destroying trees sounds like a conservation sin: but the fact was that in this case it would be a positive step forward. Rob wanted to extend the dwindling habitat of heathland, at the expense of something that was supporting virtually nothing in wildlife terms. The question is not a simple one, however. After the '73 campaign, many people are tree-conscious: they know how long it takes to make a tree, and how long it takes to destroy a wood forever. I wrote, in the first draft of this book, the lines: 'People are aware of trees, and are very reluctant to see them destroyed. People are less profligate with their trees these days.' That is true as far as it goes, but all the same, one must be wary when celebrating any good news in conservation. Since then, my next door neighbours felled a glorious silver birch glade on their land because 'it looked untidy'. So much for optimistic generalisations.

At Minsmere, there is a long-term project for regenerating woodland that dates back to the tree-planting '70s. It looks like a conifer plantation, but between the rows of conifers stand smaller rows of slow-growing oaks. The conifers have been grown simply to shelter the oaks and thus to accelerate their growth. In a mere 200 years or so, we shall have a magnificent and ancient woodland there.

I wonder if they would take that management option today. Since the Minsmere oaks were planted, many other strong positive steps have been taken elsewhere to conserve woodlands. There are many replanting schemes and woodland management schemes. The problems of dwindling woods are still considerable, but they are certainly less urgent than they were in '73. In the meantime, heathland has been destroyed at a terrific rate. That is why the 400 acres of arable land that Minsmere had acquired in 1990 were going to be heathland; perhaps twenty years ago this would have been seen as an oakwood project. Times, and priorities, change.

Rob saw the old part of the North Warren reserve, the part that had been bought for red-backed shrike, as a place to regenerate for nightjar and woodlark. 'Once we've taken out the bracken, I know we'll have a super site for nightjar,' Rob said. 'But it's woodlark that interest me particularly. There's one pair that nested just off the reserve – their territory even overlapped the reserve boundary. And I know they breed on the golf course at Aldringham Common. Woodlark have been feeding here, and I really think we could get four or five pairs breeding on the reserve.'

Most bird books are unable to give any idea as to why woodlarks should be birds that excite the passions. They are classic LBJs: the sort of bird that seems doomed to be the object of worthy, rather than gratifying conservation. The only clue to the bird's real nature lies in the Latin name: *lullula arborea*. Lullula is the woodlark's song: Latin for tralala. Woodlarks sing as well as any skylark: in fact, rather more melodiously. The skylark song is modernistic, full of challenging Schoenbergian effects and unexpected juxtapositions. A woodlark gives you an old-fashioned melody: just a damn good tune, *Love's Old Sweet Song*. Woodlarks like open glades: where skylarks fly high above open country filling the air with their bright-toned clatter, woodlarks fly around a glade and sing the sweetest and simplest song you could wish for.

'The way I've explained it, it sounds like I'm chopping the place up into watertight segments,' Rob said. 'But that's not the idea at all. It can't be. A reserve has to operate as a unit. We have a lot to offer: lowland wet grassland, acid grassland, heathland, woodland, reedbed and mixed scrub. And then we'll have the pools and the deep mere. We have the beach too: not part of the reserve, but I record what's going on there. We'll get grebes and red-throated divers in the winter, other passage birds offshore, too. It is not a reserve full of separate bits – what I'm aiming for is a mosaic, a really nice mosaic. And it's all systems go, really.'

Rob was itching to get cracking on major projects. It was all so close, he felt almost that he could reach out and touch it. The place was teeming, not with life but with potential, and it was almost more than Rob could bear not to start work. True, nice birds had already dropped by that year – no one would turn his nose up at a golden oriole, icterine warbler and bee-eater. There was even a red-backed shrike, though alas, this was just a bird on passage, no would-be breeder. A reserve's success is not to be measured by such twitcher's treats, but in the numbers of breeding birds and, in this place particularly, in the numbers of overwintering birds it supports. Some of the things Rob wanted to do were so easy, he was positively aching to get them done. 'I remember on a farm down at Pulborough one winter, there was a sluice that got stuck and they accidentally flooded a field. Within a day – a *day* – they had internationally important numbers of teal, 200 pintail, 500 mallard, 2,000 wigeon. It's staggering. You provide what they want – and whop! Straight on. They'll go for it. That's what I'm hoping, that's what I *know* will happen here.'

But the process must of necessity be slower than that. Patience is often a conservationist's virtue. All the consultations had to be gone through. Rob wanted the place thoroughly botanised before committing himself to any irrevocable steps. And he was also waiting on the report of the hydrologist, on which so much depended. Only then could he draw up his five-year plan 'like Russia'. This then had to go to Sandy, to be passed and inevitably modified and subjected to budgetary constraints. For example: could the Society afford a tractor? The Society had to work out its priorities, just as Rob had to work out the priorities for the reserve. There is no doubt that the projected ponds would bring in wildlife: but how much would the project cost in terms of manhours and equipment?

North Warren was seething with possibilities, and every line of Rob's five-year plan expressed his delight in this. So much: so close. All the reserve needed was time and money. These are two vital commodities in conservation: and they are the two commodities that keep running out. 'I tell you what, though,' Rob said. 'For the first time in my life, I'm looking forward to winter. Normally I can't wait for the spring, when everything's happening, all the birds are singing.' I remembered the whitethroat census with Rob: the scruffy brakes of gorse and bramble, the little hollow in which a whitethroat sang his sorethroat song on every bushtop. 'But the winter here is going to be good. Really rather good. Yes.' He waved the cattlestick across the grazing marsh. 'Water, that's all it takes. Water is the key.' Yes, that, and money: the stuff of life.

HERON

THE year was turning. The lapwing numbers were growing almost daily, returning from their northern breeding
grounds, anticipating winter. This was high summer,
peak school holiday time: 'All these people,' Jeremy
said. 'On their autumn holidays.' Jeremy insists that
there are only three seasons of the year. The first is winter: when
a bird simply clings on and survives, if it can. The second is
spring: arriving, breeding. And the third is autumn: fledging and
dispersal. Autumn starts round about the end of June: a gentler,
quieter time than the spring; a less desperate time than the
winter. This is the season of transition.

Jeremy went off on an autumn holiday himself, taking a couple
of weeks in Wales. I asked if he went birding. 'Not specifically. But
I never stop looking – well, you don't do you? What's nice is that
in Wales I can say, oh look, there's a red kite, isn't that nice?
Instead of, what should I be doing about that bird?'

His departure left Ian in charge. For that brief period, he was
number one warden at Britain's number one nature reserve: he
expanded contentedly into the role. As a second bonus, he changed
his accommodation. He had been sleeping in a small hut near the

weather station, and doing his cooking in the volunteers' hut. This is a place that has its essential mood forever caught uneasily between a student hall of residence and a logging camp. Occasionally, and increasingly often in recent years, the place has had the civilising presence of female volunteers, but practical conservation is still male-dominated.

Ian acquired a flat just outside the reserve, hard by the Eel's Foot, a convenience he was inclined to exaggerate. Ian showed me his place (we were on our way to the Eel's Foot, as it happens) and I was taken aback to find that the front room was dominated by two stag skulls, heads with multipointed antlers. They were displayed prominently and eccentrically: in fact, they took up the entire sofa. 'Souvenirs of your stint in Scotland?' I asked.

'Yeah. Shot 'em myself.'

'Wasn't that rather unpleasant?'

'Nope. Volunteered.'

Well, excuse me, Ian – I just thought that wading about knee-deep in gralloched stag might seem less than a barrel of laughs for someone whose business is the conservation of wildlife. I can understand that deer need to be shot ('taken off the hill' is how conservationists normally put it) and someone has to do the job. This generally means that you have to do it yourself, and it would be an odd person who did not take professional pride in doing a difficult job well. All the same, the pair of skulls showed Ian at his most Dirty Harry-like.

Occasionally birds remind you of people. At that moment I had a sudden image of Ian as a heron: not the stillness, but the intensity. No bird concentrates like a heron: boring a hole in the water with its unwinking gaze, its spearlike bill ever at the ready. Ian, behind his steely specs, possesses a glare equally unwavering. A heron does not serve his own best interests if he gets sentimental about eels: the interests of conservation are not best served by squeamishness.

Ian was involved in a project to regenerate the mountain woodland of Abernethy reserve: to put the clock back, restore the landscape, and make it once more appropriate for its location and for the wildlife it should support. The deer herd had been maintained artificially, for shooting, to the detriment of both habitat and wildlife. 'The idea was to regenerate forest back to the natural treeline at 800 feet,' Ian said. 'That would triple the size of the forest. The way to do this naturally, rather than ploughing the place up and then sticking trees in, was to reduce the deer pressure. Deer will eat any tree that starts to grow, nothing has a chance to regenerate. An artificially large deer herd was not compatible with a regenerating forest. When the Society bought the place, there were three times too many deer. It had been owned by a family who spent two weeks a year there, blasting away at the deer.

'They were entitled to do that, since it was their land. But the traditional way of doing things does not work the best for conservation. They would stalk and shoot stags with lots of points, and leave the hinds, and that was obviously detrimental to the structure of the deer community. There were too many hinds, and too many deer altogether. So the idea behind our operation was to shoot mainly hinds, and reduce the entire deer population to a third. So I volunteered. Had to be done.'

So Ian moved self and skulls into the Eel's Foot flat: not everyone's idea of domestic bliss, but Ian has his own way of doing things. The place was not exactly five-star comfort, but he had been living in hut-type accommodation for almost three years. It was nice to have something a bit more grown-up. 'All that camping out in huts is fine when you're a student,' I said. 'But you guys are entitled to something a bit better, I think.'

'Nice not to be saying, sod off, it's my turn for the gas ring,' Ian said.'Nice to have my own place. When you put in a lot of hours, you appreciate not having to worry about anybody else.'

'It's a bloody hard life,' I said. 'When I lived like a student, sharing bathrooms and cookers and things, I didn't do too many thirty-hour shifts. Nor thirty-hour weeks, come to think of it.'

'Funny you say that. You say it's a hard life. I say it's an easy life. It's easy because it's what I want to do. To find it easy, well, you've got to be totally . . .' Ian paused for a while before deciding on the word 'committed'. He was, I guessed, trying not to say 'dedicated'. Ian does not believe in fancying things up. If it's the right thing to do, you just do it. Killing deer. Chroming dykes. Thirty-hour shifts. Get on with it. Simple.

'Obviously you don't go into this sort of work for the money.

Flying in the Face of Nature

You have to do it for the love of it. Of course you do. For the love of *results*. The birds. The whole habitat that brings you the birds. Insects. Plants. The public view of the archetypal warden is male, scruffy, beard, bachelor, eccentric. And it always used to be that way. There were never any women birders. A birder's wife was like a golfer's, putting up with an absentee husband. And it's never easy to share that kind of thing. No, there are pressures in this job, but that doesn't make it a pressure job. Well, put it this way, the pressures are acceptable. You enjoy having the pressures put on you.'

Ian came into conservation work after doing a degree: more and more people on the front line of conservation have degrees these days. Very few come from a background in wallpaper shops. Ian studied biochemistry and biology, and is grateful to the experience in orderly thinking. He is irritated that prolonged exposure to study gave him a profound distaste for scientific reading. It is a personal weakness, and naturally that annoys him. A few phrases of that mystifying prose that scientists traditionally use, and Ian was either nodding in his chair or wondering which window to hurl the book through. 'Stupid,' he said. 'This mental block. Come winter, when there's less work to do on the reserve, I'll have to work through it.'

Oddly enough, when Ian was a student he spent more time golfing than birding. Over three years of study his handicap plummeted from eighteen to six, and was still falling. He was told that he had the potential to turn professional, though it was probably too late for two reasons. One was that most professional golfers start their serious competitive life in their early teens; the second was that conservation was about to claim him.

I suggested that he must have been a gungho golfer, as befits a gungho conservationist. I imagined a massive drive, and a suspect short game. 'No. Not at all. My short game was my strength.' Which is an important clue: for Ian is not a gungho conservationist at all. He is meticulous. First acquire the skill, then apply it. Apply it exactly as hard as is necessary. If you need to give it everything, do so. If you need restraint, apply restraint. Simple. 'Even now, I'll go round a golf course, and play to about seven or eight. I play when I go and see my dad. I've not played for months, and I get on the first tee and knock the ball straight

down the fairway, and my dad, who taught me to play, stands
there pigsick. He still plays off ten or eleven. Why can't *I* do that
every time, he asks me. My swing pattern is just built-in, now.
Logged upstairs.' I write a good deal about sport, and my favourite
truism, the basis of most of my writing on the subject, is that sport
does not build character. It reveals it.

Ian was a subject people liked to discuss. He is an unusual
person, one who commands the attention. Oddly enough, it was
not the Dirty Harry persona that convinced people, the man who
loves to 'tear a habitat to bits'. His appetite for work is legendary,
but that is something one almost takes for granted among the
people who lead this kind of life. Nor was it his equally legendary
physical strength that people discussed: Ian's greatest strength is
not his strength at all. It is what one might call an affinity for
habitat. That is a hard quality to define; still, wardens are used to
working in areas that are hard to define. This drives the scientific
mind wild: science is, after all, about reasons. But the reasoning
process is often shortcut, as in the eureka experience. This, at a
less dramatic level, is the method by which a warden works. Much
of the job of creating and managing a habitat, particularly the
minutiae, is done by a series of intuitive shortcuts. A warden gets
to learn what *feels* right. There is, no doubt, a reason for everything
they do to a habitat, but often it would take far too long to work
out what it was. A warden learns to *know* how to make a shingle
island that an avocet will like, or a glade a woodlark will sing in.
Ian has that gift, and combines it with huge energy, both physical
and mental. It is a combination that makes things happen.

Jeremy's absence on his autumn holiday left Ian with all the
admin., as well as the practical management. After Rob had
moved to North Warren, Jeremy had to delegate more and more
to Ian. That suited Ian well enough: 'Good fun, being in charge,'
he said. 'But frustrating. You also have to do all the petty, and to
you, unimportant things. Answering letters. Counting money. All
have got to be done, no question. But frustrating, sometimes.'

Ian's famous antipathy to people is as much a running joke as
his love of destruction. Both are poses. Ian is a very good communicator, as well as good company. He taught me a huge
amount: about birds, yes, but more importantly, about how a
habitat works. That is the key to understanding wildlife, and to

conserving it. He is a good talker: 'I have made it a policy to talk,' he said. 'When I'm in a hide, and I'm wearing the warden badge, and someone asks me a question, I always raise my voice a little. So everyone in the hide can listen, if they want to. Part of the job. People are interested: they want to learn more. I'm happy to talk to visitors. Just this morning, a couple of people sneaked onto the reserve before we opened. I found them, and explained why the rule existed. And we talked for about twenty minutes, about how the reserve works. It's all part of it.

'Twitching, too, that's important. I haven't got any time for twitching myself, not these days, though as you know I used to be keen. I know that twitchers can be a pain, but I still think twitching is good. It attracts attention. It brings people to birdwatching, and that brings them to conservation. And it's not just wildlife conservation, is it? It's planet conservation.'

Ian will admit to a life list of 'about 330', which is respectable in twitching terms, if nothing very startling. He always adds 'but it doesn't mean a thing to me.' Twitching is, after all, a mere scratching at the surface. Ian has been immersed miles deep in the business for years.

He left a part of himself in Abernethy, dead deer or no dead deer. 'It's just the hills, you know. I hate this horrible flat countryside with all its mashed hedges. Still, Lincolnshire is worse. And I've worked there, too. Might as well be in Kansas. Nothing but tractors. But I'm at Minsmere now, and that's great. It's . . . it's like Manhattan here.' I found the last bit rather cryptic, and said so. 'The intensity of the place,' he said. 'Well, there's nothing like it, is there?' That there is not.

Perhaps Minsmere mirrors something of Ian's own intensity. 'It was a shock for me, when I first became a fulltime warden here. You just don't go out and birdwatch, not as a matter of course. As a contract warden, you have much less pressure, less urgency to keep on the top of things. You wait to be told what to do, and so you have a lot more time to wander around. But the more responsibility you have, the more involved you get. With everything. You are maximising the efforts of the volunteers. Organising the work so that it gets done properly. You want everything to work smoothly and quickly. You know that if you get things wrong, you will spend weeks faffing around.'

Faffing around is, you might say, the thing that Ian loathes most in life. Lord knows why. It is not a thing he has ever done much of. I found him a perpetually surprising man: a man of deceptions, or at least of concealments. He reminds me slightly of a Catholic priest I know: a man who works in terms of practicalities, and who is almost neurotically despising of self-righteousness. Self-righteousness is a disease that comes often with religion, and with conservation: more accurately, to people on the fringes of both. At the sharp end of both areas, you are far too aware of how much you cannot do, rather than of the jolly fine things you have achieved. Here, you are more likely to find self-deprecating humour than self-righteousness: and you do. Ian's sense of humour is not obvious, but it is razor-edged. And for all his laconic ways, he is a mover and shaker in conservation. He is highly skilled with binoculars and with chainsaw. But it is the mind behind both that makes him an exceptional man.

MARSH HARRIER

MINSMERE teems with life, and every single year of its history has been a triumph. That includes the year when the Kestrel with the Schedule One Diet ate all the avocets and little terns. For Minsmere is not a business dependent for its self-respect and survival on increasing productivity. Jeremy does not face the sack if he fails to raise fifty avocets a year. Just as well, really. For he – or they – fell a long way short. He was back from his autumn holiday, and most of the birds were through with their breeding. It was a time to wonder about results. There is a tendency, naturally, to enjoy the success of any bird as a personal triumph. But this is dangerous, for there is also the tendency to travel the other way: if a bird does less well than you hoped, you have failed: failed at your job, lost your self-esteem, let the bird down and disappointed the entire conservation movement.

It is easy to see that both routes lead to madness. Because conservation ain't like that. Jeremy spent many hours, and rather a lot of money, erecting an electric fence for the avocets – and when the final results were in, it was clear that the avocets had done rather worse than they had done the previous season, without the fence. For you can control habitat, but you cannot control climate. And you can control the habitat on your reserve, but you can't control the rest of the world. You can create a perfect place for birds, but if they are being shot or poisoned next door, you are going to suffer a good deal of frustration. And shooting and poisoning have been going on for years: all over the country.

'Every year it's the same,' Jeremy said. 'Your final results all depend on those six weeks in spring. The six weeks when the birds get down on their nests and rear their young. We can influence it in various ways, like controlling waterlevels and managing predators. You can include man as a predator if you like. But after those six weeks it's going to be too late to recover the situation. You can only sit back and watch. I've learnt not to lose too much sleep over the natural disasters – but I do make sure we get our bit right. If you do that, then you don't have to feel bad about the natural disasters. We've got so much here that something's bound to do well. And we've got so much here, that something is bound to do badly.'

Alas, the avocets, the traditional superstars of Minsmere, did not have the best of years. 'We reared something like half as many avocets as I had hoped,' Jeremy said. Drought was the enduring problem of the breeding season. At one point, as waterlevels fell drastically on the Scrape, Jeremy opened a sluice and let water in from North Marsh. It was a horrible decision to have to make: the bittern were not doing at all well, and draining their marsh would make things worse. But the avocets, already put back by the cold weather of early spring, were in dire straits themselves. What is a warden to do? No matter what decision he made, it would be wrong. Conservation is a hard business: sometimes a brutal one.

One thing is obvious enough: the Scrape would have been a complete disaster that year had Jeremy not opened the sluice. The rain simply refused to fall: and so an unusually dry year slowly became a drought. Without the borrowed water, the Scrape would have turned into the surface of the moon. As it was, conditions were bad enough. The water retreated from the islands, more and more mud was exposed, dried, cracked and became beakproof. But the avocets held on, in such water as there was, and the aggressive little bundles of fluff gradually turned into incipient archangels. Slowly, they acquired their lovely sepia subadult plumage. They also acquired grace, dignity and certainty, even when they fed. The wild scythings of chickhood were set aside, and they took on the purposeful windscreen-wiper rhythm of the adults. You can see how successful a feeding avocet is: when he has caught something, he lifts his head, tosses whatever delight he has caught backwards, and smacks his bill together in satisfaction. As Jeremy's 'autumn' gathered pace – it still seemed like midsummer to me – I watched a sepia avocet feeding dementedly: clearly a bird determined to survive. At least if you asked that one, he would tell you that Sorensen got it right that year.

'But it was a poor year,' Jeremy said. 'Just about satisfactory. I won't regard it as a disaster. It was a pretty lousy performance, but bearing in mind that avocets are pretty long-lived birds, it was far from disaster. There were twenty-three chicks fledged from 102 nesting attempts. The fluctuating waterlevels on the Scrape seemed to affect the rate at which the larvae of the invertebrates were emerging. That affected the rate at which the avocets could feed on them. With less food, the chicks are slower to develop – and that means they are vulnerable to predators for a great deal longer. And the waterlevels, dear me, the waterlevels. Less and less water. With the evaporation, the Scrape has got more and more saline. It is probably saltier than the Red Sea right now. Not an ideal environment.'

But no year that raises any avocets at all can be considered a disaster. Avocets are birds made mysterious by their former extinction, their former fabulous rarity. And even as the birds fight back and grow more common, they lose nothing of their wonder. The more I returned to Minsmere, the more I took delight in them. All birds are equal, but some are more equal than others. I love their mixture of grace and high comedy. Every time they take to wing, they remind me of a Tenniel drawing in *Alice Through the Looking-Glass*, in which the table takes life, the decanters acquire dinner plates as wings and forks as legs and flap awkwardly, legs a-dangle, into the air. Avocets even use their dangling legs to clout one another in aerial combat.

But, while every individual avocet was a delight, their performance en masse was a disappointment, and it took all of Jeremy's experience not to be downcast. I was reminded of an osteopath called Gerald Lamb. He was cracking my back into shape after some fairly minor alarm. A fine man, Gez, with a healing touch, or wrench; like Ian, he is precisely as violent as circumstances require. Gez came to his profession through a late vocation. But once he had set up in practice he found life very difficult. He had felt called to heal people, but instead of finding life straight-forwardly rewarding and satisfying, he was finding it deeply frustrating. The problem was simple: he was unable to heal the whole world. You cannot perform an arise-Lazarus act on every patient that walks through the door. This was hard to bear at first. He had, he said, to learn where the boundaries of possibility lay. You must strive to achieve the extraordinary, in the knowledge that too fierce a striving for the impossible is likely to make you less, not more, effective.

'It was working on the Ouse Washes that taught me the right attitude,' Jeremy said. 'You could sometimes get floods that covered the entire area. And either you got all your nests flooded out, or you didn't. I learnt to accept it as something I couldn't control, and I got on with the things I could control.'

This was never going to be a year of plenty. The weather was too weird. The number of churring nightjars fell from forty to twenty-four, but that was nothing to get depressed about. It was an illusory decline, in some ways. The previous year's census had taken in birds churring on heathland outside the reserve. There were only five fewer birds on the reserve itself, not a significant drop. The reasons for an apparent drop on the edges of the reserve were elusive: and certainly beyond Jeremy's control. The avocet were hammered by the cold and the drought. The little tern were hammered by the black-headed gulls and wiped out by the idiot with the Land Rover. The bittern were affected by the drought even more than the avocet. One young bittern was clearly seen. But that was it.

But if you found any of this depressing, if you found that you needed any kind of cheering up at all, all you had to do was lift your eyes to the heavens. There, you looked for that menacing, floating form, drifting cruelly over the reedbeds with its wings in a shallow vee. Marsh harrier. You seldom looked in vain.

This is pretty outrageous. After all, the marsh harrier is yet another bird that went extinct in this country in the nineteenth century, mainly because gamekeepers shot them. The bird came back in the 1920s and led a troubled, fluctuating existence: the growth of a more enlightened form of gamekeepering was effortlessly countered by the ever-more-rapid pace of agricultural drainage. Marsh harriers are another of those rare examples of a bird with an appropriate name: what they like is marsh. Their physique and behaviour is adapted to a living among the reeds. If you destroy the reeds, you destroy marsh harriers. They will sometimes nest among arable crops, but they need reeds to hunt over.

When Jeremy arrived at Minsmere in 1975, only one pair of marsh harriers had bred in the entire country the previous year. They did so, inevitably, at Minsmere. In 1990, there were forty nests all over the country. Eight of them were at Minsmere – and from these, a total of twenty-seven young were fledged. Even Jeremy might find the word fabulous inadequate here. This was a complete triumph.

And what birds they are. There were times when I understood how John Denny, squinting through his 'scope in Island Mere Hide, could hardly bear to look at, or even think about any other bird. The males could certainly strike a claim for being the most handsome bird on the British list. The tricolour wings are a triumph of colour coordination: pale grey underwings, chestnut body, black wingtips. The female, creamy-headed with cream forewings, is scarcely less gorgeous.

But with raptors, it is their flight that enthralls you. To witness that mastery of the airways seems for a moment to free the watcher from an earthbound existence. Harriers do not stoop, like falcons, or hover, like kestrels, or pounce, like sparrowhawks. Harriers *quarter*. With their wings canted in that shallow vee, they patrol their reedbeds with grace and with method. But they also live a good deal of their lives below the level of the reedtops, which makes it slightly tough on the observer. You ask Glenn Tyler, the bittern man, about trying to see through reeds. But if there is an impossible thing to do, there is always one option at Minsmere: turn Ian loose. He landed the job of chief harrier watcher, mainly because he wanted to do it very much indeed. His task was to spend long hours every morning starting from dawn (which was a prelude to moving on to the Scrape and spending several more hours counting avocets) staring at the opaque reedbeds and trying to make sense of about a dozen more or less identical, widely-spaced birds. He revelled in it.

It was the sort of job that is only possible with constant repetition and familiarity: and only interesting when done absolutely exhaustively. The job quite literally required an all-or-nothing approach, and Ian is the man for that. Only if you do a great many hours does the scene before you begin to make sense: the birds rising from the reeds, sinking out of sight. They form brief associations, sometimes to show aggression, at other times quite the opposite, bringing nesting materials, and later food, down to the nests dotted about the reedbed. Slowly the complex patterns acquire a logic, and then an air of familiarity and inevitability. Ian got to know the harriers as well as the landlord knows the regulars at the Eel's Foot. It is stuff like this – not twitching – that real birding is all about.

Ian mapped the location of the eight nests, and wondered at the total. It was staggering – certainly a record. That meant eight females, but he could only count six males. Well, male marsh harriers have been known to go in for bigamy – but Ian worked out, with some bemusement, that this was not the case here. There were five orthodox couples in the reeds and the one trigamous male. Even in a monogamous relationship, female marsh harriers take on most of the work in raising a brood, but the males are still involved. They will even take over the nest and raise the brood alone, should the female be killed. But this male was clearly one hell of a bird: a great provider as well as spectacularly polyphiloprogenitive. For he and his three wives raised eleven chicks. The other ten birds in the reeds raised the other sixteen among them.

The harriers catch most of their food below the reedtops. Their game plan is to cruise above the reeds, with that gloriously leisurely flight, and when they spot something, to drop vertically. This is a gentle, almost inevitable procedure. It is nothing like the smash and grab of a sparrowhawk or a falcon. They take small mammals, mainly rodents, and also birds like moorhen.

The flight of all birds of prey is inspiring and heartlifting. Sometimes one wonders whether the bird feels something of the same thing. Is that powerful, elegant flight only ever exploited for simple utilitarian purposes? Does it represent no more than an answer to the problem of existence? Does it ever become a display of virtuosity, a revelling in the powers of flight, a celebration of the joys of existence? No one will ever have the answer: but it is true that for one short season of the year the flight of the marsh harrier serves no straightforward utilitarian purpose whatsoever. Flight becomes a vehicle for self-expression: an outrageous display of utter mastery of the airways. That is spring and the season of the Sky Dance.

The Dance is often performed at heights of 1,000 feet, sometimes higher, as high as 3,000 feet. There are moments when you find a cosy accessibility about Minsmere's birds. Even the marsh harriers can seem engagingly domestic, and obligingly easy to see. You can almost forget their wildness, their rarity, their absolute untameability. But in spring, when the treasured, cosy harriers become two little screeching dots, you begin to understand more about their true wildness: the wildness that delights one in all birds of prey.

The Sky Dance is all about courtship. It involves complex stratospheric manoeuvring: high circles as the male performs a series of mock attacks on the female. The creamy-headed female will respond by rolling in flight and presenting her talons to her energetic lover. The male, screeching dementedly, then performs a series of aerobatics: rapid descents, sharp zooming climbs. He will throw in increasingly complicated twiddly bits in the course of a headfirst descent. He will spin, slew, tumble, somersault, loop-the-loop, and appear, at times, to be totally out of control. What creamy-headed female could resist such a performance? The better you perform, and the greater your mastery of the air, the greater your chances of success with the creamy-headed ones. Young birds will arrive early and find a mate, but will get jocked off when the older birds, all more accomplished Sky Dancers, appear and outdance the callow youths. The trigamous male must have put on a series of performances that would knock you sideways: Lord knows what they did to the hearts of the creamy-headed harriers.

John Denny is, of course, an old hand at Sky Dance observations, and one thing in particular exasperates him. In a later stage of the pair formation, the harriers perform a ceremony in which the male passes food to the female in mid-air. Almost every book will tell you that the female completely inverts herself to receive this gift – something truly delicious, like a dead moorhen – in outstretched talons. Even so patriarchal an authority as *Birds of the Western Palaearctic* goes along with this, compounding it with a line drawing of an inverted female stretching for a dropped bird. John insists, and Jeremy agrees, that the Food Pass is in fact performed sideways on. The female never inverts. But once a piece of observation makes it between cardboard covers, it becomes sanctified. Often an observer sees what he has been taught to see – rather than what he actually sees. This is particularly likely to be the case when such observations require hours in a hide, and where the significant action takes place at 3,000 feet.

But the harriers just keep passing their food the same old way, sideways or inverted. And, rare birds though they are, in Minsmere they were thriving. It was a year as never before, a year with more marsh harriers raised than avocets. I speculated that the drought conditions may have helped them: that the poor growth of reeds improved visibility and made hunting easier. Surely nothing in those sparse reeds would escape the eye of a quartering harrier. But this notion was fanciful. Marsh harrier improvement is a fact of life, and has been for some years, drought or no drought. This year was not a freak peak, but gloriously enough, just another point on a rising graph. There are two main reasons for this. One is the outlawing of DDT and other dangerous pesticides: the top predators, previously 'whopped', as Jeremy would say, by the poisons in the food chain, now have a better chance. At Minsmere the sparrowhawks were thriving and so were the marsh harriers.

Another important factor is the decline of gamekeepering, and with it, the rise of more responsible gamekeepering. Jeremy is inclined to rate the change in the gamekeepering business as the most important factor in the marsh harrier increase. 'Gamekeepers these days are thinking about what they do, rather than simply doing what their grandfathers told them,' he said. It is against the law to shoot at marsh harriers, and besides, marsh harriers hardly take a single gamebird in a year. The gamekeeper's traditional task of blasting away at every predator he claps eyes on is way out of fashion, as well as illegal. Not that the problem is solved. Every year there are several cases discovered in which hen harriers' nests are stomped by gamekeepers. Hen harriers will take gamebirds, but it is still illegal to persecute them. The problem is smaller than it was: but the ancient barbarisms of privilege still linger on. 'Most important of all for the marsh harriers, and for most raptors, there are simply fewer gamekeepers about these days,' Jeremy said. 'I'd like to think we are getting nearer a time when only the intelligent gamekeepers are left.'

Kestrels are Britain's commonest raptors, and sparrowhawks fill second place: glorious enough birds in all conscience. The kestrel's frenetic hovering and the sparrowhawk's tumultuous ambushes are an increasing part of British life. But the marsh harriers add a further dimension to the splendours of British predators. They are Britain's great laidback raptors. They cruise. They quarter, on canted wings, as if they had all the time in the world. They pounce in slow motion, with scarcely a rustle of the reeds. And twenty-seven new birds left Minsmere after the finest year in living memory. Not bad. You didn't actually get Jeremy crowing about it. It was a triumph, yes, but Jeremy did not see it as a personal triumph at all. 'Brilliant,' he said. 'Brilliant year. You want to know why it's been such a brilliant year for them, well, I couldn't really tell you. You'd better go and ask the marsh harriers.'

WOODLARK

BY the time Robin Moore's stint as a Minsmere volunteer was drawing to a close, the air above the reserve must have been black and blue with bruises. Robin, big, longhaired and noisy, was accustomed to punch the air in delight, like a goalscoring footballer, whenever something especially pleased him. And practically everything about Minsmere pleased him: working endless hours, relentlessly hard, and getting absolutely no money whatsoever. Great, yeah, punch the air. It was the beginning of autumn, autumn as the world, rather than Jeremy Sorensen, knows it. I was walking through the Minsmere woods. I came on Robin and a party of volunteers, led by Ian. The scream of the chainsaw inevitably brought me to them: Robin was engaged with a spindly silver birch. It was clear he had acquired an affinity with the machine since I had seen him take his toddler's first steps earlier in the year. He cut his melon slice from the trunk ('never cut through your hinge') and, with initial reluctance and final swishing acceleration, the tree fell to the forest floor – the right way. Yeah! Robin gave the air a fierce right uppercut, and grinned in delight.

During a pause in his exertions, Robin removed his hardhat, scratched the back of his neck below the ponytail, and explained: 'This is going to be a really nice cushy little number for nightjar and woodlark. You see we have a nice southwest-facing slope, which will get warmer than other places. That's why they grow grapes on southwest slopes. We're taking out all the silver birch, leaving a decent length of trunk sticking out. That's so that Ian will find them easily later on. He will take the trunks out close to the ground, and treat all the trees, all that's left of them, with Amcide, which will kill them. Otherwise they'll come back as thick bushes. Later still we'll come back and strim out the bracken, and it will be a lovely glade in the summer. The nightjar like to display in an enclosed space. So we'll leave a few perches for them: six, seven feet off the ground. They churr on the ground, and then take off, and clap their wings. You can just see the pale patches on their wings, in the dusk. Two hundred yards off, all you see is a white patch. And with luck, we'll get woodlark singing in the glade too. Great.'

Robin was planning to stay at Minsmere till the end of the year, and then a little longer: probably fifteen months in total. He lived, for all this time, in the Vols' Hut, as the place is invariably called. For the first couple of months I was at Minsmere, I confess I was convinced it was called the Voles' Hut. I never dared to ask why. Perhaps in some walks of life, any kind of volunteer is considered a lower form of life. This is not the case in conservation, even if the physical circumstances of a volunteer are pretty unattractive. Robin's plan was to spend his fifteen months sharing not only a gas ring but a tiny room with any stranger that came along. It is not domestically ideal. But it had to be gone through. It had to be welcomed, because for Robin, as for many vols, volunteering was a career move. It is hard to get a start in conservation as a paid profession. In banking, they try to lure in the people whom they consider the right sort: they give them a very high initial salary, and offer a mortgage at a deliriously exciting rate. And before you know where you are, you are a banker. You can't afford not to be. It seems that conservation has adopted a precisely opposite approach: doing all it can to put people off: at first not paying them at all, accepting them into the paid ranks only reluctantly, and even then refusing to do anything rash like overpaying them.

No one leaves university, or any other kind of education, and walks straight into a paid job in conservation. All advertised jobs demand a good bit of practical experience. This is the same Catch-22 that affects an actor fresh out of drama school. Both areas have the same answer. Work for nothing. Actors on the dole perform in 'fringe' productions, earning nothing as they do so. Conservation volunteers live in sheds like the Vols' Hut, out in the wilds, and they chrome dykes for the same salary. It is, when you think of it, a reasonable enough way of carrying on. Conservation sounds a lovely thing to do, especially if you are twenty-one. It *is* lovely, certainly, but it is not for everybody. You must learn whether the huge rewards of practical conservation inspire you in their physical reality, as much as they did in the imagination and in a thousand dreamy discussions in students' unions. And of course, you must do it for nothing: conservation organisations are not going to try and tempt you with recklessly lavish offers of their hard-campaigned-for lolly.

Vols who intend to make a career in conservation must work in the hope of winning a six-month paid contract: the next step in the rather rickety career structure. This will generally be for the spring and summer (sorry, Jeremy, spring and autumn) when there is a need for extra hands on a reserve. You then look for another contract, making it through the winter as best you can, sometimes returning to volunteer work. Ian did seven six-month contracts before he landed his first fulltime post: you really have got to want to do this kind of work very much indeed. And when you finally reach the holy grail of fulltime employment, the salary is hardly princely. It is not the world's most attractive option for a family man: and it needs an exceptional partner to make it work. Doug, who had joined Minsmere that year, and moved into Scotts Hall Cottage in Sheepwash Lane, is one of the few wardens with a wife and children.

A lot of mid-term and long-term vols come straight to a reserve from university. Minsmere is a very good option for them. The place is immediately enthralling, and the variety makes this especially valuable: a vol can 'learn' half-a-dozen habitats during a decent spell at Minsmere. Doug came to Minsmere to look after much of the training: Minsmere, under his direction, was becoming something of a national university of practical conservation.

Many of the newly-graduated vols were doing a three-month stint for two simultaneous reasons. They were doing something important, and at the same time, for the first time in three years, they had a period in which they could think things over. Many people suffer from the bends when they emerge from university. Volunteering can be a useful buffer between education and real life. Many come into a three-month stint with science degrees, along with various hopes and ideals and problematic thoughts about compromise. Minsmere gives you an opportunity to sort out such a muddle. Many vols do not know whether to go into practical conservation or research: they are as anxious to find out about their own desires as to learn about practical conservation. Three months at Minsmere is a fine way of postponing an irrevocable decision.

But for others, conservation comes capriciously, as a late vocation. Robin was one of these. 'Basically, what I did was live in London doing lots of chronic jobs for bosses you never saw, for a pittance, trying to live in a flat on the breadline. So I went to do a City and Guilds six-month course in catering, because I liked cooking. But there I learnt that the profession mostly involves horrendous hours in steaming kitchens, and I knew it wasn't for me. I then spent a period working for British Rail, sitting in a Tadworth station, which was mostly deserted, selling tickets to about ten people a day. Then I heard about volunteering, and I did a week here at Minsmere. And I found out that I really loved it. I heard that you could become a long-term volunteer, and that if you did the job well and worked hard, you could get a six-month contract. So I left a girl I'd been with for four years, and came here. In fact, I left everything I'd known. I've never looked back. I came in with all my worldly goods, a bag of clothes and a black and white TV.

'First thing I did was to spend an intensive two months in the reedbed. January, it was. I used to have a job in a place without any windows. Now I was out there all the time. A little cold, maybe, but you look up and there's a harrier flying round . . . all those things I'd left behind, all those things that I'd been working to try and buy. I didn't want them any more. I just wasn't interested. People tell me I'm here because I can't handle real life. I'm putting my head in the sand. I can't face the real world. Well, this *is* the real world.

'Either you like it or you don't. Some people come here, and they really want to do their bit for conservation. After two weeks of being wet and cold and muddy and cooking for themselves and sharing a kitchen and the wellingtons are still soaking the next morning . . . they say, this is not for me! But I went home after the first month of being here. I remember standing at a bus stop in Purley. A group of young men went by. The *aggression* on their faces! An ambulance went by, and a fire engine, up the A23. And I thought, no, I'm never coming back to live in a place like Purley. I'm for Minsmere. And I was really happy about that.'

There are various things a long-term vol has to get right. The first of these is generally parental. Vols often explain to their parents that they need a few months to 'get it out of their systems'. And some do exactly that, leaving behind them three months or so of hard work, generally well done. But there are plenty who find, in the freezing ditches of a Minsmere winter, that they are not having a break from real life: they are coming to terms with a vocation that will last them the rest of their lives. Robin said that his parents were totally supportive. 'That was because for the first time in ten years, they saw that I was doing something I liked.' Most parents, confronted by the full force of youthful vocation, become supportive. There is no other option.

That leaves the question of money. The answer is to sign on for Social Security: but this is another Catch-22. There is an official belief at the Department of Health and Social Security that volunteering is a way of skiving: putting yourself out of the job market and having a blissful time at the taxpayers' expense. Dole-paid actors working on the fringe would have their dole money taken away if it was discovered that they were actually trying to build a career for themselves by doing unpaid work. Volunteering in conservation is a tentative, if not an out-and-out career move that will eventually lead to fulltime employment: that is an argument they have heard often enough at the DHSS in Saxmundham, and that has been generally found acceptable. It is an arrangement that is good for the future of their clients, and, as it happens, for conservation.

'You've got to stick having little money, working hard, and

getting on with lots and lots of different people,' Robin said. 'And it can be hard, living in that Vols' Hut. I mean, you get people coming in and there's something about them that you know is going to drive you *insane*. I remember one bloke that seemed to have a permanent drip on the end of his nose. Then there were some French ladies coming in and shouting about how dirty the bathroom is. You really do get some obnoxious people. You get some really nice people too, but it can be difficult. For a start, you have to share your room.

'You might get a different person every week. Any one of them might have BO. Vegans and vegetarians. Libbers for nature. But I'm not complaining. I'm hoping to get a contract in the spring. Anything. Anywhere. I'm back with the same girl I left to come here, after an eleven-month break. She has moved into conservation work as well. We've both changed. Both in the same direction. It's great, you know? For the first time in my life, I'm looking forward to the rest of my life.'

There are a good many female vols these days. Like Robin, many see the period of volunteering as an important career move. But the business is less straightforward for a woman. Eirwen Edwards spent six months at Minsmere over the autumn and winter. Why winter? 'Because I'm stupid.' Possibly she would go for a career in practical conservation. Possibly not. She has a biology degree: perhaps she would end up in research. 'It was the idea of conservation that brought me here. Not birdwatching.' She knew she had let herself in for a tough time. 'There is a very macho atmosphere in conservation work. Too many jokes. I don't know if I could live with that for ever. Because it is the outside jobs I am interested in. The Society has a good number of female information wardens, but they are people who spend a lot of time indoors talking to people. It's not what I'd like to do. But they don't take on many female contract wardens. Still fewer as fulltimers.'

In September, Minsmere had three female vols in residence, including Eirwen, all of them recent graduates. You can say what you like about university, but it certainly does not set you up for eight hours and more of physical work.

Anna Geach had spent a year before arriving at Minsmere working in a shop in Bond Street. This elicited cries of horror from the other two. Anna was pretty firm with them: she happened to need the money, at the time. So she did it. As you do, if you want independence. 'I like being outside,' she said. 'The longer I am here, the more I realise how much I hated working in that shop, squeezed into a nice little suit all day long, squeezed into nice little shoes, squeezed into a nice little personality. I'm enjoying this very much, though I haven't got any precise plans. It's not as if I have a mortgage or kids or anything. I haven't found any problems in being female – but then I haven't applied for any jobs. It's not a problem getting a vol's posting.'

Conservation is supposed to be a forward-looking business, so it needs to take a forward-looking line on women. More and more women want to be involved: reserving all the decent jobs for the traditional burly, bearded bachelor is not the way forward. And in fact, the Society took on Barbara Young as chief executive that year: life was changing at Sandy as elsewhere. Ian and Jeremy both believe it is important to involve women in practical conservation as well. Neither of them wants to see good talent leaving the Society, or worse, leaving conservation altogether. 'You don't have to be fantastically strong,' Ian said. 'You just need a little stamina. It's more important to have what's necessary upstairs. I sympathise with the women who come here. If they want to get anywhere, they have to go for everything 150 per cent.' However, I have done a fair amount of writing about women's sport, and I know that physiologically, women are tougher than men. The tougher the event, the narrower the gap between male and female performance. At the extremes, like running over the Himalayas, women outstrip men. Women have greater stamina. They are better equipped for handling both heat and cold. That makes women a pretty decent bet for running the average nature reserve.

Mike Barton was another man with a late vocation. He came for a six-month stint: he was thirty and he had been processing claims for the Social Security. Now he was on the dole himself, and an invaluable source of advice for others in the Vols' Hut making Social Security claims. 'It wasn't great, working for the DHSS. I especially hated the way that you are not allowed to tell people what they are allowed to receive. You can only give it to them if they ask specifically. I was working for them for four years, and then I got out. I'd had enough. I'm thirty, I have no academic qualifications whatsoever. So I'm trying to get in through the back door. What I need is lots of experience and very good references. And I'm here trying to get both. It's a very long and very late apprenticeship. I know it will take me twice as long as someone with a degree, but you have to hope. Sooner or later it must come to those who work. And as for the DHSS – never again. If they paid me five times as much, never again. The money is no problem: you just live within your means, don't you? I'll be staying here. Outside, I mean. I'll never go back inside.'

He looked around the woodlark glade. The floor was now littered with wood: the trees had been carved into still-uncomfortably-large hunks with assured strokes of Robin's chainsaw. The tractor could be heard in the distance: it was Ian roaring up with a trailer to take the wood away, so that the glade could be left for the birds. The next task was for Mike, Robin, Eirwen and Ian to get the trailer loaded. The autumn damp was beginning to eat in the bones, and hands were made unhandy by the chill. Soon it would be dark: time to go to the hut and cook some mess on the shared cooker. I remembered what Robin had said: and he was right. These people were not running away from real life. They were embracing it.

GREENSHANK

MINSMERE was birdless. That, at least, was how it looked at first glance, and at second glance too. The view from West Hide was nothing less than shocking. Not only were there no birds: there was no water either. All you could see was mud: mud that had baked as hard as concrete. It was deeply and fiercely cracked: you could hide a hand and more inside the best of them. Lifeless. This was drought in full grip.

I sat there for a while, rather hypnotised. It was hard to come to terms with Minsmere as a thoroughly nasty place. Then, at last, I saw one: a bird, a bird! It was a young heron, mooching about on the far side of the Scrape. It bore the appropriate expression of Ian-like intensity, but I thought it would probably need one of Ian's powertools to get through the baked mud. A moorhen walked along the edge of the reeds, wondering where the water had got to. The place was unnervingly silent: a silence emphasised by the sudden brief caterwaul of a couple of herring gulls. Right across the Scrape from me, I saw a wader, poking about in a dispirited fashion. I watched it for a while, as it traipsed around. It was a greenshank. A nice bird in a nasty place. That was all; a couple of months back, the place was heaving: you would see a thousand birds every time you glanced at the Scrape, and hear the babel of two dozen species. But now, nothing.

This was September, and it should have been one of Minsmere's busy times. The autumn wader passage was in full swing across the country, and normally you get a nice range of species making refuelling stops on the Scrape. Right now, the Scrape looked about as useful for a south-journeying sandpiper as Times Square. I saw a set of otter prints, fossilised in the mud.

Jeremy was getting a terrific volley of complaints from visiting birders. He was doing everything wrong, they said: it was quite obviously his duty to put water on the Scrape. That would soften the mud, and bring in the autumnal waders. It would, too. Minsmere is supposed to be good for rare birds, so where were the semi-palmated sandpipers? Where were the lesser yellowlegs? Jeremy's thoughts on the subject could be interpreted as 'bugger the lesser yellowlegs', though he is too much of a gent to put it quite that way. But he would point out that Minsmere is rather more than a birdtable for passing rarities.

'The drought has gone from serious to desperate,' he said. 'And I do have another card to play. The birders are actually right, for once: I really could put water onto the Scrape if I chose to. But I'm not going to. I could only put down seawater, and I've already had to put seawater onto the Scrape once this year. And if the drought continues, still more seawater would be disastrous. It would get the salinity unbelievably high by the time the next breeding season came along. And if it got too saline, that would kill off the invertebrates that live in the lagoons. So the waders would have nothing to eat, and we would have no breeding season at all on the Scrape. Next year's breeding season is far more important to us than a few rare waders passing through over the next few weeks.' As a refuelling stop for passing waders, Minsmere is useful. As a breeding ground, it is essential.

'It would be nice to have a display of waders for our visitors,' Jeremy said. 'Of course it would. But it's more important to think in terms of next spring. If someone could guarantee that we would get ten inches of rain in December and January, then fair enough, I would open the sluice and fill the place with seawater. But we might only get six inches, and that ain't enough.' The figures, so meticulously logged every day from the weather station, told the story of the drought with pedantic clarity. A wet year at Minsmere gets thirty inches of rain. Twenty-six inches is reckoned to be a little on the damp side; twenty-two inches is a normal dry year. But by mid-September, Minsmere had received a total of twelve inches. 'It's not dry, it's crazily dry,' Jeremy said. 'If we had a year like this following a twenty-two-inch year, it would be fairly serious. But it comes on top of a year with nineteen inches – and that's . . . well, it's *not* disastrous. It's different all right. But you don't have disasters in this sort of game. Take the gale of '87, when all the trees blew down. That wasn't disaster – boy, I could have wept – but if you put your mind right and you work it out, then you realise that it's very interesting. Maybe we shouldn't have a reedbed at all. Maybe we should have pratincoles nesting where the reedbed is now.' Since pratincoles go for places like arid steppe, it was clear that Jeremy was making his point by over-stating it.

'Well, who is to say that the present weather is just a blip on the chart?' said Jeremy. 'We don't know if it's part of the greenhouse effect, or whether it is something completely unrelated. Perhaps the reedbed is done for, in the long term. Perhaps the entire pattern of the distribution of rainfall is changing. Perhaps some places will get a whole lot more rain than they are used to, and others much less. We are working in the dark: we always are. All we can do is assume that, over the next eighteen months, we will get a sensible amount of rain, and plan accordingly. We have no other basis we can plan on. And if you don't make an assumption like that, if you just sit back and watch – and we know from all our past experience that we can help bird populations enormously with good management – then we will start going backwards. So, what we do, what we *must* do is to make the assumption that there is no real long-term change. And work on.'

This is not an easy matter: it gets more complicated the longer you look at it. The more you try and think long term, the greater the number of variables you are faced with. The only certainty is change: change is the essential process of life. There are indications of a gradual rise in the level of the North Sea: some people have predicted a very considerable rise. If the sea rises enough, then it will overwhelm the flood defences that line the coast, the flood defences that are at the heart of the reclamation schemes that created so much of the East Anglian landscape. Water would then pour over the seawall, and it will be goodbye, Scrape and goodbye, Minsmere New Cut. You would end up with an estuary. This was exactly how the Minsmere River met the sea before it was tamed by the land-drainers. 'And it would make a smashing estuary. So you can't lose in the end, can you?'

Perhaps Professor Pangloss is the patron saint of conservation: all is for the best in the best of all possible worlds. Certainly a Panglossian approach is better than gloom'n'dooming. The Panglossian principle is essential for any working conservationist, so long as you are talking about natural forces, like climate and waterlevel. It is when you take in human intervention that life gets problematic: the forces of development and commerce and the ever-expanding human population are potent threats to the proper order of things. And to make things worse, mankind's influence on the climate and on waterlevels becomes more apparent with every passing day.

But in natural terms, and strictly in natural terms, Jeremy's Panglossian approach is the only sane and proper way to understand things. There is no disaster in nature, only constant change. Take the great extinctions of prehistory: the most massive, the Permian extinction, the most famous, the passing of the dinosaurs. Without these disasters, we would not have the world we know today. Had the dinosaurs not met their spectacular end (after, never forget, 100 million years of dominance, which sets a useful benchmark for ambitious species), then the mammals might well have stayed what they had been for millions of years: little overlooked scraps of fur that scraped a living in the shadow of the dominant beings of the planet. No, the only disasters are manmade. If Minsmere Estuary were to be reborn, then it would certainly teem with life.

'You must strive to do what you can do for the habitat you've got. And you do that, always knowing that you might be striving for nothing. You must not ludicrously fight the natural process. You fight it, yes, you'd never build a seawall if you weren't prepared to fight it. We'd never keep our reedbeds if we weren't prepared to fight it. So you fight. But not ludicrously.' Should Minsmere Estuary arise, like a phoenix, from the grazing fields around Minsmere River and the New Cut, we would have an estuary where the RSPB was the major landowner. The estuary would probably spread the length of the reserve, as far inland as the Eel's Foot. That might even be something worth celebrating.

Jeremy was not spending the drought thinking of worst-case scenarios. His job was to continue as before: to maximise the habitats that Minsmere possesses. And, in his Panglossian way, Jeremy had decided that the drought was not a disaster but a Window of Opportunity. He decided that this was the moment to perform some spectacular management work. For it was not just the waterlevels on the Scrape that had been giving him cause for concern. He had also been losing water from Island Mere. He had expected the levels to fall in a drought, obviously, but they had fallen far more rapidly than he expected. It looked all right, if you peered out from the Island Mere Hide. But if you stepped into the areas of prohibited access, you found an alarming rim around the mere: a rim of the same cracked, dried mud you found on the Scrape. Island Mere was leaking.

So Jeremy came up with a magnificent doubleplay. He decided that he could do some important work to improve the Scrape – and that work would enable him to improve Island Mere. Both these jobs could only be performed in drought conditions. The first job was to bulldoze a section of the Scrape. This was an area that had never been finished satisfactorily: when the Scrape was first scraped out with a bulldozer, the rains had fallen too rapidly to allow them to finish the job. Now the Scrape was bare and dry again, and once again it was possible to bring a bulldozer out across the lagoon and get to work. The idea was to deepen one section of the Scrape, and to create a series of new pools and islands – 'profiling', in conservation jargon.'Quite a business,' said Jeremy. 'Using a front loader to profile the Scrape. Because you can't really see what you are doing. And it's a pretty delicate operation. The tendency is not to skim, but to dig in. And having dug in, you dig in further. That's exactly what you don't want, so you have to be careful. I wanted to leave a series of smooth undulations; actually, I've ended up with rather steep undulations. And I've deliberately put in some deeper profiles, so that the water will remain there longer than it did this year, if we have another dry summer. I've also created a few more avocet territories, by

Flying in the Face of Nature

making various angly bits and bays and inlets on the islands and the edges of the lagoon. You remember the principle of the round pond, and the wiggly pond? A round pond will have a pair at each end, a wiggly pond will have a pair in every inlet. Anyway, I've taken a load of soil from the Scrape – and I've been able to use it straightaway for something pretty important. That's very nice. I'm very pleased indeed about that.'

The next stage of the masterplan involved the construction of a track right through the reedbed, skirting the edge of Island Mere: a track wide enough to take the tractor. The track was about a mile and a half long, and by the time it was finished, it would take you from Tree Hide to the nearest point of interest in Eastbridge in half an hour: accordingly, I nicknamed it the Eel's Foot Expressway. The construction of the expressway was an inch-by-inch advance, clearing the undergrowth and scrub, and occasionally taking out willow. This had, of course, to be done tactfully: marsh harriers like to perch on small trees that stick up into the reeds, and known harrier perches, or even likely-looking perches, were left. This made the path agreeably serpentine, rather than ruler-straight. Once the project had gone deep enough into the reeds, Jeremy organised the construction of a new sluice gate about 100 yards from Tree Hide. This would enable him to control the levels of Island Mere, and give him a huge advantage here should there be another drought. Again, the dry conditions made this a moment to seize: the disastrously low waterlevels made the construction of the sluice a much simpler business than it would be with the area in full spate. The expressway builders advanced slowly along the edge of the mere, and as they went, they made good the bank. You could not take a tractor here in anything other than drought conditions: and even in the dry, there were a number of perilous moments. More than once the tractor got stuck, and had to fight its way out. On one occasion, Ian was within a toucher of turning the thing over. But the combination of good luck and good management is a potent one, and the team worked hard to make its own luck.

About three-quarters of the way to the pub, Jeremy made the great discovery: he found the trouble-spot, the place that had caused the loss of all that water from the Mere. It had started as a coypu hole. The water had found this weakness and had worked on it, in its relentless watery way, and brought about a collapse in the bank. Water had poured away from the Mere. So the tractor was loaded with all the clay that Jeremy had scraped from the Scrape during the re-profiling. It made the carefully perilous journey along the expressway to the breach in the bank, and there the bank was made whole again. It took five complete trailerloads: an awful lot of dirt. The result was that the Scrape would be better than ever, when the rains came again, and the waterlevel on Island Mere would, in the end, be higher than ever. As a bonus, Jeremy's triumphantly acquired new tractor had proved its value one thousandfold in its first few months on the reserve.

In short, the drought had been turned into a boon. We would not see the benefits of the work till the following spring, but in the meantime, the new sluice had replaced the electric fence as Jeremy's special delight. Instead of deliberately electrocuting himself every time he passed the fence ('Ooh! That's working, that is') he now felt the compulsion to thrust his hand into the chilling waters gushing through the sluice to see how beautifully everything was flowing.

The autumn was also the time for advance planning on the heathland regeneration. The first nitrate-less crop of barley had been harvested by the leasing farmer, and down on the reserve proper, the planners from Sandy wanted to carry out an experiment to work out the best way of hurrying the reclaimed arable land back into a tract of proper heathland. So a researcher came from headquarters to establish an experimental ground on the tussocky, rabbity area behind the shop. The idea was to try a series of different cultivation methods in measured strips of land. That way, it would be clear which method worked best and fastest. There was a complicated map detailing exactly how each strip should be dealt with. Every possible combination of circumstances was catered for. Some strips were to have rabbitproof fences, some would have cropped heather scattered over them: every variable they could think of was covered. Naturally, there was a special strip that had to be left alone, for control: it was marked on the map 'Control: No Treatment'. 'If this was a betting event, I'd fancy a quid or two on Control: No Treatment,' I said. 'A promising outsider, I'd say.'

'You've got to have a special strip for Control: No Treatment,' Jeremy said. 'Even though the experimental plot is surrounded by about a hundred acres of Control: No Treatment.'

Jeremy's slightly weary amusement betrays one of those great gaps that inevitably occur between people who work in the same field in a totally different way. It is an archetypal clash: in this case between the people on the front line ('idiot wardens who don't understand the first thing about experimental science') and scientists ('idiot scientists who've never got their hands dirty in their life'). The scientist came to Minsmere and laid out all the strips with impressive care, getting his boots dirty on the actual site. This was a good start. Unfortunately, he used brown string to mark the strips. This was invisible, and also, he did not put it on awfully well, so a lot of it fell off the marker pegs. The rabbits liked it, though: they chewed up a good deal of it, finding it an interesting variation to their usual diet. All of that meant that the Minsmere staff had to lay out all the strips again. The scientist had also stipulated two-metre buffer zones between each strip. This made good scientific sense. However, many of the strips also required a stout fence: the scientist specifically did not want any of the strips to share a common fence. Jeremy worked out that this was quadrupling the length of fencing the project required, quadrupling the cost in materials and, more importantly, in manhours. No chance, he decided. He had a dozen or so essential management projects to complete, including the major project of the Eel's Foot Expressway. This had to be completed in the dry, and though the drought showed no sign of abating, an intense bout of rainfall would have scuppered the project pretty effectively. So the Great Experiment had to have shared fences and like it.

Heather, laden with seedheads, was scattered across the plots that required it, according to the scientist's instructions. Within a couple of days, a spritely wind had picked it all up and tossed it elsewhere. Perhaps it went all over Control: No Treatment. Perhaps it had dropped all its seed on the right patch before it blew away. And perhaps it hadn't. And anyway, the heather had been gathered by hand: when the regeneration project began for real, the heather would be gathered by forage harvester. But you don't employ a forage harvester to gather a few handfuls of heather. So in fact, the experiment was not all that closely related

to what would actually be happening when the time came to light
the green touchpaper and turn the arable land into heath. Still,
no doubt some useful conclusions could be drawn from all this.
And no doubt at all, in times to come there would be nightjars
churring across what was now three fields of barley stubble.
Doubtless it would happen soon enough.

The year moved on. Many birders find autumn, and October in
particular, the most exciting time of the year. Many dash to the
Scillies to see what kind of wonderful windblown rarities will be
tossed their way; others take the opposite extreme and go to
Shetland and Fair Isle to tick more rarities and assorted lost souls.
Others revel in the seawatching that October brings, staring out
to sea for hours whenever the wind is favourable, wondering at
the passage of pelagic wanderers. October is a time of frenzied
birding. But in Minsmere, birdless Minsmere, with its lonely,
skulking greenshanks, it was a time for thinking about the birds
of spring: avocet and nightjar – next year's avocets, and the
nightjars of twenty years hence. In Minsmere, you are always
thinking about the spring. Spring is what the place is for.

And Jeremy, from the Panglossian school of conservation, had
harnessed drought and disaster and made it a potent ally in his
quest to improve the habitat for future seasons. 'Not Pangloss,'
said my wife, looking up from her theology books. 'Julian of
Norwich.' She quoted: 'All shall be well, and all shall be well, and
all manner of things shall be well.'

STARLING

A SPARROWHAWK wheeled over the trees of the Belt Wood: effortless mastery of the air. It attracted the attention of a pair of crows, who resented this indolent, insolent display of superiority. They opted to give the sparrowhawk the full harassment treatment. They decided to mob. Normally, two is a small number for a mob, but this is not the case with a crow. Even a solitary crow can be a mob when in the right mood. The two of them plunged and darted around the sparrowhawk, making a series of aerial passes daringly close to the beak end. The sparrowhawk glided on, apparently completely unconcerned, executing a series of very natty tight turns. Each turn left the crows flapping in his wake. They were left for dead, and made clumsy adjustments of their own, virtually making a three-point turn of the manoeuvre, before flapping raggedly back to make another pass, and once again to be treated with smug disdain.

It was clear that the sparrowhawk could leave the crows any time he had a mind to. But he stayed there, comfortably wheeling and mickey-taking, like George Best with a couple of fullbacks.

'Why doesn't he get away from them?' I asked Jeremy.'Why does he tolerate them?'

'Probably enjoying it,' Jeremy said. *Enjoying* it? Wasn't that rather flagrant anthropomorphism? And yet Jeremy was clearly at least half serious. Enjoying it? I looked up again to the sparrowhawk, the crows in hot, determined pursuit. One of them made his pass across the beak end – and this time he did so very close indeed. That changed the game completely. The sparrowhawk performed his most brilliant manoeuvre yet. In mid-air, he flipped. For a fraction of a second he was inverted, and he presented those fearsome talons to the crows in a brief, flashing instant, before flipping level again. This wigwag movement was performed in an eyeblink, but its meaning was unmistakable. Certainly the crows understood it: they backed off immediately. They performed a couple more passes, as a token gesture, but at a far more respectful distance. The game – or whatever it was – had lost its enchantment. That slick presentation of the talons had made it plain: OK, chaps, joke's over. By easy stages, the sparrowhawk flew, unmolested, down to treetop level.

A couple of hours before, I had walked down Sheepwash Lane and heard the sound of yaffling: the hearty peal of laughter uttered by green woodpeckers, a cheery sound of autumnal woodland. I knew, however, that it was not a green woodpecker. It was a good yaffle, but not quite good enough. And that made it a starling, the master impressionist of British birds. *Hahaha*: the woods echoed to the starling's merriment. As Jeremy taught me the beginnings of birdsong, I began to tune into the starling's mimicry. I remembered, back in the spring, delighting in the sound of a starling running through an entire repertoire of spring sounds: song thrush, robin and blackbird were all imitated in a single masterful burst.

I had the notion of compiling a tape for knowalls called 'So You Think You Know Birdsong?'. It would be a tape of nothing but starlings: the task of the knowall would be to work out what birds the starlings were impersonating. Jeremy liked the idea, but effortlessly topped it: 'You can tell what breeding birds you have in an area by listening to starlings. I remember when I first went to the Ouse Washes, I knew there were black-tailed godwits breeding there, because I heard starlings doing impersonations of the song the black-tailed godwits perform on their ceremonial courtship flights.' That, of course, is one of Jeremy's usual blackbelt-standard manoeuvres. But the question of starling impersonations continued to puzzle me. Why do they perform all this mimicry? Do the best mimics get the best females? What possible survival value could mimicry possess? I have a tape of a starling performing in rapid succession a swallow, a domestic hen, and a farmer whistling up his dog.

Are starlings also enjoying themselves? Are they taking the mickey, like the jinking, teasing sparrowhawk? Is the yaffle of a starling a hearty, thigh-slapping joke, a cheery two fingers to Pavlov and to everyone else who thinks that an animal is no more than a genetically programmed machine? What would a behaviourist make of a starling roaring with laughter from the woods of Minsmere?

And then I was reminded of another Minsmere incident, this time among the avocets. Again, it was in the spring. The avocets were going through their rigmarole of confrontation and dispute. The theory behind all this is to sort out flock hierarchy before the birds start nesting and establishing territories, though avocets are such quarrelsome birds they never stop picking fights and making minor adjustments to their social position. I saw one particularly vehement controversy. One bird was clearly dominating the other. It is customary in such circumstances for the loser to back down gracefully and quickly: much of the dispute behaviour of all animals is designed to produce a rapid and peaceful settlement. But this time, the loser really did not want to admit defeat. It was extremely reluctant to back down. I guessed that both birds were pretty dominant, both carrying a lot of clout in the flock. Certainly neither seemed much used to backing down. Most disputes among avocets are settled by a couple of run-and-pursuit ploys, but not this one. It went on through a dozen and more exchanges. Every time the losing bird was chased off, it insisted on coming back into the top bird's area of concern, provoking yet another dispute, and another rapid retreat. It was a long while before the top bird had made his point quite clear: one furious, headbobbing charge ended with the second bird finally taking to wing and flying across the lagoon to join the main body of the flock. I kept my glasses on the loser: he went into the flock, perhaps picking his place of alighting with particular care. On landing, he immediately set about harassing a subordinate bird: a sudden piece of utterly gratuitous bullying of a bird that had, no doubt, already had his inferior status clearly established. It was so ludicrously human, I laughed aloud in the hide. It was like someone coming home from a bad day at the office and kicking the cat.

Was I being anthropomorphic? Well, yes, obviously. Did this pattern of thought diminish my understanding of the birds? Or did it increase it?

If you have any involvement with animals, you are going to be accused of anthropomorphism. Accused? For this is supposed to be a dire sin. It is the sin of sentimentality, an affront to reason, an insult to the human condition. The implication is that we must have a completely different set of concepts for understanding humans and for understanding animals. The further implication is that the notions by which we understand people, notions like pain, anger, frustration, fear, fulfilment and enjoyment, can give us no help at all if we want to understand animals.

That is the hardline behaviourist view. People are people. Animals are mechanisms that slaver to the sound of a bell: preprogrammed Pavlovian machines. Animals do not have feelings to which people can relate. Everything must be interpreted mechanistically. If animals have subjective feelings at all, these must be as remote from our own understanding as the Creatures from Planet X, which have a flesh of solid gold and breathe pure methane.

I find such a set of beliefs unacceptable. Anyone who owns a dog *knows* this is nonsense. While it is absurd to say that a dog 'understands every word I say', it is equally absurd to say that a dog and his owner live in a state of bewildered mutual incomprehension. There is a rough-and-ready understanding in the relationship: there has to be. I shall turn here to Mary Midgley, the ethical philosopher, for some words about elephants: 'I want to point out how odd it would be if those who, over many centuries, have depended on working with animals, turned out to have been relying on a sentimental and pointless error in doing so, an error that could be corrected at a stroke by metaphysicians who have never encountered these animals at all. For instance – working elephants can still only be successfully handled by mahouts who live in close and lifelong one-to-one relations with them. Each mahout treats his elephant, not like a tractor, but like a basically benevolent if often tiresome uncle, whose moods must be understood and handled very much like those of a human colleague . . . If they [failed to take into account] the basic every day feelings – about whether their elephant is pleased, annoyed, frightened, excited, sore, suspicious or angry – they would not only be out of business, they would often simply be dead.'

The unwritten law of the mahout, then, is anthropomorphise or die. Anthropomorphism works here: and there is no other method that *does* work. Now a confession: I spend a lot of time with horses. I know how much this annoys the non-horsey world: horse people anthropomorphise to the point of nausea and beyond. All the same, anyone who treats a horse like a machine for a long period of time ends up injuring the horse or himself or both. Horses aren't human, but if you treat them as machines, they just don't work.

And so to people. Can we understand other people at all? Obviously we can, to a degree. How? We have our own feelings and emotions to work with, and use these as a guide. We make a leap-in-the-dark assumption that other people have feelings which are broadly similar to our own, and we work from there. It is rough-and-ready, but life in a community would be impossible without it. It is harder with people from different backgrounds and cultures, easier with people we know well. With a close friend, or a spouse, a subtle and accurate understanding is possible, almost as a matter of routine. But say we see a stranger take a tumble downstairs. We can see bewilderment, disorientation, pain, momentary fear. This is not presumptuous: it is obvious.

Now take a sparrowhawk zooming purposefully into a flock of starlings. The starlings see him and flee. Are they feeling fear? It is certainly easier to think of this as fear, rather than to see the starling as a running-away machine. Mary Midgley again: 'The fact that a power of understanding can be used on one's own species does not tend at all to show that it cannot work on others. It is an empirically established fact about human beings that they possess powers of expression and sympathy which make it possible for them to assess each other's subjective states, not in precise detail, but well enough to make an enormous difference to success in their understanding and treatment of each other. Where real care and attention are brought to bear, fine tuning of the common system can at times produce astonishing results. We ask next: does this work with other species? Do human beings, in their frequent interactions with other animals, manage to identify their moods and feelings too? This question can only be answered in terms of success of improved interaction, resting on interpretation and prediction of their actions. But then that is true on the human side as well. To go on using a concept successfully in a wide variety of situations *is* to have that concept. And the answer is that those who try and understand animals, and give time and attention to the matter, often come to understand them quite well. Those who do not, fail, which is also true with human beings.'

This is very nicely expressed, I think. But we are taught to be dismissive of our feelings for and about animals. It is good to hear a strong, academically certain, logical voice spell out for us what we have always *felt* was right. Mary Midgley makes it clear that you do not need to be a sentimental crank to believe that we can have some understanding of animals, or that we have certain moral duties towards them – any more than you need to be a sentimental crank to think that slavery is wrong.

For those who bring their attentions to the matter sometimes learn to understand animals quite astonishingly well. Look at Jane Goodall with chimpanzees, Cynthia Moss with elephants, Dian Fossey with gorillas, Mark and Delia Owens with lions and brown hyenas. Or for that matter, look at Jeremy Sorensen with his birds. Yet my wife told me of a philosophical discussion at her theological college, which had turned around a Jesuit's brutal question: 'How do you *know* animals suffer?' The same way I know that a human being suffers when he falls downstairs is the correct answer. Or, more brutally, consider this question again: is it acceptable to kick a tin can down the road? Is it equally acceptable to do the same thing with a kitten?

This confusion reaches its masterpiece of self-contradiction in vivisection. For years, experiments have been carried out on birds and mammals because the results are useful when they are applied to humans. You would not, after all, test your shampoo on the solid gold citizen from Planet X. But if your shampoo blinds a rabbit, then it is logical to assume it will damage a human. It is useful to experiment on a rabbit because it is *like* a human: it is considered morally acceptable to experiment on a rabbit because it is *not* like a human. Logic, please. For we are not actually talking about logic at all here, but about human self-esteem. We are back with Peter Singer's hissing term of speciesism.

We can increase our understanding of animals if we abandon the assumption that animals have nothing whatever to do with us humans. Intuition is the key: intuition backed up with logic and research. In practical conservation, this involves Jeremy's policy of 'think bird'. In terms of scientific breakthrough, it is equally important. An example: by making a small intuitive leap, we can understand how owls see in the dark. Or to put this another way, how they don't.

One of the vols had found an injured barn owl lying at the foot of Tree Hide. It was a plump bird, in excellent condition, but it had fallen into a ditch, was wet and cold, and was more or less unconscious. It carried no visible injuries, so the first assumption, that it had been involved in a punch-up with a marsh harrier, was ruled out. The problem appeared to be concussion. Ian and the vol rescued the bird, put it in a box, and left it in the warm, by Jeremy's stove to recover. But it did not, alas. It died. It had probably injured itself by flying full tilt into Tree Hide. It was almost comically pathetic.

Barn owls like open spaces for their nocturnal hunting. The Minsmere Levels, visible across the water from Island Mere Hide, are a favourite hunting ground for barn owls: though I effortlessly maintained my record of never seeing them. The open areas have the best visibility: as nightjars like to hunt open heathland, so barn owls like open grassland. The darkest and most difficult place for hunting is under the trees: this is where the tawnies make their living.

How do they manage it? The usual notion is that they have supersenses. They have phenomenal eyesight, magical orbs that are miles more acute than puny human eyes, and they have superb hearing: they can hear a wasp walking up a windowpane at a mile distance. They are miracles of adaptation.

Well, they are. Their eyes and ears are at the extreme limits of vertebrate adaption. *But so are our own.* An owl's eyes and ears are no better than a human's. Bats do, indeed, have a supersense:

their ability to fly in Stygian darkness guided by their radar sense is quite outstanding. But owls have no radar, which leaves us with the question: how do tawny owls manage to make their living in the pitchy darkness beneath the canopy? The answer is the same as the answer to the question of how a human can drive a car at night, or how a person can find his way round his own house in the dark, or why Jeremy and I can both see the same flash of feathers, and he will see a bird and name its species, while I will see a mere blur.

The answer, once again, is cognition: the education of vision. You can drive at night, even over unfamiliar roads, pretty nearly as fast as you go by day. You are driving well beyond the limits of your senses. You cannot see the surface of the road or very far ahead. But you know the pattern of British roads: you know that it is highly unlikely to throw you any surprises like, say a fifty-foot crevasse, or a river in full flood. You know the road width will remain constant, the road will follow standard radius curves, and that there will be signs to point out any irregularities in the pattern. You assume that other traffic will follow the conventions of headlights, driving on the correct side of the road, and so on. Thus you are able to process the meagre information in a useful way, and you can do so because the road is a familiar environment.

In the same way, it is no great matter to move confidently about your own home in the dark. You interpret a similarly meagre quantity of information in the same meaningful way. You see a glint of reflected light is the doorknob: you know the door must be half open. You have enough information to avoid walking into it. That darker patch is the chair, which is always in that spot, so you can now walk around it. You are home: you know all these things without thinking about them.

Tawnies act in exactly the same way. Their patch of woodland is as familiar to them as your own house is to you. Tawnies are completely sedentary birds. Once they have established a territory they will not, under normal circumstances, consider moving out. If a neighbouring territory falls vacant, they will not expand their range. There would be no point. The tawnies' edge is in knowledge of their territory: in familiarity. They know every hunting perch, all the flightpaths that lead to it, and from it. If you alarm a tawny in its own wood, and it panics, it is quite capable of flying into a tree and braining itself, as the poor barn owl did when it hit Tree Hide. But under normal conditions, a tawny owl makes its living through its ability to process meagre information in a meaningful way, and it can do so because its environment is utterly familiar to it. This enables it to exploit the nocturnal life of the woodland floor, a food source that would be unavailable to a predator that could only operate in daylight.

Similarly, a good birder is not one whose eyes are sharper, but one whose eyes are better educated. In exactly the same way, you learn to process meagre information in a meaningful way. I can amaze non-birders by identifying birds which they had hardly seen at all: Jeremy amazes me with the same luck at a higher level. And all of that means you can understand how a tawny owl makes its living by thinking about what happens when you get up in the middle of the night to let the cat in. Anthropomorphism is the key – that, and intuition.

Intuition is a working method that all practical conservationists employ. It is the fastest way of working. Research will often back up what a warden had learnt intuitively. The processes by which a warden 'thinking bird' has reached a conclusion can be retraced laboriously and logically. Good conservation allows for intuition as well as for well-documented scientific research. Anthropomorphisation is a vital tool, both for research scientists and for conservationists on the front line.

To accept the usefulness of anthropomorphisation is to lay yourself open to the charge of sentimentality. People who argue for a no-nonsense, unsentimental approach to animals and wildlife are generally rejecting not so much sentimentality as sentiment itself. This is dreadfully self-limiting. Really, I think that the people who reject anthropomorphism with the most violence are those who are most fearful of the obvious truth behind the whole business: that people are animals too.

As such, people are capable of a rewarding, two-way relationship across the species barrier, capable also of understanding how animals live their lives. Examples include mahouts, dog-owners, cat-owners, me and 'my' horse, Goodall and chimps, Moss and elephants, Fossey and gorillas, the Owenses and lions and hyenas. The point is to get away from the species-based pride. The human is certainly an unusual species, but it is still a mammal, still a

Starling

vertebrate animal. Irrational speciesist arrogance is not helpful in understanding the world in its plenty. I do not find it demeaning to share a relationship with an animal of a different species. It is an honour, is it not?

The more people who work and apply their analytical powers and their intuitions across the species barrier, the more we all grow capable of understanding and delighting in our fellow-animals. No animal that does Mike Yarwood impressions of other animals can possibly be a machine: that is Barnes's first law of animal behaviour.

GREATER FLAMINGO

THE year closed with some good news and some bad news for Minsmere and for conservation. The good news was that the RSPB bought another 100 acres of land at Minsmere, which brought the reserve beyond the 2,000-acre mark. The bad news was that Jeremy decided to leave.

This was something that took everyone by surprise. Well, he was of an age to take early retirement, and he was doing so. He was moving into a flat in Leiston, a few miles down the road, and he was going to work fulltime for the Jehovah's Witnesses. 'It's a question of leaving something you love for something you feel you must do,' he said, when we discussed it over the Slimmer's Lunch.

There is no doubt that the decision was a terrible wrench. It is not in Jeremy's nature to look backwards, but there were fifteen years of his life in that reserve. Minsmere was his life's work, his supreme achievement: and no one could spend fifteen years in the place, and then look out over those 2,000-plus acres, with their phenomenally successful breeding population of birds – *fabulous* birds – without a certain amount of satisfaction, and a great deal of anguish at leaving it. But Jeremy has always been a man who believes in doing what he thinks is right: so his decision, though very hard, was in a sense easy enough. For it was inevitable.

'You need the right kind of warden to take over,' he said. 'Got to be someone who is prepared to work. Not someone who wants a quiet life and no shop and no visitors. Of course he'll have to run the place his way; he won't run it my way, any more than I wanted to run it the previous bloke's way. I'll give him all the help I possibly can. Pass him a running ship. He'll come here with a management plan already drawn up, so he'll have time to get to know the place before the time comes for him to draw up the next five-year plan. I'll have everything on disc in the computer system by the time I go. And we'll have a month, maybe more, together, side-by-side, so he can learn how I did it. You've got to get out and look and talk, and walk every subtle inch.'

The new land the society had bought was mostly the rank meadow of the Minsmere Levels, south of the Scrape. I once saw a substantial herd of white-fronted geese grazing there: it was already a decent place for birds. 'I shan't even attempt to write a management plan for it,' Jeremy said. 'Leave it to the new bloke.' Most of the land was tufty grazing marsh, rather like Rob's new reserve at North Warren. The new land lay between the Scrape and Sizewell: Minsmere may be under siege, but it was fighting back gamely.

In the meantime, Jeremy was building his new hide. When it was finished, it would stand about fifty yards from the carpark. It would encapsulate all that is most miraculous about Minsmere. By the following May, I thought, a visitor would be able to leave his car in the carpark, duck under the whirring sand martins, and within a minute be inside the hide gazing at avocets. Jeremy was doing most of the carpentry himself. The Sorensen Memorial Hide? No, Centre Hide.

His last full year at Minsmere had been a year of great satisfactions and great disappointments: like all other years. There were 68,487 visitors, a falling-off from the previous year. This was largely because of the poor autumn: the drought-hit Scrape attracted no passing waders, and therefore few passing birders. There were ninety-six breeding species. The most spectacular performance came from the marsh harriers, with their twenty-seven young. It was a good year for raptors all round: three pairs of sparrowhawk and four of kestrel bred on the reserve. There were also enough sightings of hobby to encourage the thought that hobby had also nested on the reserve: no nest was found, but the picture was very encouraging. Since raptors indicate the health of a habitat, these figures appeared to demonstrate that Minsmere had been a howling success that year.

The success was reflected in a very solid performance from the songbirds. The total numbers of pairs were sixty-two nightingale, eighteen redstart, ten stonechat, seventy-nine whitethroat, fifty-two garden warbler, eighty-two blackcap, 135 chiffchaff and 217 willow warbler, with one each of Cetti's and Savi's warbler for good measure.

But there were many disappointments. The bitterns were perhaps the worst: three booming males, and only one definite young. The avocets, victims of the weather, performed adequately, with forty-seven pairs producing twenty-three young. The little terns were, of course, a disaster. Sandwich tern gave cause for optimism: there were five breeding attempts, and though none of them succeeded, this was a good pointer for the future. The bird has not bred at Minsmere since 1978. There were sixteen pairs of common tern, who reared eight young. The 300 pairs of screaming blackheads raised 100 chicks among them. It doesn't sound so many, but for a population to remain stable, a bird need only replace itself in the course of a lifetime. Over on the heath, the total of twenty-four churring male nightjars was thoroughly satisfactory.

There were 218 species recorded during the year, of which the superstar rarity was black stork, a new tick for Minsmere. Other 'whoopees', as Jeremy called them in his official annual report, were white-tailed eagle, white-rumped sandpiper, red-necked phalarope, greenish warbler, penduline tit and, of course, the ortolan bunting. Me, I missed the lot.

Jeremy would miss a lot the following year. That was certain. C.S. Lewis described himself as 'perhaps the most dejected and reluctant convert in all England'. There was a tiny bit of that in Jeremy's decision to man the watchtower for the Witnesses. He has lived with a vocation all his life, and it is not in his nature to resist a call: whether to conservation or as now. He was moving on because of a strong feeling of duty. The decision was based on certainty and conviction, rather than overwhelming emotion. I thought of the intrepid proselytiser who had penetrated the length of Sheepwash Lane to knock on Jeremy's door: soon Jeremy would be giving a greater part of his life to knocking on doors himself. I made a number of jokes about what I would do if he ever came knocking on my door to ask if I had ever thought about the Bible. 'I'll set the cats on you,' I said.

'That's all right,' he said. 'I'm looking for sheep. Not trying to saw the horns off goats.'

The Witnesses' gain – a very considerable one, it seemed to me – was emphatically Minsmere's, and conservation's, loss. I was, and am, extremely sad about this; I wished, and still wish, him well in whatever he does. He had given me the gift of an unforgettable year.

After lunch, we left the Eel's Foot, and Jeremy returned to his carpentry. This was going to be a cracking hide, a new design, part of the new generation of hides, the model of what a hide should be for years to come. And when it got too dark to work, he would go to the computer, where he was working on putting the entire reserve checklist on disc. ('Black stork *ciconia nigra*: an immature bird that was seen in the local area on four occasions . . .') Me, I walked the reserve.

The clouds were low and grey, hinting at snow. I started a circuit of the Scrape. I startled a stoat, which ran in front of me for twenty yards before disappearing like a snake into the bushes. I entered a hide and looked out. The Scrape was full of water again. Four inches of rain had fallen in November and early December, bringing the total up to that of a normal bad year. The mud was still cracked and hard beneath the surface, like a swimming pool, but that would change over the winter. And there was now a little fresh water in reserve for spring. That would be upon us alarmingly soon.

Lapwing was the dominant bird out there: and, thank the Lord, the place was full of birds. Minsmere looked like Minsmere again. A couple of dozen shelduck. Wigeon, the ginger-headed males adding a touch of colour to a monochrome day. Then all at once the birds took to the air, and I scanned the sky for a raptor that might have disturbed them. Hen harrier: Minsmere's winter

Flying in the Face of Nature

specialty. Two of them, a male and a female, circling round and round each other, not hunting at all. They seemed interested only in each other. Was this a hint of spring? Together, they glided down into the reeds.

I walked on to South Hide. The air was biting. A few flakes of snow were beginning to fall. A light precipitation, they would call it when they wrote the weather log. I entered the hide, took a seat, opened the viewing flap – and laughed. It was a joke: too good to be true. For there, in front of the hide, stood a flamingo. To be precise, a greater flamingo: looking as happy and as much at home here as any avocet. He looked as if England and a Minsmere winter was the only natural place for a flamingo. It was probably an escapee, but not certainly. In fact, as I was to learn later, there was a growing body of opinion that three greater flamingos seen around the coast that year were in fact vagrants from the east. The matter is *sub judice*, and as I write the British Ornithologists' Union has yet to pass judgement as to whether or not the bird was a real vagrant.

But it provided my year with a final touch of delight: a flamingo, sieving the waters of the Scrape through its daft great Roman nose of a bill, while the snow fell around it. This was Minsmere in self-parody: Minsmere in life-loving absurdity. Laughing again, I left it, and went to seek Eric the taxi, and the train home. As I went, the hen harriers rose from the reeds, and performed vast circles in the snow-filled air.

KLUUT

L IFE is a process of constant change; stasis is a kind of
death. Minsmere is not the place it was when I first
arrived there on the day of the gale. That is exactly as it
should be. It is bigger than before, having grown from
1,500 to more than 2,000 life-affirming acres. Many of
the people I met at Minsmere have left, but Minsmere itself is ever-
changing, ever-teeming.

Doug stayed on at Scotts Hall Cottage, recording bitterns and
running the Minsmere university of wardening. Neil moved on
when his six-month contract ended: he won his first fulltime post
as assistant warden at Arne reserve in Dorset, where the stars are
Dartford warblers. Robin's fifteen-month stint as a vol ended
when he won his first six-month contract in the Dee Estuary.
Mike, the vol with the late vocation who had left the Social Security
office to join Minsmere, had missed a contract that year, but he had
expected to. He was working on tractor-driving skills, convinced
as ever that he was doing the right thing. Next spring, he was
thinking, and I'll be there: a contract warden's job will be mine.

Down at North Warren, Rob continued to work on his new
reserve. He had flooded the north end of his grazing marsh that

winter, and the expected magic had happened: impressive numbers
of wintering wildfowl had zoomed in on the place. No Bewick's
swans, but just about everything else he had hoped for. He had
dug some pools to attract waders, and they were already bringing
in some cracking birds. Lapwing and redshank had bred under
the tufts of grass as the cows munched contentedly all around
them. No woodlark, but Rob was convinced they would be breeding on North Warren before long. 'Just a matter of time,' he said,
pretty contented himself.

Ian was more bullish about life than ever before, which was a
pretty awesome prospect. He had been promoted. He was now
Minsmere warden in charge of habitats, working to the new man
who came in with the title of Minsmere manager. 'It's brilliant,'
said Ian, eyes sparkling maniacally behind his steel-girdered specs.
'I can hardly sleep, I've got so many ideas. So many things I want
to do. It's those reedbeds I want to tackle most. I'm convinced
Glenn was right about them. I want to smash 'em to bits, and let
them start again. Make some new, *wet* reedbeds. I want to get
those bittern numbers back up where they should be.'

The new Minsmere manager was a man called Geoff Welch. He
was taking over from Jeremy, but the nature of the job was to
change with his appointment. Jeremy's success over fifteen years
lay in his creation and maintenance of a series of ever-improving
habitats, and his attraction of vast numbers of visitors. That
success meant that the demands Minsmere made of its staff had
changed. Jeremy had been all things. He had trained people to use
chainsaws, shot foxes, directly concerned himself with practical
management, and done all the ever-increasing amount of
paperwork and keyboard-bashing at the wordprocessor.

Now things were changing: Jeremy had departed, and the
patterns of work could be reorganised. Doug was to control the
training, Ian the practical management. Ian also took over
Jeremy's firearms license. 'Means I can shoot twitchers who sneak
onto the reserve on Tuesdays,' he said.

'That should give you some nice stuffed heads to go with your
deer trophies.'

'We had woodlark singing in that glade we made, remember
the place? It came in early March, but it went again. Never mind.
I'm convinced we'll get 'em. Next spring, maybe.'

Next spring: always another spring. Glenn, the bittern man, completed his two years with his reedbed skulkers, and his work found favour with everyone. He was then asked to make a study of capercaillie: after stone curlew and bittern, he had at last been asked to study a bird he would actually be able to *see* on a regular basis. He accepted the change with delight, once he had negotiated for himself an opportunity to continue his bittern studies for a month every spring.

Geoff was as delighted as everyone else with Glenn's work on the bitterns. 'The only pity is that he wasn't around to do it ten years ago,' he said. Geoff was as keen as Ian to start some creative management of the reedbed, for the following spring produced only a single boomer in the Minsmere reedbeds. It was very close indeed to being too late.

Geoff was approaching the challenge of the bitterns, and of all Minsmere, with great relish. For in a sense, he was coming home. Minsmere was his first love: he had spent much of his youth as a schoolboy volunteer at Minsmere, initially under Jeremy's predecessor, sleeping in a lean-to shed in the carpark. When he went to university, he spent all of every summer back at Minsmere. He was working as a vol during Jeremy's first year, and shared Jeremy's bungalow: a comparatively civilised place after the shed. After that, he was taken on as a fulltime warden elsewhere. He came to Minsmere after a long stint on the Nene Washes. He has something of Jeremy's easy affability, his good cheer, and his delight in tackling problems.

Jeremy was ensconced in Leiston: 'I was worried I would miss Minsmere dreadfully. But it's not nearly as bad as I thought. And I am so very much involved with what I am doing here.' He was in fine form, thoroughly enjoying his search for sheep. 'Geoff is a very good man. I know he'll do the job well. I am very happy to think of him running the place now, in his own way.'

I said to Geoff: 'Did you ever think, when you were sleeping in the shed, that one day you would come back here and run the place?'

Geoff laughed. 'The idea did cross my mind. But I think a lot of RSPB wardens *didn't* apply for the post, because of the size of the job. Now the job is called Manager, it means my job is basically to make sure that all the other people on the reserve have what they need to do *their* jobs. I was concerned that I might find that a little frustrating, but so far, I have not. Partly it's because I don't mind paperwork. But it's mainly because I have two big projects to get stuck into straightaway.'

The first project is a Visitors' Centre: a place where visitors will report on arrival to get their permits and hire binoculars, if they need to. The Centre will also take in the shop, and provide plenty of space for giving out information. It will include places for visual displays and a room for lectures. The parties of schoolchildren and adults – from absolute beginners to advanced birders – would be able to make better use of Minsmere than ever before. The place was marching onward. There was talk of putting in a tearoom at the Centre as well. The very suggestion has probably got the great wardens of the past spinning in their graves like tops: but Minsmere is for people as well as for birds, and that is now one of its great strengths. The RSPB exists because of the public will: and one of the finest proselytisers for conservation is Minsmere itself.

'The bittern situation is really worrying,' Geoff said. 'There has only been the one pair this year, and no evidence at all that they produced any young. No one has seen any feeding flights. And we are now convinced that this is at least partly to do with the reedbeds. The quality has gone right down. Tall, bone dry, all kinds of stuff growing there that shouldn't. So what we're hoping to do this winter is to start a major programme of rotational cutting. We will start in the main reedbed, where we have the water controlled, and once that's knocked into shape, we'll move on to North Marsh, or perhaps the section between Tree Hide and Island Mere. Glenn reckons the section between Tree Hide and the Scrape has gone so far that we will have to take a bulldozer to it.

'So I have arranged to borrow a couple of reedcutters, and we will see how fast we can go. And I have put our own machinery into next year's budget. The idea is to start a five-year rotation of cutting, but in some places we will have to isolate the reedbed, bulldoze it down below ground level, and start again. It will regenerate pretty fast: in about five years, provided the rhizomes are not too damaged. After all, the original reedbeds here only took eight years to spread from the ditches, once the area was flooded during the war.'

The reedbeds and the Visitors' Centre were the major projects, but the time would be coming soon enough for the heathland restoration. The arable fields were now growing their second crop of barley without added nitrates. The level of the nutrients remaining in the soil was being very carefully monitored. 'There has been plenty of work on restoring heathland, but no one has ever tried to create heathland from scratch before, apart from on a very small scale. The pattern we are predicting is that after the first year, when we have laid the heather clippings down, we will look at the place and think, my God, we have wasted our time here. Nothing has happened at all. And the next year it will all start to grow, and we'll be away. On some sites, they have found that heather strips are properly established in six years. So we are talking twelve or fifteen years here: the place is so big we will probably have to choose blocks within each field, and expand outwards. We won't have enough heather clippings to start the whole lot off at once.'

'There's a lot to do,' I said.

'There is. And I'm looking forward to doing it.'

Minsmere fizzes with hope. Every season is redolent with the promise of the next spring. And even after my year at Minsmere was officially over, I found myself returning. I simply couldn't keep away: I had to come and see the changeless, ever-shifting spring. Naturally, it was quite different from the previous year: naturally, the feeling of teeming expectation was the same. I went early, in the biting cold of March, and simply stayed, alternating bouts at the wordprocessor, processing these words, with long hours walking the reserve: more a matter of delight than research.

I was back at North Marsh in the dawn, and stood and listened to the lone boomer echoing forlornly across the reeds: '*Om.*' I heard the first chiffchaff chiffing and chaffing by the rhododendron tunnel. I saw the first wheatears as they arrived and flashed their flashy tails. The first sand martins swooped their way across Island Mere: these are the Big Three early arrivals, and it was a joy to be at Minsmere to greet them. The Cetti's warblers, resident all year round, woke up to spring and started to sing '*je suis Cetti*'. Three otters felt the bite of the season, and started to play elaborate and delightful games in the waters of Island Mere: every evening for a week they cavorted and writhed and wrestled and tumbled in full view of a few enthralled enthusiasts. I even caught up with my barn owl: two ghostly white shapes flitting away across the Minsmere Levels, on the far side of the Mere.

A couple of female marsh harriers had been seen, but I was there for the arrival of the first male, gloriously tricoloured. He and one of the females started energetically building a nest in the reedbeds, silently quartering the reedbeds, occasionally joining each other for a joint flight. One morning I saw the pair come together in the air, and then move simultaneously into a piece of perfect aerial ballet. Both flipped sideways, each presenting the talons to the other: such effortless virtuosity that it made your heart leap to see them.

And on the Scrape, the avocets were back, and every day as evening fell, they gathered together in a group in front of South Hide for what the books call 'loafing'. But as spring begins to rush through the avocet veins, a bunch of loafing avocets becomes a pretty restless sight. There is such a buzz in the air in late March, for it is all about to begin: the important business of the year, those crucial six weeks of the rearing of the young, was almost upon them.

Some birds stood on one leg and tucked their bills out of sight, affecting sleep. But others preened away with great self-absorption. A couple were feeding. In front of me, one pair was preening with unusually vigorous, synchronised movements. As I watched, the preening became less and less effective, more and more obviously a form of ritual. It was clear that they were not intent on their individual selves, but on each other. The exact arrangement of their feathers was not the main thing on the avocets' minds at all. The female then cocked her head on one side, as if intent on the feathers high to the left of her snow-white breast: for it was, you see, now obvious which was the male and which the female. Differentiating the sexes can be a problem for avocet observers, but not, apparently, for avocets. As the female continued her formal breast-preening, the male began to perform a series of half-circles around her, splashing the water rather dementedly with his beak as he did so. It looked like a parody of the avocet feeding technique. Time and again, he ducked under the female's white stern, which she lifted fractionally and invitingly.

And then all at once it happened. The male mounted, and as he did so, he dramatically raised his wings on high so that for a moment he looked, and no doubt felt, like an archangel. 'Lovely copulation, bliss on bliss', wrote William Blake, and who am I to argue? Spring was fizzing through Minsmere, and every bird could feel the force of it flowing through his veins. I thought of Dylan Thomas: 'The force that through the green fuse drives the flower . . .' Here at Minsmere, the green fuse had been lit, and it was sizzling away like fury. The very air of Minsmere was crackling with life: it was hardly surprising that it took only a second to turn an avocet into an archangel.

The rest of the avocet flock was profoundly disturbed by this pair's display of the passions of spring. A feeling of restless impatience spread through the gathering. Roosting was forgotten. The urge to move, to do something, almost anything, was strong in all of them. One by one, the birds untucked their heads from their wings, lowered the second leg back into the water and started feeding furiously, as if this were mid-day rather than the charcoal-grey light of near dusk. This was owl time, barn owl time, as I could now say with insouciance, not avocet time, but the green fuse, fizzing in the veins, allowed them no rest. Soon half the flock were feeding, scything through the water with windscreen-wiper strokes. The rest began energetic preening, often in close association with another bird. There was no more mating, not then, but the mood was all of anticipation, and the air was full of sexuality. Restless birds picked quarrels with each other, threatening rivals with head-bobbing charges, and backing down with brief, hopping flights. Not until it was almost completely dark did the flock come together again, and slowly wound down from all this restless loafing into something more appropriate for the time of day: a slow roosting, jockeying for best sleeping positions, and waiting for another teeming day of another teeming spring.

FURTHER READING

These books have all contributed to the background of my own, and a good few of them to the foreground as well.

A. G. Cairns-Smith, *Seven Clues to the Origin of Life*. Cambridge University Press 1985.

Paul Colinvaux, *Why Big Fierce Animals Are Rare*. George Allen and Unwin 1980.

Stanley Cramp (chief editor), *Handbook of the Birds of Europe, the Middle East and North Africa: The Birds of the Western Palaearctic*. Volumes 1–5. Oxford University Press, 1977–1988.

Charles Darwin, *The Origin of Species*. John Murray 1859.

Richard Dawkins, *The Selfish Gene*. New edition, Oxford University Press, 1989.

    The Blind Watchmaker. Longman 1986.

Alan Feduccia, *The Age of Birds*. Harvard University Press 1980.

Dian Fossey, *Gorillas in the Mist*. Houghton Mifflin 1983.

Stephen Jay Gould, *Ever since Darwin*. Burnett Books 1978.

    The Panda's Thumb. W. W. Norton 1980.

    Hen's Teeth and Horse's Toes. W. W. Norton 1983.

    The Flamingo's Smile. W. W. Norton 1985.

    Time's Arrow, Time's Cycle. Harvard University Press 1987.

    An Urchin in the Storm. W. W. Norton 1987.

    Wonderful Life. Hutchinson Radius 1989.

    Bully for Brontosaurus. Hutchinson Radius 1991.

Donald R. Griffin, *Animal Thinking*. Harvard University Press 1984.

Aubrey Manning, *An Introduction to Animal Behaviour*. Edward Arnold 1979.

Graham Martin, *Birds By Night*. T and A. D. Poyser 1990.

Peter Mathiessen, *The Tree Where Man Was Born*, William Collins 1972.

    The Snow Leopard. Viking Penguin 1978.

    The Cloud Forest. Viking Press 1961.

Mary Midgley, *Animals and Why They Matter*. The University of Georgia Press 1983.

Cynthia Moss, *Portraits in the Wild*. Second edition, University of Chicago Press 1982.

    Elephant Memories. Elm Tree Books 1988.

Bill Oddie and David Tomlinson, *The Big Bird Race*. William Collins 1983.

D. F. Owen, *What is Ecology?* Oxford University Press 1980.

Mark and Delia Owens, *Cry of the Kalahari*. Houghton Mifflin 1984.
Jonathon Porritt, *Seeing Green*. Basil Blackwell 1984.
Jonathon Porritt and David Winner, *The Coming of the Greens*. Fontana 1988.
David Quammen, *The Flight of the Iguana*. Delacorte Press 1988.
Oliver Rackham, *The History of the Countryside*. J. M. Dent and Sons 1986.
Harriet Ritvo, *The Animal Estate*. Penguin 1987.
Tony Samstag, *For Love of Birds: The Story of the RSPB*. The Royal Society for the Protection of Birds 1988.
Peter Singer, *In Defense of Animals*. Basil Blackwell 1985.
  Animal Liberation (Second Edition). New York Review of Books 1990.
Colin Willock, *Wildfight*. Jonathan Cape 1991.

Systematic Species List –
Minsmere 1990
Compiled by Jeremy Sorensen

NOTE: The figures concerned with location (e.g. c09) refer to biological compartments.

RED-THROATED DIVER (*Gavia stellata*)
Again, as in 1989, very few records in January; however, the peak Winter count on Jan 14th was 138. The first Autumn record was of a single bird flying North on Sept 25th.

GREAT NORTHERN DIVER (*Gavia immer*)
The only record was of one offshore on Nov 9th.

LITTLE GREBE (*Tachybaptus ruficollis*)
Peak count of 11 on Apr 1st was a good indication of the number of birds on the reserve; breeding is thought to have occurred, with a max of 6 pairs holding territory.

GREAT CRESTED GREBE (*Podiceps cristatus*)
Two pairs bred on Island Mere with one pair successfully rearing 2 young. Good numbers were seen offshore in Jan with a peak of 22 on the 7th. 18 on the sea on Nov 14th was the highest post-Summer count.

FULMAR (*Fulmarus glacialis*)
Recorded offshore from March 21st to September 16th with a peak of 17 on June 10th.

MANX SHEARWATER (*Puffinus puffinus*)
One bird going South on June 10th was the first record of the year. Other singles were seen on Aug 17th, Sept 11th, 15th and 20th; 2 flying North on Oct 3rd constituted the last records for the year.

LEACH'S PETREL (*Oceanodroma leucorhoa*)
Only one record of a single bird on Oct 13th.

GANNET (*Sula bassana*)
Recorded from Jan 28th to Oct 21st with a peak of 78 on June 10th.

CORMORANT (*Phalacrocorax carbo*)
Recorded in all months with a peak of 64 at Island Mere on Aug 13th. The island was cleared of vegetation in December; hopefully this will attract more birds to the roost.

BITTERN (*Botaurus stellaris*)
A poor breeding season for this secretive bird; 3 booming males were located in May/June and a flying juv. was seen in N. Marsh on Aug 25th. First booming was on March 14th.

LITTLE EGRET (*Egretta garzetta*)
Only one record of a single bird seen on the Scrape early on the 16th of May.

GREY HERON (*Ardea cinerea*)
Recorded throughout the year with a peak count of 8 on several dates. Predation by this species was minimal this year.

PURPLE HERON (*Ardea purpurea*)
Only a very brief view of an adult bird, from Tree Hide on June 6th constitutes the only record; this was not submitted because of the brevity of the observation.

BLACK STORK (*Ciconia nigra*)
This species was the only addition to the reserve bird list in 1990. An immature bird that was in the local area during August was recorded on 4 occasions all in August, on the 4th, 6th, 8th and 17th. All of these records were fly-overs; the bird was not seen to land.

SPOONBILL (*Platalea leucorodia*)
An early first record of a single bird flying over on March 10th was followed by an abundance of records, particularly in May when 3 birds were seen together from the 29th–31st. Last record was a single bird on July 31st.

MUTE SWAN (*Cygnus olor*)
2 pairs bred rearing 6 young. Peak numbers were recorded from Jan to March, with a max of 41 on Jan 14th.

BEWICK'S SWAN (*Cygnus columbianus*)
Recorded in Jan, Feb, Oct and Nov, with maxima of 32 on Oct 22nd and 15 on Feb 6th and 20th.

BEAN GOOSE (*Anser fabalis*)
The only record was of a single bird on Jan 26th.

PINK-FOOTED GOOSE (*Anser brachyrhynchus*)
8 on Nov 23rd probably constitutes the only genuine record; however, singles were recorded in Jan (1 date), April (3 dates) and Oct (1 date).

WHITE-FRONTED GOOSE (*Anser albifrons*)
The usual trend of numbers increasing from January and tailing off in March was again noted this year. Monthly maxima were: 25/Jan 4th, 86/Feb 14th, 55/Mar 8th. The first returning birds were 10 on Dec 2nd.

GREYLAG GOOSE (*Anser anser*)
2 pairs bred on the Scrape rearing a total of 12 young, and 2 pairs on Island Mere raised 7 young. The peak early year count was 200 on Jan 3rd, and 200 on Oct 8th was the peak in the latter half of the year.

CANADA GOOSE (*Branta canadensis*)
2 pairs on the Scrape reared 9 young, and a maximum of 3 pairs bred on the Island Mere complex. 235 on Jan 7th and 188 on March 11th were the highest counts.

BARNACLE GOOSE (*Branta leucopsis*)
All records refer to the feral birds frequenting the area. The peak count was 4 birds.

BRENT GOOSE (*Branta bernicla*)
Thin on the ground early in the year, with 17 on Jan 1st being the peak. Strong

easterly winds in October from the 12th to 22nd displaced many birds. Daily highs were 1500/13th, 500/14th and approx 10000 on the 21st.

EGYPTIAN GOOSE (*Alpochen aegyptiacus*)
The only record was of an adult on the Scrape on July 6th.

BAR-HEADED GOOSE (*Anser indicus*)
All records refer to a single bird; probably an escapee; from April to June.

SHELDUCK (*Tadorna tadorna*)
2 pairs bred on the Scrape rearing 14 young. A pair were also seen prospecting in c19 around the pool. Peak counts were 60 on Feb 6th, 48 on April 1st, and over 1000 flew past on Oct 21st.

WIGEON (*Anas penelope*)
2 pairs bred successfully on the Scrape rearing 1 and 3 young respectively. The peak early year count was 350 on Feb 4th and over 5000 were recorded flying past on Oct 21st.

GADWALL (*Anas strepera*)
3 broods of 6, 2 and 9 were seen on the Scrape and a minimum of 4 broods were seen on Island Mere. Early season counts suggested a possible breeding population of 24 pairs. Feb and June were the best months with respective peaks of 78 and 96. A record of 96 birds on Sept 19th is noteworthy.

TEAL (*Anas crecca*)
Only one brood was seen on the Scrape (9). However, early season counts suggested the population was much higher. The early season peak was 640 on Feb 4th and numbers rose later in the year to a maximum of 550.

MALLARD (*Anas platyrhynchos*)
Again a very successful season with over 20 broods located; the breeding population was estimated to be 52 pairs, from early season counts. Peak counts included: 237 on Jan 14th, over 700 on Oct 21st, and 381 on Dec 16th, which included 180 in c40.

PINTAIL (*Anas acuta*)
An early season max of 13 birds on Feb 4th was higher than last year's peak, however, over 140 birds flew past on Oct 21st during the prolonged easterly blow. Again as in 1989 a single bird was recorded in July on 4 dates.

GARGANEY (*Anas querquedula*)
The first returning birds were a pair on March 11th. A male was present for most of April and there were regular sightings through all the Summer months. The last record was of a female on Aug 23rd.

SHOVELER (*Anas clypeata*)
Approx 23 pairs were thought to have bred on the reserve. The highest count of the year was 68 on Feb 9th, but otherwise numbers were low: 60 on Jan 27th and 57 on March 11th were the only other decent counts.

POCHARD (*Aythya ferina*)
At least one pair bred successfully on Island Mere, a female was sighted with 5 young on May 15th. Good numbers were recorded in Feb and early March, with 20 on 2 dates in Feb being the season's peak.

Flying in the Face of Nature

TUFTED DUCK (*Aythya fuligula*)
Good numbers in early March and April suggested breeding could have occurred, however this was not proven. 18 on Feb 4th was the season's high; most of the other records were in the first half of the year, with a very poor showing after May.

SCAUP (*Aythya marila*)
The only record is of 2 birds on Aug 9th.

EIDER (*Somateria mollissima*)
Only recorded on 4 dates; 3 offshore on May 12th, 1 on Oct 21st and 3 on Oct 22nd and 7 on Nov 28th are the details.

COMMON SCOTER (*Melanitta nigra*)
A flock of over 200 offshore on June 16th was the peak count. Good numbers were noted in Oct, 174 on Oct 21st was again associated with the large movement of wildfowl at that time.

GOLDENEYE (*Bucephala clangula*)
Well represented in Jan, Feb and March, 2 males and 6 females on Jan 16th being the highest count. 10 offshore on Oct 21st and 2 on Nov 29th were the only records in the latter half of the year.

SMEW (*Mergus albellus*)
A female on the Scrape on Nov 8th constitutes the only record.

RED-BREASTED MERGANSER (*Mergus serrator*)
Only recorded on 3 dates, the first being a male offshore on Jan 1st; 2 flying South on Oct 13th and 5 on Oct 21st are the other sightings.

GOOSANDER (*Mergus merganser*)
2 records, the first being 3 on Jan 30th, and the other a female on Nov 12th.

RUDDY DUCK (*Oxyura jamaicensis*)
The only record is of a male on May 6th.

WHITE-TAILED EAGLE (*Haliaeetus albicilla*)
A 3rd-year bird was seen on three occasions: Feb 4th and 15th, and Mar 12th, all sightings were around the Scrape/reedbed.

MARSH HARRIER (*Circus aeruginosus*)
Once again a fabulous breeding season for this species. 27 young fledged from 8 nests. One male paired with 3 females and this section reared 11 young, all the other pairings were 1:1. Up to 2 birds were regularly sighted in Jan and Feb apart from a record of 3 birds on Feb 1st. The first male returned on March 17th and most juveniles were flying by the end of July. Dispersal was rapid in August, and by the end of the year 2 females were left as the Winter population.

HEN HARRIER (*Circus cyaneus*)
The highest roost count early in the year was 6 birds (2M, 4F), and birds were sighted regularly at least until the end of March, the final record of the Spring being a female on May 19th. The first bird back in the Autumn was a female on Oct 18th, and the highest roost count at the end of the year was on Dec 16th when 9 birds (4M, 5F) were noted.

Systematic Species List

MONTAGU'S HARRIER (*Circus pygargus*)
Recorded on 5 dates; a female on May 24th, June 16th and 19th, and a male on June 20th/21st. All records were of birds hunting/quartering over the levels and fields around Eastbridge.

GOSHAWK (*Accipiter gentilis*)
4 records all in October of a male seen around c51/55 were the only sightings.

SPARROWHAWK (*Accipiter nisus*)
3 pairs bred in c08, 17 and 28, the nest in c17 raising 3 young. This particular species was numerous both on and close to the reserve, and from records taken throughout the Summer an approximate total of 9 pairs bred in the local area.

BUZZARD (*Buteo buteo*)
There were 5 records, all of single birds over-flying the reserve: April 13th, May 28th, June 17th, August 31st and October 19th.

ROUGH-LEGGED BUZZARD (*Buteo lagopus*)
Only one record of a single bird on Oct 25th (per Philip Burton).

OSPREY (*Pandion haliaetus*)
2 records of adult birds, both of which circled the reserve for about half-an-hour; May 7th and June 1st.

KESTREL (*Falco tinnunculus*)
As with the other breeding raptors on the reserve this species was very successful. 4 pairs held territory, 1 pair in c19 raised 4 young.

MERLIN (*Falco columbarius*)
Only one record of a single bird seen on the October Hen Harrier roost on the 27th.

HOBBY (*Falco subbuteo*)
Recorded throughout the Summer/Autumn. 2 juvs seen on Aug 8th and afterwards could suggest this species bred for the first time, this year on the reserve; however, this was not proven.

RED-LEGGED PARTRIDGE (*Alectoris rufa*)
14 territories were located on the reserve, mainly on the heath/arable land. From the numbers of birds seen later in the year whilst monitoring the progress of the arable land this species had a very successful year.

GREY PARTRIDGE (*Perdix perdix*)
5 territories were located, all being towards the edge of the reserve. As with the Red-legged Partridge this species seems to have been quite successful this year.

PHEASANT (*Phasianus colchicus*)
The peak count was 30 on Nov 13th. As with the other gamebirds, this species has had a good breeding season.

WATER RAIL (*Rallus aquaticus*)
An approximate count of 25 squealing birds in the whole reedbed suggests the population of this species in 1990 was good, and from the number of sightings of immature birds the breeding season was a good one also.

Flying in the Face of Nature

MOORHEN (*Gallinula chloropus*)
Numbers were again low, with the peak being 70 on March 11th. Predation by this species on the Scrape was not observed this year.

COOT (*Fulica atra*)
Once again the best counts of this species were in July, the high being 75 on July 29th. However, as with the Moorhen, this species seems to be in decline.

OYSTERCATCHER (*Haematopus ostralegus*)
3 pairs bred on the Scrape this year, from these nests 6 young were reared. Present in most months with a peak of 14 on May 22nd.

AVOCET (*Recurvirostra avosetta*)
A very mixed season for this species, due mainly to the fluctuating weather conditions and varied waterlevels during the breeding season, which affected the rate of growth of the young. There were 102 nesting attempts, from which only 23 young fledged. The first returning bird of the year was on Feb 20th, and numbers peaked at 115 on April 13th. Most birds disappeared very early with only 2 records after Sept 5th.

LITTLE RINGED PLOVER (*Charadrius dubius*)
Only 2 Spring records, both of single birds on April 27th and May 7th. Most numerous in August with a peak of 8 on Aug 22nd.

RINGED PLOVER (*Charadrius hiaticula*)
Of 6 nesting attempts on the Scrape only 1 was successful, raising 2 young. The same was true on the beach/dunes where approx 10 pairs had limited success due mainly to visitor pressure. Recorded in most months with a high of 20 on several dates.

KENTISH PLOVER (*Charadrius alexandrinus*)
The only record is of a male which was seen for only 1 min. on the Scrape on May 4th.

GOLDEN PLOVER (*Pluvialis apricaria*)
Still a scarce bird at Minsmere: recorded on only 28 dates this year, with a peak of 29 on Oct 14th.

GREY PLOVER (*Pluvialis squatarola*)
May and October were the best months for this species, with 26 on May 2nd and over 80 on Oct 21st being the seasonal highs.

LAPWING (*Vanellus vanellus*)
19 nesting attempts were made on the Scrape and 10 attempts between the Sluice and Reckford Bridge on the Levels. From the number of chicks seen this species seems to have had a reasonable season, suffering from the same problems encountered by the Avocets.

KNOT (*Calidris canutus*)
7 birds were present on the Scrape on 5 dates in May, this being the season's high. The post-breeding high was 6 birds on Sept 2nd.

SANDERLING (*Calidris alba*)
The first record was of 2 birds on the Scrape on April 21st, with a peak of 10 on May 2nd. Very few records later in the year.

Systematic Species List

LITTLE STINT (*Calidris minuta*)
A poor Spring passage with only 3 records all in May. Best numbers were recorded in Aug and Sept, the peak counts being 12, 10 and 10 on Sept 2nd, 3rd and 4th respectively.

TEMMINCK'S STINT (*Calidris temminckii*)
Only one Spring record of a single bird on May 13th. A juvenile was present from Aug 30th to Sept 4th.

CURLEW SANDPIPER (*Calidris ferruginea*)
Recorded on only 6 dates in May with a max of 2 birds. Autumn passage started on July 16th with a peak of 18 on July 27th. The last record of the year was of 2 birds on Sept 19th.

PURPLE SANDPIPER (*Calidris maritima*)
Only one record of a single bird on May 12th.

DUNLIN (*Calidris alpina*)
Recorded in all months. The early season peak was 135 on Feb 27th. Numbers started to build up in July and the late season peak was 225 on Oct 14th.

WHITE-RUMPED SANDPIPER (*Calidris fuscicollis*)
An adult was on the Scrape from Aug 24th to 30th inc.

RUFF (*Philomachus pugnax*)
A male on Feb 25th was the first record of the year, numbers built up thereafter and peaked at 20 on May 5th. Autumn passage was mainly in July and the first half of August and the high was 28 on July 28th.

JACK SNIPE (*Lymnocryptes minimus*)
Only 4 early season records all of individual birds. The first bird of the Autumn was seen on Sept 24th and the peak was 6 birds on 2 dates in October.

SNIPE (*Gallinago gallinago*)
Again as in previous years 2 pairs bred on the Scrape and 2 pairs on the Levels. Early season highs were 140 on Feb 23rd and 160 on March 13th, 150 on Nov 10th was the post-breeding peak.

WOODCOCK (*Scalopax rusticola*)
A good breeding season with a max of 8 roding birds in May/June. The peak count was 10 birds, seen on Nov 17th.

BLACK-TAILED GODWIT (*Limosa limosa*)
The first Spring record was a single bird on Feb 10th. Spring passage was fairly poor, 111 on April 1st being the high. Poorly represented after July, 105 on July 7th was the post-breeding high. 90 birds were blown in on Oct 21st during the strong spell of easterlies.

BAR-TAILED GODWIT (*Limosa lapponica*)
A short Spring passage from mid-April to mid-May produced a peak of 131 on May 5th. Very few records later in the year with a peak of 5 on Aug 4th.

WHIMBREL (*Numenius phaeopus*)
Records relate to the period April 14th to Aug 29th, with highest numbers in May, 22 on May 12th was the peak.

CURLEW (*Numenius arquata*)
Fairly well represented in the early months, 12 on May 3rd being the high. Good numbers were present in June, 27 on the 20th and 33 on the 24th were the season's highs.

SPOTTED REDSHANK (*Tringa erythropus*)
No more than 6 birds were present in the Spring period, but this species was recorded on most days in April and May. Numbers increased from mid-June onwards to peak at 90 on Aug 5th and 7th. The last record was a single bird on Nov 22nd.

REDSHANK (*Tringa totanus*)
There were 18 nesting attempts on the Scrape; as with Lapwing and Avocet the success was limited by climate. The breeding population on the Levels was around 8 pairs, and several families were seen approaching the Scrape to find suitable feeding conditions, as the Levels were bone dry. Highest numbers were recorded in March and April and peaked at 36 on April 3rd.

GREENSHANK (*Tringa nebularia*)
Recorded between April 13th and October 20th. The Spring high was 6 birds on May 6th, and the high Autumn counts were 9 on July 4th and 8 on Sept 4th.

GREEN SANDPIPER (*Tringa ochropus*)
Singles on Jan 14th and Feb 19th were the only Winter records, and Spring passage consisted of records on only 9 dates. In the Autumn the peak months were July and August, when the high was 10 birds on Aug 30th. A single bird was seen on Nov 2nd.

WOOD SANDPIPER (*Tringa glareola*)
1 on May 1st, 2 on May 7th and 1 on June 4th were the Spring records. Autumn passage started on July 16th and the species was recorded on 10 dates, the last being a single bird on Oct 13th.

COMMON SANDPIPER (*Actitis hypoleucos*)
First recorded on April 27th, the Spring max being only 2 birds on several dates in May. Autumn passage was excellent in July and August with a max of at least 20 birds on July 28th. The last record was on Sept 19th.

TURNSTONE (*Arenaria interpres*)
Recorded on 21 dates in April and May with a max of 9 birds on May 2nd. Autumn passage, however, was very poor with only 12 bird days and a high of 8 birds on July 17th.

RED-NECKED PHALAROPE (*Phalaropus lobatus*)
The only record is of an adult on the pools in front of the large public hide on Aug 22nd.

POMARINE SKUA (*Stercorarius pomarinus*)
2 records, the first being an adult offshore on July 9th; the other was also a single bird on Sept 19th.

Systematic Species List

ARCTIC SKUA (*Stercorarius parasiticus*)
Recorded on 7 dates all in the Autumn, with a high of 4 birds flying South on Sept 21st.

GREAT SKUA (*Stercorarius skua*)
Only one record, that of a single bird flying South on Oct 13th.

MEDITERRANEAN GULL (*Larus melanocephalus*)
Recorded between March 24th and July 12th on 18 dates. All records apart from 3 were of the same 2nd Summer individual. The other 3 records were of a different 2nd Summer bird on one date and a 1st Summer bird on April 23rd and May 7th.

LITTLE GULL (*Larus minutus*)
5 birds on Feb 8th and an adult on the 4th and 10th were the first records of the year. There were 5 records in May with a max of 3 on the 5th, and a 1st Summer bird was present from 12th to 15th June. All Autumn records were in October and were associated with the easterly winds. The highest counts were 18 on the 21st and over 30 on the 22nd.

BLACK-HEADED GULL (*Larus ridibundus*)
A large increase in numbers breeding on the Scrape this year was attributed to the increased effectiveness of the electric fence. There were approx 300 nesting attempts and around 100 young fledged. Mortality was high due to predation by Lesser Black-backed Gull. There was a noticeably higher number of gulls on the Scrape this year compared to previous years. These were actually roosting overnight, something that has not happened in recent times. Approx 1000 birds on Feb 24th was the early season high, and 1100 on Sept 18th was the post-breeding max.

COMMON GULL (*Larus canus*)
Good numbers were recorded in Feb with highs of 260 and 250 on the 25th and 26th respectively. The Winter max was 40 on Nov 6th.

LESSER BLACK-BACKED GULL (*Larus fuscus*)
First recorded on Feb 9th with an early season peak of 63 on June 10th. Very scarce later in the year when the peak was 13 on Oct 2nd.

HERRING GULL (*Larus argentatus*)
A very poor year for this species with a max of only 43 birds on March 23rd.

GLAUCOUS GULL (*Larus hyperboreus*)
The only record is of a single bird on April 22nd.

GREAT BLACK-BACKED GULL (*Larus marinus*)
As with Herring Gull, this species was poorly represented this year, the highest count being 25 on Oct 5th.

KITTIWAKE (*Rissa tridactyla*)
Recorded on 12 dates in the first half of the year with a peak of 11 on June 10th. Over 70 were seen offshore on Oct 22nd and 22 on Nov 26th is also notable.

SANDWICH TERN (*Sterna sandvicensis*)
As in previous years this species attempted to breed late in the season; however, this year there were 5 nests. Unfortunately all were unsuccessful. All the nests were on

Flying in the Face of Nature

island 47. The first record of the year was on March 19th and the season's peak was 85 on July 11th. Most records were between April and July with the last sighting on Sept 28th.

ROSEATE TERN (*Sterna dougallii*)
The only record is of an adult on the Scrape on July 11th.

COMMON TERN (*Sterna hirundo*)
16 nesting attempts were made all on East Scrape, and 8 birds reached the fledging stage. Predation was quite high because of the number and proximity of Black-headed Gull nests. A single bird on April 3rd was the first record of the year and numbers steadily built up during May. The last record of the year was of a single bird offshore on Nov 6th.

ARCTIC TERN (*Sterna paradisaea*)
Quite a good year for this species with records on 8 dates. The first was a single bird on April 23rd, and one on May 15th. 2 birds on June 14th were followed by an adult between the 8th and 11th of July. The last record was of 3 birds on Aug 23rd.

LITTLE TERN (*Sterna albifrons*)
This species suffered heavily from predation and disturbance in 1990. Numbers built up steadily during May to peak at 97 on the 17th. However, all 21 nests on island 65 were predated in the last week of May, the culprits being Black-headed Gulls. 20 pairs made a second attempt down near Sizewell power station just beyond the reserve boundary, but were destroyed later in that month by a jeep driving over the nests. The last record was of 2 birds offshore on Aug 5th.

BLACK TERN (*Chlidonias niger*)
Considering the large influx in May there is only one record of a single bird that flew in off the sea on May 1st.

GUILLEMOT (*Uria aalge*)
Recorded on 14 dates with a max of 7 South on Oct 13th.

LITTLE AUK (*Alle alle*)
One record in Nov of a single bird on the 4th. Passage in mid-December was very good with 14 on the 13th, 1 on the 14th and an unusual record of 1 bird on the Scrape in front of East Hide on the 16th.

STOCK DOVE (*Columba oenas*)
More numerous this year, the peak count being 61 on Feb 24th.

WOODPIGEON (*Columba palumbus*)
Mostly recorded in Jan and Feb with highs of 630 on Jan 14th and over 1000 on Feb 25th. Numbers late in the year were relatively low with 350 on Oct 21st the highest count.

COLLARED DOVE (*Streptopelia decaocto*)
Only recorded on 6 dates; the highest counts were of 3 birds on May 8th and 25th. Not thought to have bred in 1990.

TURTLE DOVE (*Streptopelia turtur*)
A drop in the number of territories this year with only 24 pairs. First record was of 2 birds on April 22nd, with a high of 10 on July 8th. Last seen on Sept 2nd.

Systematic Species List

RING-NECKED PARAKEET (*Psittacula krameri*)
Recorded on 3 dates: all single birds on Aug 13th and 18th, and on Nov 7th.

CUCKOO (*Cuculus canorus*)
Quite numerous this year with a max of 10 birds on several dates. Seen most often in the reedbed and around c55. Recorded between April 15th and Sept 26th.

BARN OWL (*Tyto alba*)
A pair bred in Eastbridge again using c41 and 40 as part of their hunting area. Seen regularly during the year with a few records of 3 birds suggesting more than one territory in the locality.

LITTLE OWL (*Athene noctua*)
A pair bred again just on the edge of the reserve by c05, and most of the records were from that part of the reserve.

TAWNY OWL (*Strix aluco*)
11 territories were located on the reserve this year, a drop of 2 on last year. Recorded in all months.

LONG-EARED OWL (*Asio otus*)
One pair bred in c10, and an adult with 2 juvs were seen flying along the main ride by c10 on the 6th and 9th of July. A migrant bird was in North Marsh on the 13th/14th of Oct.

SHORT-EARED OWL (*Asio flammeus*)
Very scarce in the first quarter with only 6 records of single birds. The same was true later in the year with only one record of one bird on Sept 5th. There was, however, much activity in April and May, and it was thought at one stage that a pair was going to breed, as they were displaying on the Levels. Unfortunately nothing came of the attempt; 5 birds on July 19th is notable.

NIGHTJAR (*Caprimulgus europaeus*)
24 churring males were located this year compared to 40 in 1989. This represents a drop of only 5 actually on the reserve, because the study in 1989 included several birds just beyond the boundary. In fact not a single bird was heard churring on the N.T. reserve!

SWIFT (*Apus apus*)
The first record of the year was the earliest ever on March 21st, the next being 1 on May 1st. Highest counts were 300 on June 22nd, 600 on July 5th and 200 on July 7th. The Autumn peak was 80 on Sept 1st, and this species was last recorded on Oct 5th.

KINGFISHER (*Alcedo atthis*)
2 pairs bred this year, one pair at the Sluice and one pair on the edge of c41. Recorded in all months, showing excellently from North Hide, and along all the Scrape dyke systems.

WRYNECK (*Jynx torquilla*)
Not seen on the reserve but a bird was on Dunwich Heath on May 4th/5th.

GREEN WOODPECKER (*Picus viridis*)
17 territories were located, an increase of 3 on 1989. The highest count was of 8 birds on April 2nd and Oct 19th.

GREAT SPOTTED WOODPECKER (*Dendrocopus major*)
No change in the population with 18 territories again this year. The highest count was of 10 birds on April 5th.

LESSER SPOTTED WOODPECKER (*Dendrocopus minor*)
Again no change in the population with 9 territories, with 3 each in c19 and c54.

WOODLARK (*Lullula arborea*)
Only one record of a bird singing in c55 on April 17th. Hopefully management work done late in the year specifically for this species will attract it to nest in 1991.

SKYLARK (*Alauda arvensis*)
The breeding population of this species on the reserve in 1990 was 61 pairs, which is double that in 1989 and shows the usage of the arable compartments (60's), and the dune system from the Sluice down to Sizewell. Peak counts were 103 on Jan 27th, 112 on Feb 1st and over 100 on Oct 13th and 21st.

SAND MARTIN (*Riparia riparia*)
18 holes were occupied in the carpark colony early in the season, but this increased to 60 when the 2nd broods were started. An electric fence erected around the car-park colony was 100% successful in keeping stoats out. 75 holes were being used on Dunwich Cliffs during the Summer. First record was on March 11th and the last on Oct 13th, with a peak of 150 on April 30th.

SWALLOW (*Hirundo rustica*)
A total of 15 pairs bred in the hides and there were 2 pairs in the Sluice. The first record was on April 3rd and 800 on Aug 14th was the Autumn peak. The last record was of a lone bird flying over Westleton Heath on Nov 18th.

RED-RUMPED SWALLOW (*Hirundo daurica*)
Only the second record for the reserve. A single bird was seen from North Hide for half-an-hour on April 13th and then again the next morning between West and South Hides.

HOUSE MARTIN (*Delichon urbica*)
2 birds on March 23rd were the first back. Very few Summer records but good numbers passing through in Sept and Oct with a peak of 50 on Sept 6th.

TREE PIPIT (*Anthus trivialis*)
A good breeding season with 16 territories. March 29th was a typical first record, as was the last sighting on Sept 2nd.

MEADOW PIPIT (*Anthus pratensis*)
The population remained stable at 24 territories. High early season counts were 52 on Jan 11th and 58 on Feb 11th. Far from numerous later in the year, 60 on Dec 14th being the peak.

ROCK PIPIT (*Anthus spinoletta*)
Only 2 records both in October; 2 on the 14th and 1 on the 16th.

WATER PIPIT (*Anthus spinoletta spinoletta*)
Recorded from Jan to April and from Oct to Dec. A very good showing from this species this year, most records being of birds on the Scrape. Early in the year

Systematic Species List

between 1 and 3 birds were seen regularly on most days with 8 on Feb 7th the highest count; the last record in the Spring was on April 20th. 3 birds on Oct 26th was the first Winter record, and a new high figure of 9 birds on Nov 10th was recorded.

YELLOW WAGTAIL (*Motacilla flava*)
Spring records commenced on April 10th and peaked at 4 birds on April 28th and on May 4th. Recorded in the Autumn from July 29th, reaching a high of 10 on Aug 27th.

GREY WAGTAIL (*Motacilla cinerea*)
Only 2 Spring records, both in March, singles on the 21st and 29th. 2 juvs were on the reserve from the 16th to the 18th of July, and latest record of the year was a single bird on Oct 14th.

PIED WAGTAIL (*Motacilla alba varrellii*)
Breeding was again noted at Scott's Hall Farm. Peak roost counts at Island Mere were 90 on March 20th and 50 on Nov 6th.

WHITE WAGTAIL (*Motacilla alba alba*)
4 Spring records, 2 on April 2nd and 25th and on May 7th, and 1 on April 30th.

WAXWING (*Bombycilla garrulus*)
Two records in Jan; 1 on the 3rd and 2 on the 13th were of birds flying over. 2 birds on Nov 14th were seen feeding on Hawthorns below East Walks Bungalow, but the 4 on Dec 16th were recorded flying over the heath during the Hen Harrier roost count.

WREN (*Troglodytes troglodytes*)
Very common and widespread.

DUNNOCK (*Prunella modularis*)
Widespread and common.

ROBIN (*Erithacus rubecula*)
This species was not surveyed this year, but from casual observations the population appears to be very healthy.

NIGHTINGALE (*Luscinia megarhynchos*)
62 territories were found again this year but the season was a very short one, with records only between April 15th and June 29th. Again highest concentrations were in c19 and c54.

BLACK REDSTART (*Phoenicurus ochruros*)
Recorded on 10 dates with all but one of the records being of single birds. 3 females on Oct 18th was the peak.

REDSTART (*Phoenicurus phoenicurus*)
Once again there was an increase in the population of this species, 18 territories were found this year, concentrated around c19 and c08. A typical first date was a male on April 18th and the last occurrence was on Oct 19th.

WHINCHAT (*Saxicola rubetra*)
A good year for this species with 4 Spring records and 12 Autumn records. In Spring 5 birds were seen between the 2nd and 7th of May. 3 on July 15th were the first

Autumn records and over 15 birds, most of which were in c59 on Sept 9th, was the season's peak.

STONECHAT (*Saxicola torquata*)
The breeding population doubled to 10 pairs this year. This is probably due to the recent mild Winters. 6 of these territories were in the dune system (c49, 58, 59) and most of these pairs raised 2 broods. The peak count was 16 on March 30th.

WHEATEAR (*Oenanthe oenanthe*)
Breeding was not proven this year. Records are for the period March 16th to Oct 14th on 55 dates. The peak was 11 on March 25th.

RING OUZEL (*Turdus torquatus*)
Recorded on 17 dates in the Spring with 8 on April 28th the highest count. Autumn passage was restricted to 7 dates in October, 6 birds on the 19th being the peak.

BLACKBIRD (*Turdus merula*)
Widespread and common.

FIELDFARE (*Turdus pilaris*)
Present in good numbers in both the early and late parts of the year. The peak count in Jan was 250 on the 11th, and the last record was on April 24th. The first Autumn record was on Sept 29th and numbers built up dramatically in Oct during the easterly blow, to peak at over 2750 on the 22nd.

SONG THRUSH (*Turdus philomelos*)
The breeding population dropped to 20 territories this year, which is slightly unusual looking at the next-but-one species.

REDWING (*Turdus iliacus*)
Fairly good numbers were present early in the year, the peak being 55 on April 12th. Sept 22nd saw the first Autumn bird returning and numbers built up to peak at 300 on Oct 19th.

MISTLE THRUSH (*Turdus viscivorus*)
15 territories were found this year, an increase of 50% on last year. 25 birds on Feb 16th and July 31st was the highest count.

CETTI'S WARBLER (*Cettia cetti*)
One pair is thought to have bred in c32 and there may have been a possible second territory near to Tree Hide, as there were several sightings from this part of the reserve during the year. Singing males were recorded in April and May and on odd days in Nov and Dec, again in c32.

GRASSHOPPER WARBLER (*Locustella naevia*)
A slight drop to 19 territories this year. First arrival was a little late – April 18th, and departure was early too with the last record being on Aug 10th.

SAVI'S WARBLER (*Locustella luscinioides*)
One pair managed to avoid all our survey efforts and raised 3 young in North Marsh. The first certain record was on July 15th when an adult was seen taking food to 2 young birds, then a bird was heard singing on the 16th. On the 18th 4 birds were definitely seen, again this appeared to be an adult feeding 3 young.

Systematic Species List

SEDGE WARBLER (*Acrocephalus schoenobaenus*)
162 territories were located along the reedbed edge this year, an increase of 32 on last year's mark. This is the only way to survey this and the other reedbed warblers, and is obviously an underestimate of the true population. However, as this method is used every year, a comparative study shows population trends. The first Spring record was 2 birds on March 29th and the last on Nov 6th was very late.

REED WARBLER (*Acrocephalus scirpaceus*)
The first sighting was on April 23rd, and as with the Sedge Warbler there was a marked increase in the population this year, with 84 territories being located along the reedbed edge, an increase of 40% on last year. The last record for the year was on Oct 1st.

LESSER WHITETHROAT (*Sylvia curruca*)
Only 25 territories were located this year which is not particularly worrying as last year's figure was remarkable. The first record was on April 22nd and the last sighting was on Sept 24th.

WHITETHROAT (*Sylvia communis*)
A slight increase to 79 territories this year is probably due to the increase in mature scrub after the '87 blow, c55 and c05/04 are still the choice breeding areas.

GARDEN WARBLER (*Sylvia borin*)
A similar increase this year compared to last year, with 52 territories being located. Most of these territories were in the c57-c19-c54 triangle. Records for this species were for the period April 23rd to August 23rd.

BLACKCAP (*Sylvia atricapilla*)
Another Sylvia warbler which has had a good season. 82 territories were found, which is an increase of over 30% on last year's figure. A male on April 1st was the first returning bird and the peak count was 20 on April 25th. A male and a female in the Sluice bushes on Oct 26th were the last sightings.

GREENISH WARBLER (*Phylloscopus trochiloides*)
Visitors to the reserve in late August had the opportunity to see 2 rare birds in one day, when this individual was found in the scrub in c59, between the Sluice and Sizewell. It remained in this area from August 27th to 30th, and represents the second record for the reserve and only the third for the county.

WOOD WARBLER (*Phylloscopus sibilatrix*)
Only one record this year of a single bird singing in c19 on May 15th.

CHIFFCHAFF (*Phylloscopus collybita*)
Another species to show a marked increase with 135 territories compared to 101 last year. At least one bird overwintered, evidence being two records in Jan. Spring passage started in earnest on March 10th and records were obtained in all months. Again a few birds were thought to be overwintering, as several were present on the reserve into Nov and Dec.

WILLOW WARBLER (*Phylloscopus trochilus*)
The population remained stable, 217 territories being located this year. The first Spring arrival was on April 1st and the last record was of 5 birds on Sept 24th, a little later than last year.

Flying in the Face of Nature

GOLDCREST (*Regulus regulus*)
The breeding population dropped to only 47 pairs this year, most of these being in
c08, 15, 16, 17, and 18. Passage in October was very good, double-figure records
being obtained on 13 days in the month with a peak of over 80 on the 19th.

FIRECREST (*Regulus ignicapillus*)
Singles were recorded on 4 days in mid-March, and on 5 dates in April where 4 on
the 2nd was the year's peak. There was one record in May on the 4th, and two
further records in October, 3 on the 19th and 1 on the 26th.

SPOTTED FLYCATCHER (*Muscicapa striata*)
Only 6 territories were found this year, 4 in c19, 1 in c16 and 1 in c25. Records
were obtained for the period May 12th to Sept 3rd.

PIED FLYCATCHER (*Ficedula hypoleuca*)
Only 3 records all of single females on Aug 13th, 19th and 26th.

BEARDED TIT (*Panurus biarmicus*)
No large gatherings were noted in the Autumn but lots of activity was apparent
throughout the year, many pairs successfully rearing 2 and even 3 broods.

PENDULINE TIT (*Remiz pendulinus*)
The only record was of a male seen behind West Hide on April 4th. It was present for
about 4/5 hours and fed on Typha heads and Phragmites.

LONG-TAILED TIT (*Aegithalos caudatus*)
Very abundant this year, 56 territories were located, an increase of 11 on last year's
figure. Highest concentrations were in the c19/c54 area. Most visible early in the
year, 45 on Feb 4th being the peak.

MARSH TIT (*Parus palustris*)
A remarkable recovery for this species in 1990, the number of territories rising from
19 in 1989 to 32 in 1990. This is encouraging as the number of records during the
Summer were few and far between. Numbers were noticeably high in the Autumn and
early Winter.

WILLOW TIT (*Parus montanus*)
Only recorded on 2 occasions during the year, both sightings were in c54 near the
crossroads of paths. This species is thought to have bred as the second sighting in
April was of a pair visiting a nest site.

COAL TIT (*Parus ater*)
40 territories were located this year, mostly in c08 and c16, 7, 18, 19. Otherwise
fairly widespread on the reserve.

BLUE TIT (*Parus caeruleus*)
Widespread and common on the reserve, some early breeding attempts failed, and
several broods of young were found dead in the nestboxes; this was thought to be
due to the cold weather affecting the food supply.

GREAT TIT (*Parus major*)
The same comments apply to this species as to the above species, widespread and
common.

Systematic Species List

NUTHATCH (*Sitta europaea*)
6 territories were located all in c19. Very little was seen or heard of this species in 1990, and how successful the breeding season was is difficult to assess.

TREECREEPER (*Certhia familiaris*)
A slight increase in the breeding population to 32 territories this year, most of these were concentrated in c19 where 17 were located.

GOLDEN ORIOLE (*Oriolus oriolus*)
2 records both in May of single birds seen from Island Mere flying over the reedbed towards Eastbridge.

GREAT GREY SHRIKE (*Lanius excubitor*)
The prolonged easterly winds in October probably accounted for the record of a single bird in the North bushes on the 21st.

JAY (*Garrulus glandarius*)
A fairly widespread and common bird. No great influx was noted associated with the large movement of Thrushes in October.

MAGPIE (*Pica pica*)
Fairly large numbers were recorded in the first three months of the year, most records are from the 60's (arable land). Peak counts were 56/Jan 3rd, 58/Jan 11th, 51/Feb 1st and 58 on Feb 8th.

JACKDAW (*Corvus monedula*)
A few pairs bred in c19 again. The peak count was 100 on Feb 19th and 25th.

ROOK (*Corvus frugilegus*)
Almost all of the records for this species are from the arable land. Peak figures were in April with 40 on the 26th and 45 on the 28th.

CARRION CROW (*Corvus corone corone*)
The highest counts were 45 on Feb 25th and 33 on April 12th.

HOODED CROW (*Corvus corone cornix*)
Only one record, that of a single bird flying over c69 on Oct 19th.

STARLING (*Sturnus vulgaris*)
Most numerous in October perhaps indicating some movement from the continent, the peak was 5000+ on Oct 21st. A fairly common breeder on the reserve with most of the reserve buildings supporting at least one pair, and as in previous years several pairs bred in c19.

HOUSE SPARROW (*Passer domesticus*)
Quite a common species on the reserve, most records are associated with birds in/on the reserve buildings and on the arable land. Peak count was 55 on Feb 11th.

TREE SPARROW (*Passer montanus*)
Unfortunately this species has become very scarce on the reserve in recent years. There were only 6 records in 1990, all of single birds flying over the reserve.

CHAFFINCH (*Fringilla coelebs*)
The breeding population was not studied in 1990, but there did not seem to be any great changes from simple casual observations. Good numbers were present on the arable land from Jan to March with a peak of 110 on Feb 11th.

BRAMBLING (*Fringilla montrifingilla*)
Recorded on 14 dates during the year. There were 4 records of single birds in March, and 2 were present from April 24th to 26th. The first Autumn arrival was on Oct 14th and 2 were seen on Oct 21st.

GREENFINCH (*Carduelis chloris*)
The population remained fairly stable, 12 territories were located. Good counts were obtained from the arable study, peak figures were 132 on Jan 18th, 300 on Jan 27th and 340 on Oct 21st.

GOLDFINCH (*Carduelis carduelis*)
10 territories were located this year and a post-breeding group was feeding on thistles between South Hide and the Sluice in August and September; this flock peaked at 110 on Sept 1st.

SISKIN (*Carduelis spinus*)
The highest count early in the year was of 70 birds on several dates, and numbers were good between Jan and March. There were only 3 records of single birds in April and a female on May 1st was the last of the Spring. A single bird flying over Westleton Heath on July 5th was unseasonal and it wasn't until November that the main Winter population arrived.

LINNET (*Carduelis cannabina*)
39 territories were located mostly in c59 and c20. Spring passage was evident from mid-March to mid-April with highs of 75 on Mar 29th and 150 on April 2nd; this species was very scarce later in the year.

TWITE (*Carduelis flavirostris*)
Only 2 records both in October on the Scrape, 1 on the 10th and 6 on the 20th during the 'Rake to the Scrape' event.

REDPOLL (*Carduelis flammea*)
7 territories were found as follows: 1 in c07 and c11, 2 in c29 and 3 in c08. Very few records for the early part of the year, but by November the usual Winter flock was feeding in S. Belt, peaking at 50 on Nov 17th.

CROSSBILL (*Loxia curvirostra*)
A pair on March 22nd were the only early season records. Most records were from mid-June to early October and were due to an influx of birds from the continent, 13 on Sept 10th was the highest count.

BULLFINCH (*Pyrrhula pyrrhula*)
There was another appreciable increase in the breeding population again with 36 pairs holding territory. Now quite widespread on the reserve but rarely more than 15 birds were counted on any one day.

LAPLAND BUNTING (*Calcarius lapponicus*)
The first record of the year was a single bird flying over the reedbed on Jan 22nd; the other 3 records were also of single birds on the 3rd, 4th, and 8th of November.

Systematic Species List

SNOW BUNTING (*Plectrophenax nivalis*)
The highest count of the year was 23 on Jan 1st; this record was followed by sightings on 7 more dates in the early Winter period, the last being a single bird on March 25th. The first returning birds were 2 on Oct 10th and a flock of up to 7 birds were to be seen in the dunes on several dates in Nov and Dec.

YELLOWHAMMER (*Emberiza citrinella*)
68 territories were located this year which is very similar to last year's figure of 71. Large flocks were to be found on the arable land in Jan and early Feb; peak counts were 185/Jan 3rd, 132/Jan 18th, 172/Jan 27th, 170/Feb 4th and 150 on Feb 11th. Numbers later in the year were very low, the high being 31 on Nov 19th.

ORTOLAN BUNTING (*Emberiza hortulana*)
A male was seen from May 3rd to 5th around the SE corner of c51 and on the North Wall. It was quite tame and could be approached easily. The 6th record of this species for the reserve.

REED BUNTING (*Emberiza schoeniclus*)
In all 31 territories were found this year and as with the other reedbed species this is only a relative figure as only the fringe territories were recorded. The peak count was 36 on Jan 27th.

CORN BUNTING (*Miliaria calandra*)
Only 2 records, the first was of 4 birds flying North on May 7th and the other was of 1 bird over c61 on June 15th.

ESCAPES

GREATER FLAMINGO (*Phoenicopterus rabar*)
An adult was recorded on 15 dates between Oct 7th and Dec 21st. All records were from the Scrape.

BLACK SWAN (*Cygnus atratus*)
Recorded on 6 dates in March, only one bird involved.

INDEX

Shankly, Bill, 84, 85–6
shelduck, 75, 191, 205
Shepherd, Dudley, 73, 82
short-eared owl, 213
shoveler, 75, 205
Singer, Peter, 86, 184
siskin, 220
Sizewell, 2, 11, 74, 87–8, 128–9, 130–4
skylark, 142, 214
snew, 206
snipe, 209
snow bunting, 221
song thrush, 78, 216
songs, 22–8, 41–4, 75–80
Sorensen, Jeremy, 8–12, 100–4, 117–23, 188–91, 194, 195, *et passim*
sparrowhawk, 4, 20, 26, 61, 64–70, 160, 178–9, 182, 190, 207
spoonbill, 81, 204
spotted flycatcher, 79, 218
spotted redshank, 210
starling, 79, 179–80, 182, 219
stoats, 47
stock dove, 79, 212
stone curlew, 107
stonechat, 81, 190, 216
Suffolk Ornithological Group, 63
Suffolk Wildlife Trust, 72, 82
swallow, 214
swift, 213

tawny owl, 72, 75, 184–6, 213
teal, 75, 136, 143, 205
Temminck's stint, 209
territory, 43–4
Thomas, Dylan, 199
Tomlinson, David, 25
tree pipit, 214
tree sparrow, 67, 219
treecreeper, 78, 219
tufted duck, 206

turnstone, 81, 210
turtle dove, 212
twitchers, 53–60, 148
twite, 220
Tyler, Glenn, 106, 107–15, 139, 156, 195

Visitors' Centre, 196
voles, 49
volunteers, 162–8

wardens, 119–23
water pipit, 214–15
water rail, 44, 139, 207
waxwing, 215
Weinberg, Alvin, 134
Welch, Geoff, 194, 195–7
wheatear, 81, 197, 216
whimbrel, 210
whinchat, 215–16
white-fronted goose, 136, 204
white-rumped sandpiper, 190, 209
white-tailed eagle, 190, 206
white wagtail, 215
whitethroat, 42–4, 80, 143, 190, 217
whooper swan, 137
wigeon, 81–2, 136, 143, 191, 205
willow tit, 218
willow warbler, 44, 45, 80, 190, 217
wood sandpiper, 210
wood warbler, 217
woodcock, 77–8, 209
woodland, 140–1
woodlark, 142, 162, 194–5, 214
woodpigeon, 78, 212
wren, 5, 78, 215
wryneck, 213

yellow wagtail, 215
yellowhammer, 79, 221
Young, Barbara, 167